AN
AUTUMN
HUNTING

Also by Tom Callaghan

A Killing Winter
A Spring Betrayal
A Summer Revenge

AN AUTUMN HUNTING

TOM CALLAGHAN

Quercus

First published in Great Britain in 2018 by

Quercus Editions Ltd
Carmelite House
50 Victoria Embankment
London EC4Y 0DZ

An Hachette UK company

A CIP catalogue record for this book is available
from the British Library

HB ISBN 978 1 78648 239 6
TPB ISBN 978 1 78648 236 5
EBOOK ISBN 978 1 78648 237 2

10 9 8 7 6 5 4 3 2 1

Typeset by Jouve (UK), Milton Keynes

Printed and bound in Great Britain by Clays Ltd, Elcograf S.p.A.

For
Mam and Dad

The hardest thing for anyone is to be a human being every day.

Chingiz Aitmatov

Chapter 1

She hadn't managed to pull the syringe out of her inner thigh before the heroin slammed into her nervous system with the mindless ferocity of the snowstorms that race down from the Tien Shan mountains. Her body sprawled across a chaos of unwashed clothes, grease-stained pizza boxes, crushed Baltika beer cans; all the garbage junkies accumulate when nothing else in life matters but cooking up the next shot. Her cheap unbranded jeans were baggy and bunched around her knees, so I could follow the progress of her addiction by the track marks riding up and down her left leg like cigarette burns.

She might have been a pretty girl once, dreaming of true love and the next party, but that was all history now. Not for her the first kiss, summer evenings with friends by Lake Issyk-Kul, the rich scent of cut lilies, the crunch of fresh snow underfoot. Now a different kind of snow had consumed her, buried her under a blizzard that blasted death across Central Asia and on into Russia.

The raw stink of iodine told me at least one person in the squat had been brewing up *krokodil*. Easy enough to make at home; all you need is codeine, mixed with iodine, red phosphorus from matches, a subtle hint of gasoline, and whatever other poisons you can lay your hands on.

Inject *krokodil* and your skin is transformed into something green and scaly as infection and gangrene bite. Hence the name. Your flesh dies and rots away, leaving unhealing sores that chew through tissue and muscle down to the bone.

The tracks on the girl's leg were too distinct to be the tooth-marks of the crocodile. More likely to be from smack; perhaps she was an old-fashioned sort of girl, kept her knees together except for the thrust of a hypodermic. I knew Kenesh Usupov would have the answer; Bishkek's chief forensic pathologist has seen it all, sliced it up as well.

In my career as inspector with the Murder Squad, I've found enough OD bodies to know 'victim' is the wrong word. As far as I'm concerned, injecting poison into yourself is an act of folly at best, and perhaps in the coiled and hidden recesses of the mind, a desire for suicide, a final ending. I prefer to save the 'victim' word for people who don't bring their death upon themselves, people whose unfortunate paths collide and end with someone else's greed or cruelty or lust. Harsh? Maybe, but you're not the one clearing up the consequences. I haven't lost my compassion for the dead, but it's not a blanket coverage any more.

'Inspector.'

I turned round as Kenesh Usupov joined me to stare down at the shipwreck of what had once been a human being. I wouldn't call Usupov a friend – he's too humourless and dour to imagine going for a drink or a meal with him – but we've worked together for a long time, and we respect each other's skills. I could never spend my days opening up skulls, weighing parcels of meat. On the other hand, the people he encounters at work don't try to kill him. To each his own.

'The apartment's empty, I suppose?'

I nodded. Standard procedure is to have a uniformed *ment* go through the scene, gun in hand, checking there's no crazy guy with a hypo brimming with HIV and looking to share. Hygiene and tidiness aren't the only things an addict gives up on; they don't hang around to face difficult questions from some disapproving police officer. Compassion for the body in the room leaves by the door and runs down the stairs.

We were in Alamedin, near the railroad tracks, in one of the old *Khrushchyovka* apartments, the prefabricated concrete blocks that sprang up throughout the Soviet Union in the aftermath of the Great Patriotic War against Hitler.

Every morning in the summer, you can hear a train trundle dispiritedly on a five-hour trek through Alamedin and the Boom Gorge towards Balykchy on the shore of Lake Issyk-Kul, only to make the return trip the same evening. Further east, the lake is beautiful, clear calm water ringed by snow-topped mountains, but Balykchy is a festering shithole you wouldn't want to visit twice. I sometimes think if you're Kyrgyz, you can travel – after all, we've traditionally been nomads – but you always end up coming back to where you started. I've never known if that's a good or a bad thing.

Kenesh and I crouched down, squatting by the body, my knees protesting as I did so. Just one more sign I'd been doing this too long. This close, I could smell the acrid urine from when her bladder had betrayed her. I felt a sudden wave of

3

pity, guessing how ashamed and humiliated she would have felt with the emptying of her body displayed for the relentless, impersonal gaze of strangers.

Long streaks of damp stained the rough plaster walls, torn linoleum scuffed and scarred, dirt ground into it until any original pattern had become a faint ghost of a memory, the faded photograph of someone long-forgotten. A cheap wooden kitchen chair lay on its side; I guessed the girl had been sitting there when she took the hot shot and dived head first into death.

Usupov tapped my arm, pointed at the girl's groin. A few dark flecks of dried blood had sprayed across white pants.

'Significant?' I asked.

Usupov shrugged.

'Hard to say. Maybe her period. Not from the syringe; that's still in place. I'll know once she's on the table.'

'Think this is a suspicious death?'

Usupov turned to me, shrugged. Pale autumn sunlight through the window flared off his glasses, hid his eyes.

'Unusual, is the word I'd use. Something not quite right.'

I looked back down at the corpse, couldn't see anything out of the ordinary. The dark blue stain of lividity where gravity had pulled her blood back towards earth, the swelling and puffiness of pallid skin where old scars and blemishes traced the map of her life. I'd seen it all too many times.

'Look at the injection sites on her leg,' Usupov said. 'All fairly recent. It's my guess she was right-handed, since the tracks are all in her left leg. Easier to shoot up.'

He reached over, pulled at her arm.

'This is what's unusual. No tracks on either arm, not even skin-popping. Most people only start hunting for fresh veins on the legs when the arms give out.'

It was my turn to shrug.

'So she didn't want people to know she was using, maybe Mummy and Daddy wouldn't approve. Maybe she was vain, proud of her soft skin and smooth forearms. It all seems a little thin to me.'

'I'll know better at the autopsy,' Usupov said. 'You're welcome to watch. If you can be bothered, that is.'

I stood aside to let the stretcher men go about their work. Below the belt, Chief Forensic Pathologist, I thought. But maybe some truth in it.

The horrible brokenness of death revealed itself in dangling limbs and a head thrown back. As the body was lifted up, I saw the dark smudge of a bruise on the left of her forehead.

'What do you think?' I asked Usupov, pointing at the mark.

'Perhaps when she hit the floor? Her heart needn't have stopped beating straight away, which would explain why she could have a bruise. But again, I'll know more when she's under the knife.'

The body hauled away, I could smell something else in the room; fear and despair, bitter and raw on the tongue, making the eyes water but not with tears. I knew better than to say anything to Usupov; he would have looked at me as if I'd gone mad and started spouting allegiance to Comrade Stalin.

Instead, I filed the thought away in the dark recess where I store impressions, hints and dreams.

'I'll do the cut tomorrow morning,' Usupov said, making for the door, 'ten o'clock.'

I nodded, waited until I heard his boots on the landing, began to look for clues. Murder confessions, crumpled notes with dealers' addresses, mysterious telephone numbers written in cheap lipstick. I'll grab at any straw, I'm not proud. I was hunting through the pathetic remnants of a life when my phone beeped.

A text: 'Meet soonest.' Sent by Mikhail Tynaliev. Minister of State Security. Every meeting I'd ever endured with him had been the start of grief and the very real possibility I'd end up dead.

So I knew I was going to find myself up to my chin in shit.

Chapter 2

An hour later, I was in Tynaliev's house, in the ornate drawing room he uses as his private office when he doesn't want the ministry grapevine spreading the news. I'd been there before; it got no more enjoyable each time, the ritual always the same.

Waved through a high-tech scanner by sullen guards whose fingers stray worryingly close to the triggers of their Kalashnikovs, and whose eyes beg for the chance to use them.

Sitting for an hour in an overheated antechamber on an ornate gold-painted chair that manages to be both ugly and uncomfortable, before being ushered into the presence.

Then face to face with the most dangerous man in Kyrgyzstan.

Mikhail Tynaliev and I have a history together and it doesn't make for comforting reading.

I'd found out who murdered his daughter Yekaterina Tynalieva, then stood by and said nothing while Tynaliev had the man butchered like a hog.

I'd tracked down a vicious paedophile killer with high connections, then ignored Tynaliev's order to let the matter drop 'in the interests of the state'. Instead, I'd attached a bomb to the killer's car, blown him to hell.

And most recently, I'd tracked down Tynaliev's mistress in

Dubai, after she'd 'liberated' ten million dollars from his secret bank accounts. I recovered most of his money, but not without a lot of blood and death along the way.

All of which meant Tynaliev used me for his dirty work, but didn't trust me. I knew too many of his secrets. Not a reassuring position to be in.

Tynaliev stared at me, eyes unblinking, intense. A bear of a man, shorter than official photographs suggested, jacket drawn tight over massive shoulders, muscles stretching the cloth out of shape. His hands slept on the desk in front of him, knuckles scarred and brutal. Easy to imagine him interrogating some poor soul in the soundproof basement at Sverdlovsky station; a slap, a punch, a kick, blood lashing across the tiled walls, a broken tooth lying on the stained floor.

The long silence grew more uncomfortable as the seconds dragged by. Just as I was ready to confess to whatever Tynaliev thought I'd done, he jerked a thumb in my direction.

'Sit.'

I did as I was told. The minister picked up a sheet of paper, read it in silence. My price for having recovered his money from his former mistress had been a demand for reinstatement into the Murder Squad. I wondered if this was confirmation. Of course, Tynaliev being who he was, it might just as easily have been a sentence in Penitentiary One in the hope I'd catch TB or HIV from one of the other prisoners. If I didn't catch a home-made shiv first.

'You were at a suspicious death earlier,' he said, not looking up at me.

8

'A young woman. OD. Probably heroin,' I said, adding 'Sir,' to be on the safe side.

'Suspicious?' he asked.

I shrugged. I wondered at his interest, but there was nothing concrete to suggest anything more, and with Tynaliev, it's always better to say as little as possible.

Tynaliev shook his head, dismissing her death as unimportant, just another statistic, and at best a one-paragraph entry on an inner page of *Achyk Sayasat*. That's one of the differences between the two of us, and it maybe explains why I never became a politician. As far as the dead are concerned, I believe either they all count or none of them do.

'You're off that case,' Tynaliev announced, putting the sheet of paper down staring at me.

'So I'm back in Murder Squad?' I asked. 'As inspector?'

Tynaliev pursed his lips, stabbing a meaty forefinger onto the paper in front of him. The room was very warm, airless. I could sense panic rising in my stomach, did my best to look expressionless.

'Not exactly,' he said.

He pushed the paper towards me, gesturing for me to read it.

The paper was headed 'PRESS RELEASE'. It went downhill very rapidly after that.

A prominent member of the Bishkek Murder Squad is under investigation, accused of crimes against the state, including murder, corruption, extortion and blackmail. The serious nature of these allegations means the officer has been relieved of all duties and is suspended with immediate effect, without pay. If the allegations are proven to have substance, the officer will be named, brought to trial, and faces severe punishment.

Signed, Mikhail Tynaliev, Minister of State Security.

I read the statement, my face a mask to hide the shock and anger boiling up inside me. I didn't need to ask who the unnamed officer was. I screwed the paper up, tossed it back onto Tynaliev's desk.

'This is just bullshit. Sir,' I said, failing to keep the rage out of my voice. Now it was Tynaliev's turn to shrug. He smoothed out the sheet of paper, read through it once more, locked it away in a desk drawer, together with my career.

'Just be glad I didn't name you,' Tynaliev said. 'Yet.'

Tynaliev's security team were wise to confiscate my Makarov at the scanner, or I'd have been tempted to press the barrel hard against his head, maybe even pull the trigger. But I was already wondering why Tynaliev had decided to break the news to a lowly inspector, rather than hand the task over to a police station chief. As always with the minister, the cards you saw in his hand were never part of the real game.

'Personally, I know you're too honest – or too stupid – to get up to this sort of nonsense,' he continued, a gesture of dismissal underscoring his words. 'And believe me, I'm not your enemy. Which doesn't mean you don't have any.'

I understood the logic behind his words; only a very confident or foolish person would take on the whole state apparatus that stood behind Tynaliev.

'I'm afraid it gets worse for you, Borubaev,' he added, pouring a shot of vodka, not offering me one, throwing it back in a single practised move.

'In a few days, during our investigations, we'll uncover positive proof you've been involved in smuggling heroin, and you took on the case of today's tragic OD of an innocent young girl to cover up your tracks. And hers, of course.'

Tynaliev smiled at his witticism, poured another shot.

'You may even have administered the fatal dose yourself, to shut her up,' he added.

'So put me up against a wall and shoot me,' I said, 'but I don't understand why you're doing this. Is this to do with Natasha Sulonbekova?'

Tynaliev winced at the mention of his former mistress and his disappearing fortune, shook his head.

'You handled that moderately well, and you've kept your mouth shut,' he said. 'No, this is something else entirely.'

His smile did nothing to reassure me. Neither did his next words.

'Of course, you may end up being put up against a wall and shot, but not before enjoying a little torture and mutilation first.'

Chapter 3

'I take it you don't approve of heroin smuggling, Inspector? Or, in the light of imminent events, should I say Mr Borubaev?'

Tynaliev's face wore an expression of genuine enquiry and concern. I wondered how long he'd practised in the mirror. I guessed it was a trick question, decided to play it safe.

'It's against the law for a start, Minister, and the destruction and misery it causes is a real threat to the stability of society, as well as funding criminal elements,' I said, choosing my words with forensic care, as if reading from a departmental manual.

'I thought you would say something pompous like that,' Tynaliev said. 'Maybe you should be teaching at the American University, telling the world how backward Central Asia is, how we're nothing but ignorant shitheads who only know how to sell heroin to rich foreigners.'

I said nothing, but wondered if some of the nine million dollars I'd recovered from Natasha Sulonbekova had grown in Afghanistan's poppy fields. Being even an unwitting accomplice is a burden on the soul.

'It's never been a business interest of mine,' Tynaliev said, as if reading my mind. 'Too much attention, too much pressure from the Kremlin, the White House and everywhere in between. And too many open beaks all looking to be fed with a constant supply of juicy morsels.'

He shook his head, as if dismissing a far-fetched business proposal.

'Caution and cover work better in the long run, wouldn't you agree?' he said.

'In my line of work, you don't survive long without them,' I agreed, wondering if Tynaliev's caution extended to giving me an unmarked grave somewhere between Bishkek and Lake Issyk-Kul.

'I'm surprised you've survived at all,' Tynaliev said. 'Particularly since the Circle of Brothers still think you put two bullets into Maksat Aydaraliev.'

A shockwave of nausea rose up into my throat, and I wondered if I was about to vomit.

Aydaraliev had been the *pakhan*, local boss of the gangsters who feed on Russia and Central Asia like starving wolves in the depths of winter. Investigating the murder of Yekaterina Tynalieva, I'd found myself working with an Uzbek agent, Saltanat Umarova. It was Saltanat who had arranged the bullets for the *pakhan*, one in the back of the head to show he'd been executed, one in the mouth to show he'd talked. My problem? He was shot immediately after meeting me, so I knew where the finger of suspicion pointed. It didn't help that the finger was almost certainly tensed against a trigger.

I didn't know if Tynaliev believed I'd executed the old man, or if he knew Saltanat and I had become lovers in a semi-detached sort of way, but silence was still my most likely escape route.

'The world will know you've been kicked out of the force in disgrace. You'll probably need to get out of the country before the prison bars slam behind you, and the people you put there welcome you with open arms,' Tynaliev said.

'You won't have the protection of a badge any more, but that doesn't mean you won't still be useful to certain people,' he added.

'Which certain people in particular?' I asked, increasingly worried this was leading to a deep hole in a cemetery and a marble headstone with an engraving of my face.

'You never wondered why the Circle didn't avenge the *pakhan*'s death?' Tynaliev asked. 'Why you've survived with fingers, toes and brains relatively intact?'

'Presumably the new leader is very happy someone cleared the path and helped him step up to the throne?'

Tynaliev nodded.

'Still a detective, I see, if not in name any more.'

I ignored the sarcasm. Did Tynaliev really believe I'd think he was going to all this trouble simply for the benefit of the country and his fellow citizens?

'Spend time in the Kulturny, make contacts you can use in your new career,' Tynaliev said, and my heart sank like a rock towards my boots. The Kulturny is probably the roughest bar in Bishkek; they don't let people in unless they have a port-folio of prison tattoos or at least one concealed weapon. Even the name is a joke; the place is as anti-*kulturny* as it's possible to get. No welcoming signs, no neon lights, just a battered steel door scarred and scuffed from attacks with boots, pickaxes and, on one memorable evening, a Molotov cocktail. The door has no handle, and behind the spyhole that gets you admittance the bouncer is probably drunk or stoned, certainly armed. But I'd been there in the past; to pick up dirt on your shoes, walk where the mud is.

I was with Saltanat the last time I'd visited the Kulturny. There had been gunplay, with a couple of bodies to dispose of when the shooting stopped, so I'd decided I'd drink my orange juice somewhere else. If Tynaliev wanted me there, he'd have a good reason. Good for him, that is; probably bad for me.

'New career?' I asked, not looking forward to the answer.

Tynaliev jerked his head towards the exit, turned to his paperwork, dismissing me. As I reached the door, he looked up, hit me with his hardest stare.

'You're going to become a drug baron,' he said, and his smile didn't even try to reach his eyes.

Chapter 4

I've never been particularly good at obeying orders, even when they come from as exalted and dangerous a person as the minister. So I walked into Sverdlovsky District Morgue just after dawn the next morning, to watch Usupov hone his scalpels and his skills on yet another corpse. Of course, I wasn't investigating the case I'd just been fired from, merely popping by to see my old friend, the chief forensic pathologist, maybe enjoy a breakfast glass of *chai*. How could the minister possibly object to that?

The temporary occupants of the morgue don't seem to mind the stained concrete walls, the flickering lighting, the ever-present scent of freshly butchered meat. Even the living in Bishkek can't be too choosy about where they call home, and the dead never bother to complain. No rent or bills to pay either.

At first glance, you might think you were at the entrance to an underground car park beneath some dismal shopping mall, until you spot the small weather-beaten sign. The morgue doesn't advertise its presence; not many people visit, and those who do usually arrive on their back rather than on their feet.

I walked down the broken-tiled steps and along the corridor, where the emerald-green stain of mould grows bigger every winter when the snows break in, looking for shelter. As always, every other light fitting was missing a bulb, but I could still see the metal doors at the far end, smell the stink of raw flesh.

Usupov was already hard at work, transforming the young woman I'd seen the day before into the leavings of a butcher's shop. Spatterings of blood stained the steel slab, along with other juices I preferred not to think about. It's a truth of my job that beauty often hides ugliness inside, and a truth of Usupov's profession that he sees beauty and order in the internal coilings and twistings of the body.

I didn't ask for an overall; I wasn't intending getting close to the corpse, and I wasn't wearing anything a decent second-hand shop would put in the window in pride of place.

'Nothing unusual in the manner of death. Drug overdose,' Usupov said, before I'd even asked the question. 'Her blood pressure crashed, and she suffered the heart attack that killed her.'

He held up a hand for my inspection.

'Bluish nails, all pretty standard, Inspector, exactly what I'd expect.'

Usupov inspects bodies for effects that he then uses to deduce their cause; I examine them for hints, clues, secrets. The girl's nails were coated in expensive clear varnish, although the edges were chipped and torn. She'd still had enough pride in herself to make an effort to look good, which put her at least one level above the street *prostis* that loiter around Panfilov Park at night.

'No tattoos?'

Usupov shook his head. 'The only things that have ever been stuck in her are the needles that killed her.'

He nodded at my raised eyebrow.

'Yes, she was a virgin. I've not had one of those on my table for a long while,' and Usupov even smiled at his own joke.

The news instantly threw my speculations into the same tray where clumps and gobbets of discarded flesh were piling up. Not a working girl, either on the street or in a massage parlour. Not married, probably not even dating. That surprised me; she was pretty enough to have been bride-stolen, spotted by some randy pimply young bastard, grabbed off the street and taken to his mother's house for approval and an enforced marriage. That suggested a certain social status. Not every father can be with the apple of his eye twenty-four hours a day, or employ a bodyguard to keep her safe. The case was starting to look ominous, with possible headlines and consequences, none of them good. And my continued involvement wasn't going to make Tynaliev any more of a fan.

I let the thought fester at the back of my brain, tried another tack.

'Any clues to her identity?' I asked, the way they do in all the TV cop shows.

'Apart from the unique ten-carat diamond earrings and the black pearl tongue stud, no,' Usupov said, and I even stared at the body for a few seconds, then looked at Usupov. Humour has never been Usupov's thing, and I wondered if he'd acquired a lookalike comedian from somewhere, sent him along in his place.

'A couple of things might interest you though,' he said. 'For a start, the blood stains on her clothing.'

Usupov might have been discovering humour late in life, but he was still too prim to utter the word 'pants'.

'Her blood group and the stains are not the same,' he said. 'She was blood type O, and the droplets are A Rhesus positive. No way they could match.'

At least I now knew the girl probably hadn't been alone at the time of her death. But A Rhesus positive blood isn't rare, and I didn't know how her pants became soiled.

'It's not much of a start,' I grunted.

'A couple of other things,' Usupov said. 'One of them I've never encountered before.'

'Go on.'

'She didn't die from the usual heroin, cut to hell and back with baby laxative and brick dust.'

'Pure?'

'Pure all right, but it wasn't heroin or *krokodil.*'

I looked at Usupov. I didn't have time to play cat and mouse, and my face told him not to delay his surprise information.

'Ever heard of carfentanil, Inspector?'

I shook my head. Obviously a pharmaceutical of some sort, and not the sort that relieves headaches or toothache.

'It's a synthetic opioid, maybe ten thousand times stronger than commercial morphine. Originally created as a general anaesthetic for elephants.'

'And people take something that strong?'

Usupov looked down at the butcher's slab between us.

19

'As you can see.'

I shook my head, as ever amazed at the things people will do to themselves.

'I take it you don't need a lot of this carfentanil to win a place on your table.'

'A dose roughly the size of a grain of salt, that's all. Not something I've seen before; our addicts tend to be traditional-ists.'

Usupov paused, reached into the pocket of his white coat, pulled out a small, crumpled piece of paper, handed it to me.

'Hidden in the lining of her bra,' he said. 'The left cup, if that makes any difference. I wouldn't know, you're the detective.'

I smoothed out the paper, began to read.

Chapter 5

I've read a few suicide notes in my time, most of them written by men, to justify their final irrevocable departure. I guess most women lead such a barren, dismal existence they don't need to spell out the life-ending reasons obvious to everyone. As with most things in life, women just get on with it.

In the same way that suicide is the most personal act one can ever take, so each note is different, in tone, in style, in length. Bleak despairing accounts of a life that's finally run out of hope. Page upon page of hastily scrawled accusations. Explanations of the conscious decision to end the pain of terminal illness. Acts of sorrow, of revenge, carried out in moments of anger, drunkenness, heartbreak. But I'd never read a poem written by a suicide before. The handwriting was elegant, calm, not the desperate end-of-life scribble I'd seen so many times before. All the desperation was locked into the words.

> Let me tell you how this works; the heart,
> Drunk on reckless might-have-beens,
> Tiptoes past kisses still sweet but fading.
> Dawn scrambles through the window,
> Hunting for home.

'What do you think? A suicide note?' Usupov asked, behind his imperturbable manner as bewildered by this unexpected poem as I was.

'Well, I'm no critic, but she's not the next Anna Akhmatova,' I said, trying to collect my thoughts and wondering quite what a 'reckless might-have-been' was. 'Maybe she got one rejection slip too many.'

I read the poem again; it made as little sense the second time. When my wife Chinara was alive, she devoured book after book of poetry: Blok, Esenin, Pasternak, even Yevtushenko. She would have decoded the dead woman's poem, stripped it of its hidden meanings in seconds, the way I could field-strip my Yarygin in the dark. But Chinara was in a hilltop grave overlooking a valley and the mountains beyond that defend us from China, and I was alone, left with my memories of kisses still sweet but fading, fading.

'Maybe our victim didn't write this. We'll look very stupid if it turns out to be a famous poem in all the anthologies.'

'You think that's likely?'

I considered, shook my head. Perhaps because the poem was handwritten, but I sensed it had some significance for the dead woman lying in pieces in front of me, that it provided a clue to her life and death. Sometimes you let your instincts guide you in the absence of any evidence.

I was about to fold the paper and put it away in my wallet, decided to photograph it first. The poem might have been why the woman ended up with her skin being kissed by Usupov's scalpel. And if that was the case, perhaps there would be others for whom the poem was more of a threat than a memorial. My wallet would be the first place a heavy with fists like smoked hams would look; what were the odds he'd also check my phone?

'I'll send you my report,' Usupov said.

I shook my head, gave a lopsided grin.

'Hadn't you heard? The grapevine must be getting slow in its old age. I've been taken off the case, suspended, and in all likelihood about to go on trial.'

Usupov stared at me: we'd worked together a lot over the years. Though he knew I would sometimes cut corners when it suited me or the case I was working, he knew I was relatively straight. I gave a rueful nod, headed towards the door and the clean air outside. I planned on polluting it with a couple of cigarettes while I worked out exactly what I was going to do next.

'Someone from Unexplained Deaths will be in touch. Murder Squad aren't going to touch this, not without more evidence.'

I pushed the door, the metal cold in my hand.

'One more thing, Kenesh – the heartfelt verse? No need to put it in the report, eh? We don't want to start a wave of copy-cat lyric suicidal poems, do we?'

With that, I left the stink of blood, bowels and brains behind me, along with the tatters and scraps of a once-pretty girl who'd slipped away from life sixty years too soon.

Chapter 6

It's a long walk back from the morgue to my apartment on Ibraimova over on the east side of the city, even longer with the route I chose. But the day was still cool before the last of the summer's heat swept over us, and I needed the exercise. I do some of my least misguided thinking when I'm plodding along broken pavements, avoiding potholes, wondering why my feet hurt so much.

Sovetskaya was already busy, cars, trolleybuses and *marshrutki* minibuses battling it out for space on the roads. The pavements were beginning to fill with young women taking advantage of the last of the summer to show off their figures in short dresses and knee-length boots. But the bright summer days were turning to the muted shades of autumn, and the air would soon be as cold and heartless as the corpses in Usupov's morgue.

There was something off about the woman's death, a hint that didn't tally with the average overdose. It nagged at me, something glimpsed in the corner of my eye for a split second. But it wasn't my case any more, and I had other problems to obsess over, namely my career translation into drug dealer, mafia hood and common criminal.

Maybe this was Tynaliev's way of dealing with the

troublesome problem called Akyl Borubaev. No one would investigate if a corrupt police inspector didn't survive a prison sentence locked up with the people he'd put there.

I had no illusions about how long I'd last in Penitentiary One. If I made it until the gruel and stale bread they call dinner, I'd be very surprised. Even if some all-powerful *pakhan* boss inside was looking out for me and providing protection, a *torpedo*, a killer looking to make a name for themselves, would have been paid enough to melt a toothbrush handle, embed a razorblade into the plastic. A single slash across my neck and I'd bleed out before help could arrive.

I walked virtually the length of Sovetskaya, turned right onto Toktogul. This close to the city centre, the shops were smarter, a lot more expensive. Many of them even wore English names to show their sophistication and elegance of style. I didn't bother window-shopping; there was nothing I wanted to buy, even if I could have afforded it.

Finally I reached Ibraimova, known as Pravda during Soviet times. It had always amused Chinara that a Murder Squad inspector had found himself living on a street named Truth. She'd claimed it was wishful thinking on my part. Privately, I'd always hoped it was true.

Down the street, I could see the two circular hemispheres of the municipal *banya*, the bathhouse where you could get everything from a scalding shower and a choice of steam rooms to a brutal massage and a vigorous beating with birch twigs to help the circulation.

I'd avoided the *banya* ever since I'd drowned an assassin

sent there to kill me. It hadn't exactly been a fair fight because he wore a plaster cast on his hand, thanks to the earlier encounter we'd enjoyed. That had evened things up a little. I'd watched his body sink to the bottom of the ice-cold pool, thankful he was dead, guilty I'd done nothing to help him in the moment when his anger turned to terror as the water flooded his lungs.

I may be paranoid but it made sense to stay away from the scene of the crime, in case my presence triggered someone's memory and they ran through the exterior CCTV tapes once more.

I didn't think it was likely. So it came as a surprise when they picked me up as I was outside the entrance to my apartment building, activating the electronic door chip.

They were good; they had me bundled into an unmarked, windowless van before I'd had time to protest or throw a punch. No uniforms, but you can't disguise that flat-faced impassive stare. It wasn't the first time I'd ridden in a police wagon, but never wearing handcuffs before, one cuff on my wrist, the other locked onto a steel D-ring set into the bare metal seat. I didn't know either of the officers who sat on my right and left; the senior *ment* sat opposite and practised his most terrifying stare. I was meant to feel intimidated.

The air was thick with the sweet perfume of piss and sweat, with an underlying note of puke inadequately hosed out at the end of each shift. Perhaps it got the passengers prepared for the stink of the cells.

I fumbled for my cigarettes, awkwardly reaching over for

my pocket because of the handcuff on my wrist. The *ment* opposite shook his head. '*Ne kurit*,' he said, and emphasised the point by lighting up himself and blowing the smoke in my face. I wasn't sure which smelt worse – the cheap nicotine or his sour breath. Sometimes the clichés are so great you have to smile, but you keep the grin to yourself in case the arresting officer decides you're laughing at him, takes offence. That's usually when all grinning stops.

'Sverdlovsky, I suppose?' I said, not expecting an answer. Sverdlovsky station is where the soundproof basement works wonders in solving cases, usually with the guilty party confessing to whatever's on the table. It's not always easy to understand what they're saying, due to splintered teeth, split lips, dislocated jaws. Broken fingers don't make it easy to sign statements either. But everyone agrees it's a very effective way of bringing down the crime rate.

I glanced at my watch, which had rather inconveniently stopped. I'd been in the van for three or four hours, yet the watch lied and said less than ten minutes. But even ten minutes should have been more than enough time to get to Sverdlovsky station; we were going somewhere else. I shut my mind to the possibility we going to pull up in a side road between Bishkek and Tokmok, where an unploughed field would have an Akyl-sized hole waiting to be filled. Better to assume I was currently too useful to be disposed of.

Either we'd left a main road or the potholes had got a great deal deeper, because the van began to bounce and veer from side to side. With my wrist held tight by the cuffs, and with no way of bracing myself against the shocks, my back would look as if I'd been worked over by experts. Assuming that wasn't about to happen anyway.

Finally, the van stopped, the driver's door opened, a fist pounded against the back. The sunlight dazzled me for a few seconds, as the cuff attached to the D-ring was opened, snapped on my other wrist. At least my hands were in front of me, so I was able to balance myself as I was pushed into the open air.

I recognised where we were straight away: in Ala-Archa National Park, up in the start of the Tien Shan mountains, some forty kilometres south of Bishkek. We were at the point of the gorge where the road runs out and the backpacking trails begin, parked outside the area's only hotel, a curious building shaped like an inverted V. Whoever built it obviously liked the look of the Alpine hotels in Switzerland and had tried to replicate them without spending any money. The exterior looked worn and shabby, with an air of having tried and given up. I felt pretty much the same.

At this altitude, the air felt thin and crisp, even though the sun burnt down on us, the metal of the van's sides warm to the touch. Two months later, and the first snows would have already started to make the journey longer and more difficult, and by the end of the year, the hotel would have closed until the spring, its staff back in their home villages.

I was relieved we weren't parked outside the back entrance to Sverdlovsky station, but that didn't mean my troubles were over. You can torture someone anywhere, and it doesn't take much equipment to get results. A pair of pliers, a sliver of wood, a plastic bucket half-full of water: use those and you'll get the answers you want. It only depends on what you're pre-pared to do to get them. And permanently disposing of a problem is even easier. The only hard bit is getting rid of the body.

The senior *ment* jerked his head towards the hotel. His two sidekicks each seized an arm, led me to the front door. I won-dered about trying to break free and head for the treeline, dismissed the idea. You can't outrun a bullet. It struck me that perhaps these weren't policemen at all, that I was stumbling towards my execution. A wave of fear tugged at my belly – no one wants to be shot with their trousers full of shit and terror. I must have tried to pull back, because the two men tightened their grip, started to drag me forward. Once I would have welcomed the prospect of dying, ending the grief caused by Chinara's cancer. But you move on, live with loss the way you survive with a missing limb, the absence of an eye. And at that moment, nothing had ever smelt as fresh and sweet and alive as the cold air sweeping down from the mountain.

'Don't fuck me about,' the *ment* snarled. In that moment of clarity, I noticed one of his eye-teeth was missing; it gave him the look of an unpredictable dog debating whether or not to bite. 'If we were going to do you, you'd have been roadkill an hour ago.' His smile didn't reassure. 'No one's going to hurt you,' he added. 'Unless we have to.'

He pushed the hotel door open, and I was thrust inside with all the dignity of a sack of winter coal being delivered.

The lobby was dark, the lights turned off, the hotel obviously commandeered for the day. Even the clock behind the reception desk had downed tools and gone to sleep. Tynaliev sat at a long low table, flanked by two more guards whose hands never strayed far from their weapons. He sipped at a cup of coffee, pulled a face at its bitterness, added three more sugar cubes. I stood there, waiting for him to speak, to shout, to give the order to hurt me.

'You're an arsehole, Inspector. But you already know that.'

Tynaliev never let anger and disappointment creep into his voice; he instilled so much fear he didn't need to. The Kyrgyz people learnt that lesson during Stalin's time, when people 'disappeared' and ended up tumbled together in a burial pit in Ata-Beyit. But there are times when you have to speak out, even if it costs you everything. And this was one of those times.

'Minister, I respectfully suggest your bodyguards withdraw out of earshot. After all, it's not as if I can do you any harm.'

I held up my handcuffed wrists, to prove my point. Tynaliev stared at me, assessing how much of a threat I could pose, before nodding at his guards. After a brisk yet thorough frisking, the guards walked outside, leaving the senior *ment* far enough away not to hear but still able to watch my every move.

'You say I'm an arsehole, Minister. Very possibly – no, almost certainly – you're right.'

Tynaliev said nothing, simply stared.

'But then that makes two of us,' I said. I knew the risk I was taking in insulting the minister, but I didn't see any other way out of my situation. Buckle under, cave in, and I knew I wouldn't be returning to Bishkek, unless it was to check into Hotel Usupov, rooms always available.

'A rather dangerous conclusion to reach, wouldn't you say?' Tynaliev said, the menace in his voice silken and smooth.

I shrugged, gave a half-smile.

'You're not a man who lets his heart rule his head, Minister. I've been useful to you in the past, and from where I'm standing, I still am. But all this handcuffs and back of the van stuff, it doesn't scare me or impress me. You either had me brought here to kill me or to brief me. And I can't see you going to all this trouble just to put one in the back of my head.'

I paused, tried to control the shaking in my legs, the shaking in my voice. Tynaliev stared, shrugged in his turn.

'You're not important enough to kill, Inspector,' he said, 'but you're what Lenin called a useful idiot. You have a certain number of skills I can use. After that . . .?'

It was his turn to shrug, then gesture to the guy who'd brought me in, made an unlocking motion with his fingers.

The *ment* wasn't too happy with that, but no one profits from arguing with the Minister for State Security. He did as he was told, making sure he wrenched my arms as he took off the cuffs. I smiled at him, gave him one of those winks that hints at meeting in a dark alley when there's no one around and time for payback. His scowl got a little darker as he stomped back to the door.

Tynaliev gestured at a nearby chair, watched as I dragged it over, a curious smile on his face.

'You've got balls, Inspector, I'll grant you that,' he said. 'There aren't many people who've had the nerve to call me an arsehole.' He paused, stared up at the ceiling. 'In fact, I think you may be the only one. Still alive, that is.'

Tynaliev lit a cigarette, blew smoke over his shoulder, pushed the packet towards me as an afterthought. I shook my head, not wanting my hands to betray me.

'I had you brought here so we can avoid inquisitive ears. I have my enemies, as you know. This is a secure place to brief you on your next mission.'

He paused, gave me the death stare.

'If it leaks to anyone – the press, your friends, the man in the number 122 *marshrutka*, you can sleep easy, knowing that if the people I'm sending you up against don't kill you, I will. Not quickly or painlessly either.'

He stubbed out his cigarette on the table top. I could smell the acrid fumes of the burnt varnish. I knew Tynaliev was serious as death.

Chapter 7

For the next two hours, I listened as Tynaliev worked his way through a pack of cigarettes and most of a bottle of Kyrgyz Aragi. He knew me well enough not to offer me a shot. By the end, he was twenty-five per cent drunk and I was a hundred per cent horrified. The odds against me surviving even a couple of weeks under his plan were so slender I would have been better off walking down Chui Prospekt and jumping off the top of the Tsum shopping mall. Painful, but at least quick.

Finally, Tynaliev screwed up the empty cigarette pack and threw it over his shoulder, not caring where it landed as long as it was nowhere near him. Probably the same attitude he had towards me.

'Well. What do you think?' he asked.

'Frankly?' I said.

Tynaliev nodded.

'It would be easier to shoot me now, save some time and a lot of money.'

'That's not the answer I want, Inspector,' he said. 'And . . .'

'And it's not as if I have a choice,' I said, finishing his sentence. 'Because you have the evidence that links me to the death of that paedo, Morton Graves.'

'The murder of that wealthy, foreign, well-connected businessman, Morton Graves,' Tynaliev corrected.

'And if I don't do what you want . . .'

Tynaliev nodded, gave another of his wolfish smiles.

'Exactly,' he said. 'I'll see Penitentiary One has a special welcoming committee for you.'

Tynaliev then surprised me by standing up and extending his hand towards me. I took it, felt my bones squeeze together under his grip. Middle-age and a desk hadn't softened him any. They hadn't softened his attitude either.

'Look at it this way,' he said. 'You're a widower, and no woman is going to take on an obvious candidate for a burial shroud. You get laid only when your Uzbek lady friend – probably an enemy of the Kyrgyz people, in case it had escaped your notice – decides she wants a quickie and can't be bothered to find a real man. You live in a shitty apartment, you've got no friends, you're broke. What have you got to live for that's so special?'

Tynaliev let go of my hand and cracked his knuckles, the sound oddly loud in the room. I wondered how they would sound against my face.

'This way, you have a bit of fun, spend some money, maybe even come back in one piece,' he continued. 'What's a career in Bishkek Murder Squad compared to that?'

I could only nod my agreement, but couldn't help wondering what Saltanat would make of my latest capitulation, for that was how she would see it.

'Let's head back into town,' Tynaliev said. 'Time you loosened up, moved on from mourning your wife. You should go and eat, even have a few drinks. I'll introduce you to some very entertaining girls, if you like. Even you can't live like a monk for ever.'

Eat, drink and fuck, I thought, for tomorrow I turn into fertiliser. It seemed a pathetic ending to a life where I'd at least tried to make a difference, to help the dead find some sort of peace in their graves, brought those responsible to justice, however flawed.

'I'll skip the party,' I said, gestured towards the door. 'But I would prefer not to ride back in the shit wagon with those three clowns.'

I could sense the *ment* by the door stiffen with anger, but there was nothing he could do about my insult, not in front of the minister. Tynaliev nodded and gestured towards the door.

'Sir's limousine awaits,' he said, his face deadpan. I wondered if he had a sense of humour after all. Maybe it only crawled from under a rock once every ten years.

At the door, the *ment* held up his hand, wanting us to wait while he checked everything was clear outside. After a few seconds, he was back, a puzzled look on his face.

'Strange. No sign of the officers. At least one of them should have been outside the door at all times.'

Almost before the words had left his mouth, he yawned. One of those cavernous gaping affairs that suggest you haven't slept for a week, or you're monumentally bored. Or at least, for a second or so, it looked like a yawn. Then a noise like an unexpected cough was followed by a thick crimson rope that belched out of his throat and across the doorframe.

I was first to react to the *ment* having been shot: I pushed Tynaliev hard against the wall, out of sight of the windows.

The wounded policeman lay sprawled at my feet, his jaw hanging by his ear, torn away by the impact of the bullet. His left heel drummed a relentless tattoo against the floor, his chest snatching at the air in a vain effort to breathe, as the blood pumped out of his neck and the light faded in his eyes.

'An ambush?' Tynaliev said, more to himself than to me.

'Well, it's not a group of walkers on a nature tour, looking for rare tulips,' I snarled, trying to focus beyond the shock and horror of the man dying at my feet. 'Who knew you were going to be here, without your usual protection squad?'

Tynaliev shook his head, shock already replaced by a look of calculation.

'No one that counts,' he said. 'No one who could organise something like this.'

'Only one answer then,' I said, and pointed down at the body. 'He knew, sold you out, arranged for a team to be waiting here.'

Tynaliev considered that for a moment, reluctantly nodded. He aimed a kick at the man's stomach, careful not to get blood on his shoes, then gathered up phlegm and spat on the broken face. The thud of shoe leather against dead meat made me want to retch, but I knew there was no time for indulgences. I took the man's Makarov from its holster, trying not to get his blood on my fingers, only partly succeeding.

'We've only got a few seconds, Minister,' I said, pulling him away from the body. 'Is there another way out of here?'

'How the fuck would I know?' Tynaliev said, anger raising his voice. 'My team work out such things. I have more important things to do.'

It might have been unimportant to you once, I thought, but it could be a lifesaver now, and not just his life but mine as well.

I pointed at the gun on his hip, a Makarov like the one in my hand.

'You can use that?' I asked.

I saw a fleeting glimpse of uncertainty on Tynaliev's face, as he wondered if I was part of a team sent to kill him. Then his jaw set in the suppressed rage that had terrified so many people in the Sverdlovsky basement. If he was about to die, he was determined he wouldn't be the only one.

'It's been a while,' Tynaliev said, 'but you don't forget how to point and pull a trigger.'

'Maybe it's not you they're trying to kill,' I suggested. 'After all, I was the one they think shot the *pakhan*, not you. Maybe I'm the target.'

'Does it matter?' Tynaliev shrugged. 'You ever hear of the Circle of Brothers leaving any witnesses alive?'

I nodded; our home-grown mobsters make the Italian Mafia look like teenagers celebrating the end of the school year. We had no way of knowing how many men we were up against, or where they were. Perhaps on the slopes on either side of the hotel, hidden in the treeline, or maybe across the road, crouching beneath the vehicles we came in. There was only one way to find out.

'You're parked nearby?' I asked. 'And you've got the keys?'

Tynaliev shook his head, pointed down at the body. I fumbled through the dead man's pockets. Keys in hand, I stood up, edged towards the open door. I could already feel cross-hairs on my forehead.

'When I say "Run", move as fast as you can. And keep behind me.'

'You want to shield me?' Tynaliev asked. 'Why? You're not my bodyguard. You're not even police any more.'

I shrugged. Old habits die hard, I guess, and this was one where I might also die quickly.

'Don't argue,' I said, and took a couple of deep breaths.

We burst out of the doorway like Olympic sprinters, albeit elderly, slow and overweight ones. I was waiting for the bullets to punch holes into me, but we reached the Mercedes parked nearby without a shot being fired.

The car sat heavily on its tyres, thanks to the armour-plating and bulletproof glass Tynaliev would have insisted upon. Once we were inside, we would be safe from anything less than a bazooka. I pressed the button on the key fob, heard the locks retract. A second button started the engine. We were crouching on the passenger side, but I figured a crawl across the leather seats would beat standing up and running around.

The world takes on a peculiar clarity at such moments, a sense that the regular rules of time and motion have been displaced, replaced by something altogether more vivid and disturbing. Birds are suspended in mid-air, leaves hang as they fall to the ground, the branches of the trees are caught in a perpetual wind that never varies. You could almost see the bullets on their way to take your life, have time to sidestep them and watch them smash harmlessly into the ground.

All nonsense, of course, but imminent and painful death has a way of clearing out irrelevant thoughts. I waited but only silence came from the treeline. Whoever had fired the sniper shot was probably long gone, with no possibility of pursuit. I heard a car further down the track, looked to see a police car careering towards us, bouncing from side to side as it smashed over the potholes in the road. Presumably, Tynaliev or someone had triggered an alarm system that brought a high-speed rescue.

It was time.

'Stand up,' I said to Tynaliev, gesturing with the gun. As he started to rise, I pulled at his collar, dragged him off-balance, and with a sidestep and a twist, I was behind him, one arm around his throat, my gun at the side of his head.

'What the fuck?' he snarled, trying to get out of my grasp, but I simply tightened my grip.

'Sorry, Minister,' I said. 'We've been through so much together. But, well . . . orders are orders, as I'm sure you're the first to appreciate. After all, you're the one who gave them to me.'

I fired a shot into the air at random, felt the mechanism jam, snatched Tynaliev's gun from his hand to make sure I wasn't unarmed.

I let go of him, pushed him forward so he stumbled, regained his balance. I dived across the passenger seat, pulled myself forward by the steering wheel, found the pedals with my feet. I started to move out, but not before following the orders I'd been given.

And shooting the Minister for State Security twice in the back.

Chapter 8

I didn't wait to watch Tynaliev dying, or for the police to start shooting. Instead, I took the road back to the city as if I were escaping a tornado or an earthquake. If a *babushka* had been crossing the road as I sped through the nearby villages, there would have been one more tombstone in the local cemetery the next day. But I reached the outskirts of Bishkek and slowed down without adding to the day's casualties.

My heart pounded, tearing itself out by its roots in my chest, panic tight around my throat, as if I were about to be garrotted. I couldn't go back to my apartment: it would already be ringed with snipers, and a *Spetsnaz* team waiting to take me down with maximum commitment. Which would mean doubling my body weight with all the bullets they'd pump into me. I was fucked, not for the first time, but never this comprehensively before.

The only thing to do, apart from going home to commit suicide by sniper, was to stick to my original plan and head for the Kulturny. I dumped the car with the doors unlocked and the keys in the ignition. It was going to be somebody's lucky day, at least until they were stopped and discovered they were driving a stolen car involved in a murder. Their day would go downhill very fast after that.

I didn't expect a warm welcome, and I wasn't disappointed. Once I'd got through the steel door and the inept frisking by the duty thug, I walked down the stairs through the delicate aroma of piss, cheap beer and *pelmini* dumplings. Still thinking I was police, the thug hadn't tried to take Tynaliev's Makarov, a dead weight tucked into my belt at the back, pressing into my kidneys. It's never been a good idea to go into the Kulturny looking as if you're unarmed.

The torn poster on the wall showing a dead-eyed, drug-ravaged teenage girl was still there, with the headline, BEFORE KROKODIL, I HAD A DAUGHTER. NOW, I HAVE A PROSTITUTE. Someone had added a mobile phone number, followed by ONLY $10 FULL SERVICE. Good to know the spirit of enterprise was alive and well, if not free. I tore off the phone number, screwed it up, threw it to join the rest of the rubbish on the floor. Sometimes, small things are all you can do to try to improve the world.

I didn't recognise any of the faces clustered at the bar; the informants I'd known in the past were either dead or behind quite another sort of bars. I could still pass for police, unless the word was already out I was now not just little people but a wanted *prestupnik* into the bargain.

I walked to the bar, my feet sticking to the beer-sodden floor, waved the barman over. He was new since my last visit, which was probably just as well. But he could recognise what I was, even if not by name, and his attitude announced he didn't like law in any form.

'*Privyet, kak dela?*' I asked, smiling as if looking for a new best friend.

The barman said nothing, giving me his hardest stare, the one that said, 'If you weren't law, there's a baseball bat under the counter just waiting to kiss you.' I didn't give a fuck about that, and he quickly knew it, because he set about wiping a dirty glass which he placed in front of me.

'*Nyet*,' I said, shaking my head to the unspoken question. He raised an eyebrow, shrugged, pushed the glass to one side.

'I'm looking for someone.'

'So join a dating agency,' he muttered.

'You want to join one?' I asked. 'How about smashedup-face.kg or kickinballs.com? They work for you?'

He tried for a snappy comeback, decided it wasn't worth the grief.

'A lot of people come in here,' he said, turning the dirty glass in front of me upside down. 'Maybe whoever you're looking for doesn't come here.'

'The clientele too upmarket, you think?' I asked, pointing at two elderly *prostis* in the corner, at a table of *alkashi* so far from reality they thought they were sipping champagne in the Hyatt Regency.

'If they can pay, they can drink here,' he said. 'This is a free country, last time I looked.'

You didn't look very hard or very long, I thought, but then, who does? It pays not to rock the boat. I wondered what the probable penalty would be for killing a state minister. I imagined it would depend on whether he was in favour or not.

'Like I said before, I'm looking for someone.'

'And I can help how, exactly?'

I didn't like his tone. I didn't like the baseball bat under the counter. So I used one hand to seize his shirt and pull him over the bar. He fumbled for the bat, and I shook a finger in his face, scarily close to his eyeball.

'We seem to have got off to a bad start,' I said, my voice quiet and calm, the way I used it to scare suspects into a confession. 'I suggest we start again.'

I looked around the bar; no one seemed to have noticed our little disagreement. But then, when you're in the Kulturny, someone else's business is definitely none of yours. Interfere and a world of pain lies in wait.

'Whatever you say, officer.'

The staff at the Kulturny learn to recognise the look of law very early on. I pushed him back, gave his cheek a condescending little pat.

'That's much better,' I said, giving him the Sverdlovsky basement smile. 'Now, my colleagues needn't check everything's legal and above board here. No bottles without tax labels, no smuggled cigarettes, no working girls, that sort of thing. Everything's peaceful, everyone's happy.'

I checked out the *alkashi* quietly working their way through a bottle of the very cheapest stuff. Petrol is less lethal, and probably tastes better. I jerked my thumb in their direction, nodded at the barman.

'Give them another. On my bill.'

We both knew there would be no bill, but it's always good

to keep an audience sweet, or in this case, oblivious to the world around them.

'I'm looking for Kanybek Aliyev,' I said.

The barman flinched, looked around in case someone was keeping an ear cocked at our conversation.

'That's not a very good name to drop around here,' he said. 'Some people like to keep themselves to themselves.'

'And some people like to keep themselves in one piece,' I said. 'Preferably not sharing a cell with people who don't appreciate a loose tongue.'

I could smell fear coming off the barman, the way a ripe cheese or rotting meat starts to stink.

'You're afraid of him. I understand that,' I said, 'but he's not here, I am. And you'd do well to be afraid of me too.'

I pushed myself away from the bar, made for the door.

'I'll be back in a couple of hours. Make a quiet phone call, suggest a meet. It's to everyone's advantage. Especially yours.'

And with that, I headed towards the stairs, wondering how to stay out of trouble for the next two hours.

I walked up to the Russian Embassy on Manas Avenue, found a seat in Sierra, the expensive coffee shop next door. I figured the last place people could find me would be sipping cappuccino, nibbling at a slice of over-moist, overpriced cherry tart. Being so close to the embassy might even be a bonus; not that I could seek asylum, but the embassy guards might deter manic gunplay.

The coffee shop was packed with smartly dressed customers all staring at their expensive smartphones or even more expensive laptops, a world away from my usual existence. Perhaps the corruption and vice and murder I dealt with on a daily basis took place on another planet in a distant galaxy, where 'hit me again' didn't mean add another shot of espresso. But it wasn't a world where I could ever belong. The dead have too much claim on my time, and they don't carry laptops.

The coffee did nothing to steady my nerves, and I relived the moment when Tynaliev's bodyguard died at my feet, the stink of his death still fresh in my nostrils. You should never get used to it, even as a Murder Squad inspector; if you do, then it's time to look for a new career. In an abattoir perhaps.

Finally, I couldn't bear the waiting any longer, flagged down one of the taxis waiting outside, and headed for Time Out, a restaurant on Togolok Moldo, two or three minutes' walk from the Kulturny. He wasn't pleased at the short ride, but then there's never any pleasing Bishkek taxi drivers. A short fare and they grumble about leaving their favoured spot; a long journey and they complain about not getting a fare back. Every few months, a taxi driver is found dead at the wheel, shot or stabbed or strangled. I'm only surprised it's not every week.

Outside the restaurant, we went through the ritual haggle about the fare. As he drove away in a gust of bad-tempered blue-black exhaust smoke, I made the call.

'*Da?*'

I recognised the barman's voice, unwelcoming as ever.

'*Tovarich*,' I said, keeping my voice neutral. He knew who was calling, because I heard the phone clatter onto the bar, listened to the buzz of gibberish and swearing they call conversation in the Kulturny. After a moment, a new voice came on the line.

'You want to speak to someone?'

'To meet someone,' I said. 'Not the same thing.'

I'd expected the voice of a thug, foul-mouthed, barely articulate, hoarse from a hundred cigarettes and a daily bottle of vodka. Instead, I heard the calm, soothing tones of a late-night radio host or a therapist advising his patients to relax and consider their problems from a new perspective. The voice told me I was up against someone considerably more intelligent and dangerous than I'd hoped for.

'A philosopher, I see. A mind capable of making distinctions. Not one of the usual Kulturny clientele. Most of them can't distinguish between reality and delirium tremens.' He paused. 'Of course, that is reality for some of them.'

'I want to meet Aliyev. Alone,' I said. No humour in my voice.

'So do a lot of people. A popular fellow, Mr Aliyev.'

'I'll be outside the Derevyashka bar in seven minutes. I'll wait for three.'

'I'd love to oblige, but without an introduction, I'm sure you understand the difficulties. Problems of security, timing. Impossible.'

'Tell him Akyl Borubaev will be waiting for him,' I said, adding a little menace to my voice.

'The Murder Squad inspector?' The mocking tone was gone.

'Your seven minutes starts now, don't waste it,' I said, and broke the connection.

It's only a couple of minutes' walk from Time Out, and one advantage of choosing Derevyashka as a meeting place is that it stands to one side of a small park with a few sparsely spread out trees and bushes, a single road running past the one entrance. A statue of the writer Maxim Gorky, wearing a moustache whose bushiness would have made Stalin jealous, looks down on the proceedings with an air of indifference. Perhaps he knows better than to get involved.

I've always believed the notion that events fundamentally change who we are is too simplistic. Yes, we're not the same person at forty as we were at fifteen, but to say that experience alone is responsible doesn't accept that we might have 'progress' built into us. We might not want children when we're teenagers, yet crave them in our thirties; change is our only constant.

Shooting Tynaliev may not have been my smartest idea, but we reach our own conclusions about morality and codes of ethics without realising it, until circumstances call upon us to act on them. And it would be that morality and code of ethics that would determine how I dealt with the Circle of Brothers mafia, their stranglehold over organised crime, the Bishkek police, anyone else with an interest in seeing me dead.

It would be impossible for Aliyev to arrange an ambush in such a short time, just as hard for his men to appear without my spotting them first. It may not have put the odds in my favour, but at least it wasn't an attempt at suicide on my part.

I lit a cigarette, swore yet again to quit, leant against a wall hoping to look like someone waiting for his blind date to show. I'd been there nine minutes, having smoked my way down to burnt fingers, and was ready to leave, call and make another assignation, when Aliyev appeared at the far end of the park. I'd read his file at the station, remembered his photograph, taken through a car window as he entered a smart restaurant, bodyguards beside, before and behind him. He'd taken a detour, away from the direct route from the Kulturny, and I gave him extra points for caution.

He wasn't a blind date exactly; his eyesight was fine. But he walked with a limp, his left leg doing a drag and a twist with each step, as if caught in a net. He used a thin black cane to support his weak side, and I wondered how he'd managed to gain the top seat in the Circle of Brothers. Brains, I decided, uncertain whether they were a good or a very bad thing as far as I was concerned.

As he approached Derevyashka, he'd spotted me, made me as law. But I admired the way he walked past, not giving me a second glance. Just a middle-aged cripple out for a couple of beers, a bowl of *pelmini* soup, and a 'whatever happened to' chat with the regulars.

I waited until he'd pushed the door open, then followed him inside.

Chapter 9

Derevyashka means 'wood', and when you see the place, you understand why. Imagine a mad Siberian's attempt at building a log cabin, designed under the influence of some particularly potent vodka laced with magic mushrooms. Aliyev had taken one of the tables furthest from the door, facing the room, close enough to the exit into the beer garden to provide an escape route if it all turned tits up. I sat down opposite him, slid my gun onto my lap, gave a barely perceptible nod. Seeing him close up, he seemed fragile, insubstantial. Most of the Circle of Brothers crew I'd encountered over the years had been big guys, fists like boulders, bellies like barrels, hair shaved down to stubble, prison tattoos staining mottled flesh as a testament to their crimes. I'd obviously been dealing with the lower orders.

I ordered coffee, Aliyev asked for green tea. For once, the service was immediate, and I didn't think it was because of my presence. We sat in silence until the drinks arrived, which gave me the chance to inspect him more closely. Obviously Russian by family, which made his position at the top of the tree even more unusual. Once Kyrgyzstan got its independence, a lot of Russians decided there'd be better pickings back in Moscow or St Petersburg or Novosibirsk. And since crime, just as much as nature, abhors a vacuum, the local element quickly rose to the top, did their best to make sure they stayed there.

Aliyev's eyes were the washed-out blue you see in the sky above the mountains, on those clear sun-blasted autumn days that feel brittle and fragile, ready to snap at the slightest movement. The lobe of his left ear was missing, possibly a punishment cutting from his youth, but he wore his hair swept back, making no attempt to hide the missing flesh. Strong jaw, clean-shaven, no surplus fat on his face. A mouth as thin and brutal as a carp, elderly and cunning.

His hands were heavily veined, the nails trimmed back, with long thin fingers that looked as if they would be equally at home chalking algebra equations on a blackboard or tightening around a rival's throat. He could have been any age between forty and sixty, and it was clear he hadn't stayed alive this long by being stupid. I didn't know what he could tell about me; not even my mirror tells the whole truth of who I am. But he didn't blink, look away, or drop his eyes. He had the gaze of a surgeon or a psychopath, impossible to read.

My coffee was watery, bitter, and Aliyev's tea didn't look any more appetising. I didn't add sugar, didn't want him to think I couldn't take whatever was served to me.

Finally, he spoke.

'Maksat Aydaraliev.'

I nodded, showing I knew the name, admitting nothing more. The *pakhan*, the boss Saltanat and her colleagues had gunned down and dumped in the snowdrifts outside the Kulturny that dark freezing night.

'I believe it's you I have to thank for his unfortunate demise, Inspector,' he said, his voice as free of emotion as if he were reciting the Trans-Siberian Railway timetable. I raised an eyebrow, to suggest I had no idea what he was talking about. He gave a sardonic smile at my reaction, bluff and counter-bluff.

'No need to be coy, Inspector, we're all friends here.'

His eyes moved left, and I followed his glance to an SUV parking a little way down Ryskulov. I couldn't see through the tinted windows, but I was willing to bet it wasn't some high-society matron taking her poodle for a ride.

'You'll notice I'm keeping my hands on the table. All my cards as well,' he said, 'but you clearly don't trust me enough to put your gun away.' He cocked his head to one side, raised an eyebrow.

I shrugged, nodded, left my gun where it was. Men like Aliyev will apologise for ripping your head off even while they're pissing down your throat. It comes with the territory.

'Thank me for what?' I asked.

'You took care of Maksat Aydaraliev, didn't you?'

I shook my head, but I knew he didn't believe me. Someone had killed the old *pakhan*, and it made sense to decide I was the one responsible.

'You know about the alpha male in the pack, Inspector? Lions, wolves, whatever. When the alpha male gets old, starts to weaken, he can't lead the pack as well as he once did. He stands in the way, so the pack dispose of him, to ensure their survival. He's removed for the continuance of the pack, the tribe, the gang.'

Aliyev took a sip of his tea, savoured the aroma.

'With humans, the ways that once served Maksat became old-fashioned, last-century, not fit for today. He was a survivor, tough, until it was time for him to move on, for a new face, new ideas, to take over, lead the way ahead.'

'Goodbye, Maksat, hello, Kanybek?' I asked, injecting a little sarcasm into my voice.

'Maksat believed in the old ways; the fist, the boot, the bullet. Lead or gold, *da*? Fine for those days, when you could see your enemy face to face. You remember his right hand? Broken in twenty-eight places by your colleagues, he used to say, and his fingernails torn out. Down in that basement no one ever talks about. That was the world then. Do it to me and I do it to you, twice.'

He paused, inspected his own fingers. Nothing broken or mutilated, nothing old-school about him. Yet.

'But now your enemy might be anywhere in the world,' Aliyev continued. 'Nothing but an email address, a Facebook photo, a warning sent as a text message. What good are muscles and Makarovs then?'

He sat back in his chair, sipped at his green tea.

'New times, new ways, Inspector. You either move with history or you are history. Which are you, I wonder?'

'It's my history I'm planning to change, now I'm no longer Murder Squad, not even a lowly uniformed *ment*. That's why I wanted to meet you,' I said, then fell silent and stared over his shoulder, weighing up the situation. A couple of tables away, four elderly men wearing ill-fitting suit jackets and felt *kalpak* hats were working their way through a bottle of vodka and a plate of pickled gherkins. Two of the waitresses were texting their friends as if the only way they could ever communicate was via their fingertips. An Asian woman carrying a large shopping bag was making her way to the toilets at the back. No one was paying us any attention, just two more middle-aged men with time on their hands and no particular place to go.

'A pity. You'd have been useful to me on the inside, pissing out of the yurt, not into it, opening your beak to sing to me, me feeding you scraps in return. But now . . .'

Aliyev shrugged, held his hands wide in one of those 'what can I do' gestures.

'You've terminated your employment in the police force almost as quickly as you terminated the Minister for State Security.'

I did my best to appear surprised he already knew about that afternoon's events, but he merely smiled.

'I heard about you shooting Tynaliev before the sound of your shots had stopped echoing from the mountains,' he said. 'Did you really think I'd have agreed to meet you otherwise?'

'So why did you agree?' I asked, knowing my chance to implement my plan depended on his reply.

Aliyev said nothing for a moment, dropped a couple of sugar cubes into his tea, stirred then sipped. For a couple of seconds he looked oddly melancholy, as if his life was also dissolving into nothingness.

'Why do people want to join my organisation?' he asked.

I shrugged, rubbed my thumb against my first two fingers, the universal sign for cash.

'You're right, of course,' he said, 'although only up to a point. I've no use for people only looking to make enough money to get laid or stoned or drunk. Any street robber can do that. I look for certain qualities in a man, to ensure he'll be a smooth-turning cog, working for the good of the whole machine.'

Qualities wasn't exactly the word I'd choose for people prepared to rob, rape, murder; men willing to take out an entire three generations of a rival's family to avenge a perceived slight or a business deal gone sour. It takes a certain determination to walk up to a man you've never met and fire two shots into his head. But it's also barbaric, a sign our species hasn't progressed much, if at all.

I've killed people, usually when they were trying to kill me. Sometimes I see their faces as I turn a corner, or see a reflection in a shop window. They don't disturb me: I know why they died – them or me – and I believe they deserved no better. It's at night when victims visit me, their open staring eyes asking why I haven't solved their murder or brought them justice yet. They are the ones who haunt me, the ones I've failed, the ones who remind me I have to do better.

Aliyev tapped on the table. I shook myself out of my reverie and stared back at him.

'Of course, it's easy to find people to do the muscle work, the threatening, and, sometimes, the finishing, the wet work,' Aliyev continued, 'but they don't use what little brains they have. They can't even spell initiative, let alone use it. Then there are the ones who see themselves as criminal masterminds, future *pakhans*. But they generally have no spine, no balls when it comes to pulling the trigger, putting death through a man's eyeball or slashing a throat to stain a white shirt red.'

'Maybe you need a better recruitment agency?'

Aliyev gave a dry smile to show he appreciated the joke.

'You're a man of action, but you temper it with thought. You're honest, but not too honest. And you're looking for a job, right?'

I nodded. 'I thought you might help me get out of the country, and fast. After all, you wouldn't be sitting at the top of the table if Maksat Aydaraliev was still around, pulling out fingernails and counting out banknotes. So you owe me.'

Aliyev nodded, his gaze never leaving mine.

'You're right, I owe you. But the thing is,' and he dropped another sugar lump into his tea, watching the ripple hit the edge of the cup, 'I also own you.'

He smiled at my puzzled look.

'Can you imagine how many favours I'll be able to call on if I hand over the man who gunned down the Minister of State Security? That's worth twenty million *som* in the bank. It's just a question of deciding if you can be more useful to me than all those get-out-of-jail-free cards.'

'Not much use to you if I shoot your balls off while you're deciding what to do,' I said, rapped the underside of the table to prove my point.

'You could do, but you won't, because it doesn't benefit you to do so. Brains trump action.'

'On this occasion,' I said, nodding at the strength of his logic. I looked around the bar, wondering how it was my life had become thrown into such disarray. The vodka-drinking men had finished their bottle and were trying to catch the attention of the waitresses, who remained resolutely immersed in the digital world. The Asian woman was making her way towards the door, obviously unwilling to spend any more time in the bar than she had to. In her haste, she'd forgotten her shopping, and I wondered if she'd realise her mistake before walking outside.

'So?' he said, leaning forward. 'What's your answer? Job or jail?'

I opened my mouth to speak, but he never heard my reply.

Because that was when the bomb went off.

Chapter 10

An irresistible hand lifted me up and threw me backwards, bringing the table down on top of me. The windows behind me turned to sheets of ice that fractured and split, throwing diamond sparkles high into the air. Someone had poured hot wax into my ears, then punched both sides of my head; all I could hear was a distant bellowing, as if someone on the other side of the park was shrieking nonsense through a bullhorn. I put my hand to my thigh, found it wet, wondered if I'd been shot, put my fingers to my lips, tasted tea.

I scrabbled on the floor for my gun, found it where I'd dropped it, the weight reassuring in my hand. I cocked the hammer, ready for whatever would come next. Aliyev was sprawled against a pillar, the same one that had spared me a lot of the blast. He hadn't been so lucky. His forehead had been ripped open, probably by a wooden splinter, and his face wore a scarlet mask. His eyes were swollen and bruised, his pupils dilated with shock. He mouthed something at me, but I couldn't hear anything above the bells tolling endlessly in my head.

I looked around at the wreckage, hoping to catch sight of the bomber, saw a woman's coat on the ground, shredded and part covering what had once been a body and was now a butchered carcass. Either she'd intended a suicide bombing, or her willingness to die had failed her at the last minute and she'd triggered the timer too early to make a clean escape. Either way, she wouldn't be answering any questions down the station.

Over by the bar, next to the till, one of the pretty waitresses was trying to glue her face back onto her skull, while her friend did her best to comfort her, saying over and over again it was just a scratch, nothing serious. I couldn't hear the words, but I recognise the comfort of lies all too easily.

We had to leave before the police and ambulances arrived. They would certainly know Aliyev's face, and every officer would have seen my ID photo, labelled 'SHOOT ON SIGHT'. I hauled Aliyev to his feet, using my sleeve to wipe away the worst of the blood on his face, and together we crunched our way over shards of glass and spears of wood, stumbled through the devastated bar and out onto the street. The air was full of the stink of smoke, burnt wood, half-cooked flesh.

Aliyev's bodyguards were running towards their boss, fifty metres too far away, sixty seconds too late. The leading two pushed me aside, took Aliyev's arms and half-dragged, half-carried him towards the car already moving towards us. The third man grabbed my arm and collar, propelled me towards the SUV. I was thrown into the back seat, then we were racing at speed down Togolok Moldo, past the football stadium, towards Jibek Jolu.

We crashed through the red light, turned right, ignoring

the cars around us that slid to a halt or slammed into each other. A car as expensive as this one, driven like this, means only one thing to the average Kyrgyz motorist; these are people you don't want to get involved with or you might end up with something far worse than a dented bumper.

Aliyev was starting to come round out of the shock. The wound on his forehead screwed his face into a grimace of pain. The nearest bodyguard held a cloth to his boss's forehead, doing his best to stop the blood pouring down over his cheeks. But scalp wounds are messy, with so many blood vessels close to the surface of the skin. You end up bleeding like a slaughtered goat, with the wound looking far worse than it actually is. Aliyev would be able to boast a striking scar, would probably use it to bolster his reputation as a *pakhan* that took no shit from anyone.

I could tell the bodyguards were uncertain about me; they knew I was law, but they'd also just seen me rescue their *pakhan*. Time to hold back in case I was important, until Aliyev recovered enough to give them orders. I wondered about pulling the door open, rolling out and taking my chances in traffic. But we were going way too fast for that, and any attempt to get away would look like a confession to having been party to the bombing. My hearing was starting to return, and I could make out the driver asking where to go. Aliyev was barely conscious, so it was time I took control, to prevent my being pulled out of the car at the roadside and taking two shots to the head.

'Tokmok,' I ordered, as if no other choice was sensible or

safe. The driver turned around, as if to question my destination, stared at me, nodded, put his foot to the metal. I realised I was still holding the Makarov. Sometimes even a simple command needs a little extra encouragement. And Tokmok was seventy kilometres away, which gave me some breathing space to think and plan.

By now, we were on the outskirts of the city, and I gestured to the driver to slow down. He saw my signal in the rear-view mirror, lifted his foot a little off the accelerator. There was no point in getting stopped by an officious traffic cop looking to earn a little lunch money. The guys in the car weren't the sharpest knives in the box, and they would be worried, suspicious, ready to shoot it out with anyone who stopped them, especially if they wore a uniform. There had been enough violent death for one day, and I didn't intend becoming an addition to the total.

'Where are we taking the boss?' the biggest thug asked. I looked at his tattooed knuckles, at the weight of his fists, wished I had an answer.

'The safe house, of course,' I improvised. The network of the Circle of Brothers stretches all the way across central Asia and Russia, and when you're shipping industrial-sized amounts of heroin around the region, it pays to have several choices for storage and somewhere to hide. Tokmok was far enough out of the city to serve as a bolthole in time of trouble, but not so far away someone might get ideas about usurping the throne.

'What about a doctor?' he added, gesturing at Aliyev, who

groaned and closed his eyes. 'Someone to stitch his head, check for brain damage?'

'You don't have a tame *doktor sharlatanov*?' I asked, fake incredulity flooding my voice. 'I thought this was a serious outfit.'

'The boss will know someone,' he said, scowling at my insult.

'And he's in a fit state to tell us?' I asked. 'Don't bother both your brain cells, you don't want to wear them out, I'll sort something.'

Tokmok doesn't have a lot to recommend itself to a visiting tourist. Once you've seen the town's main attraction, a Soviet Ilyushin bomber perched on a pedestal as if in the throes of take-off, all that's left is the usual collection of drab shops selling fruit or vegetables as a sideline to shifting bottles of vodka to a dour population. We drove around until I spotted an *apteka*, a pharmacy whose windows were as heavily barred as the State Treasury. The sullen woman inside directed us to a doctor's house a couple of streets away, off the main road to Issyk-Kul.

The bodyguards helped Aliyev into the shabby waiting room stocked with mismatched chairs, while I explained to the doctor that our friend had been in a car crash and needed stitches. Judging by his wary gaze and clear nervousness, I could tell he didn't believe me, but when I showed him the Makarov, he quickly remembered his Hippocratic Oath.

Twenty stitches later, Aliyev's forehead looked like a badly sewn curtain, but the bleeding had stopped. I persuaded the doctor to forget we'd ever been there, and he couldn't have been more eager to do just that. He didn't forget to take a fistful of notes for his time and trouble though; doctors are the same wherever you go.

After a couple of hours, Aliyev began to regain some semblance of his old self, even managed to tell the driver where to find the safe house, an hour or so further on, just as the lake appeared over on our right.

Lake Issyk-Kul doesn't reveal itself all at once, with the kind of boastful drama you might expect from the world's second-largest mountain lake. Like the Kyrgyz people, the lake first appears with an abashed reticence, looking like nothing so much as a marshy puddle, before expanding to fill the gap between two sets of snow-capped mountains. The water is clear, placid, never freezing even in the most brutal winter, while the mountains on the horizon remain impassive, indifferent, unconcerned. It's a landscape, or rather, a lakescape, that reveals us as the small and insignificant creatures we really are. And it was to this place of austerity and beauty we came to hide and plot, perhaps even to die.

Chapter 11

The safe house was tucked away at the end of an unmarked track leading away from the town of Cholpon-Ata and up towards the mountains. We had to drive halfway along an abandoned airport runway, avoiding the worst of the potholes. Weary-looking bushes pushed through the broken asphalt, then regretted their decision. On either side, decaying buildings showed the punishment two decades of Kyrgyz winter had inflicted. I had the feeling I'd fallen into one of those movies set in a post-nuclear world, where men revert to animals and gangs roam abandoned cities looking for prey. Knowing I was travelling with a gang not so very different didn't make me feel any more comfortable.

After five bone-shaking minutes, during which I'd repeatedly slammed my head against the car roof, we pulled up outside a dilapidated single-storey farmhouse, the once-whitewashed walls grey with dust and the window panes cracked and repaired with tape.

'There's no place like home,' I said, and this certainly didn't look like any home I'd want to stay in.

'You were expecting a gangster villa, Inspector?' Aliyev asked. 'A luxury pool with bikini-clad silicone beauties sipping cocktails and eating Beluga caviar?'

I shook my head; I knew Aliyev was too clever to fall for all the usual trappings of criminal success, the ones that shrieked 'Arrest me!' to any policeman who wasn't dipping his beak in the pot. Even so, the farmhouse seemed too primitive for anything but the most basic peasant existence.

The car parked, we clambered out and one man handed Aliyev a new cane. Perhaps when you live the life of a *pakhan*, you need a constant supply. I watched as one of the bodyguards unscrewed the number plates, took new ones from under the driver's seat, attached them with a speed that suggested much practice. Aliyev didn't believe in taking the chance of a random police patrol spotting them and calling in a specialist team of snipers.

'I think I'd better have your gun, Inspector, don't you? To avoid any confusion or uncertainty.'

I didn't see how I could disagree, simply nodded. One of the bodyguards relieved me of the Makarov; I shrugged one shoulder, as if to say my jacket sat better without the gun's weight dragging one side down. Unarmed, I knew the only option I had was to sit back, win Aliyev's trust, and work out how to explain what I wanted without getting killed in the process. Simple.

'We're going to stay here? In this shithole?' I asked, and the incredulity in my voice wasn't entirely faked. It might have been safer than the Hyatt Regency in the centre of Bishkek, but it was also a hell of a lot less comfortable.

'Just for a couple of days,' he assured me, leading the way towards the front door. 'Just until we can assess the situation properly, decide what steps to take.'

That sounded like a roundabout way of saying 'retaliate in blood', but I nodded as if I agreed. The driver pulled open the farmhouse door, hinges squealing like a village pig being slaughtered, and Aliyev gestured for me to enter. I felt the hair on my neck prickle; it was one of those moments when it's very easy to put a bullet into the base of someone's skull, smashing through the spinal column and creating instant death. But I didn't have a choice, so I stepped over the threshold.

The inside of the farmhouse lived up to my expectations. It was clear no one had lived there since the collapse of the Soviet Union, perhaps even earlier. The place stank of urine, damp earth and rotting food. Two stained mattresses lay on the floor, not far from an overturned stove. The room looked as if two of the local brown bears had broken in, thrown a wild party, got drunk, then had a running battle, before sleeping it off and skulking back to the nearest nature reserve.

I turned to Aliyev, catching his arm to steady him as he skidded on the grimy grease-soiled floor.

'Which mattress do you prefer?' I asked. 'And would you mind if I slept in the car?'

Aliyev didn't answer, merely gesturing to the bodyguards, who used their boots to kick one of the mattresses aside. I had to admire Aliyev's cunning; the mattress was filthy enough to stop anyone discovering the trapdoor beneath.

'I think we can do rather better than that,' he said, waving his cane. The trapdoor was lifted, to reveal a flight of steep steps leading down into a cellar. I wondered if this had originally been a vegetable or potato store; it had certainly been cleverly concealed to deter the casual searcher.

'Will you be able to manage?' I asked, looking down at the cane on which Aliyev was supporting his weight.

'This?' he said, and handed the cane to one of the bodyguards. 'I think so.'

And with that, he stepped over to the stairs, turned around, and climbed down into the darkness with a great deal more agility than I could muster.

It never hurts to have your enemies, real or potential, underestimate you, and his pretending to be lame had certainly fooled me. I made a mental note to take nothing about him for granted, followed him down the steps, towards whatever fate was lying in wait for me.

Chapter 12

The steps went down for three metres, enough to ensure this underground hideout would be soundproof. Fire a gun down there and it wouldn't be heard outside. It was likely someone had done just that, and not as an experiment.

The basement was huge, stretching far beyond the footprint of the farmhouse above. Recessed lights illuminated a plain wooden floor, with a long table and chairs at one end of the main room. A corridor at the rear led off to three bedrooms, two bathrooms, a small room stacked with guns, a well-stocked kitchen and a storeroom full of tinned food. The air smelt musty, disused, as if it had been a long time since anyone had come down here. The dust in the air tasted metallic, harsh the way silver foil feels on metal fillings. It made me think of the underground bunker in Berlin that the German High Command retreated to as the Red Army approached to end the Great Patriotic War. The place was sterile, impersonal, but like the basement at Sverdlovsky station, I sensed it had seen its share of begging, beatings and blood.

'Where does the power come from?'

'We have a concealed generator a little way away, and reserve batteries, of course.'

'You could withstand a siege here,' I said.

'The point of building this was so we wouldn't have to,' Aliyev replied. 'My predecessor, the late unlamented *pakhan*, believed in showing the world how tough he was, how he would end in a blaze of glory. He'd consider this a cowardly way to live. Well, look how he ended up. Face down in a snowdrift, his jaw shot away. Me? I prefer to stay alive. Once you're in the grave, you can't spend money, drink, eat, fuck. From the outside you wouldn't have seen anything other than a squalid and decrepit ruin. Which makes this safe.'

'But once you're down here, you're trapped. All the police or army have to do is sit up top and starve you out.'

Aliyev simply gave an enigmatic smile, so I guessed there would be a hidden exit, a tunnel with an entrance emerging a few hundred metres away. With the kind of wealth and influence he had at his disposal, digging it would have been no problem, and the workmen would be too afraid to talk. When Genghis Khan was finally buried, all the people who'd built his tomb were put to death, to ensure his body could never be found. I imagined Aliyev would have reminded everyone of that, as a precaution against loose tongues. We Kyrgyz have never been called talkative people; good money together with the threat of a painful death clamps most mouths tight shut.

I headed for the bathroom, used the chemical toilet, checked my mobile: no signal, not that I expected one, which explained why they hadn't confiscated my phone along with my gun. Back in the main room, my new friends were watching the television news, the sound turned down low.

Aliyev beckoned me over to the table, pointed to a seat. I

sat, uncomfortably aware my back was towards the body-guards. Aliyev sensed my unease and smiled as he poured out two shots of vodka, pushing one towards me.

'I'd rather have tea, if it's all the same to you,' I said. 'Vodka doesn't agree with me.'

'I'd heard you'd stopped drinking after your wife died. Strange, most men would drink more.'

'I wasn't celebrating.'

The *pakhan* thought about my comment, simply shrugged. Perhaps I'd shown him a weakness he could later exploit, or a strength he needed to know.

I wondered how much more information was in the dossier Aliyev had obviously compiled about me, or whether it was just common knowledge among the low lifes I'd dealt with in the past. Either that, or he had filled the beak of someone at Sverdlovsky station. The look on my face must have been enough for Aliyev to seize his advantage.

'I know a lot about you, Inspector. You don't hold your palm out for breakfast money, your bank balance wouldn't keep a sparrow alive, and you occasionally fuck some Uzbek tart. I don't have positive proof you killed Maksat Aydaraliev, but I know his last meeting was with you. Your old boss, the chief, the one who was "killed in a tragic accident" – I'm sure you know more about that than the newspaper stories revealed.'

Aliyev raised his glass in an ironic salute, drained it, pushed the bottle away. He obviously didn't subscribe to the trad-itional belief that once opened, a bottle had to be emptied.

'You're an intelligent man, Inspector. Resourceful. A man

of principles, but willing to have those principles bent from time to time, if the cause is worth it. Which raises a few questions in my mind.'

He cocked his head to one side and raised an eyebrow, as if debating some unusual problem, or trying to solve a difficult crossword puzzle.

'Questions I hope you can answer,' he continued, 'so I can settle any nagging doubts I might have. I'm sure you'll agree that's only reasonable.'

He steepled his hands, then pointed his forefingers at me. I was relieved he wasn't aiming a gun, but that was short-lived. Because a forearm coiled itself around my throat, forcing me back into my seat, and I felt the cold metal kiss of a gun barrel just behind my right ear.

Chapter 13

Aliyev leant forward, his gaze suddenly brutal, driven. Now I saw the strength of will that had lifted him to the heights of the Circle of Brothers.

'I'll ask you one question at a time; I wouldn't want to confuse you. But I will have the truth, you understand? Otherwise the consequences may well be fatal.'

I managed to nod my head, the arm around my throat making it hard to speak.

'To begin, who told you to lure me to Derevyashka? Who was responsible for the bomb that almost killed me?'

For a moment, thought escaped me. Panic swelled like vomit in my throat. Keeping calm and rational was my only hope of survival.

'Why would I do that?' I said. 'I was with you when the bomb went off; I could have been killed as well. Why would I risk that?'

I saw him consider what I'd said, but the arm around my neck remained as relentless as ever.

'And who says it was a bomb, anyway? They cook with gas cylinders there: an explosion, an accident, who knows?'

'You arranged the meeting. You organised the venue. Maybe

you thought it would be a simple hit, a couple of copper jackets in my head, not a bomb to wipe you out as well.'

'What would I have to gain?' I said. 'You dead, the next in line steps up to the throne, and the wheel turns just as always. Anyway, you're no use to me dead. Not with the situation I'm in.'

Aliyev gave a single low chuckle, one of those laughs without humour that tells you just how stupid he knows you are. He nodded, and the arm around my neck loosened its stranglehold.

'On the run, every cop in the land seeing your head as the route to promotion? You honestly think you're an asset, not a liability?'

I took my time fumbling for my cigarettes, ignored his frown, lit up, rocketed blue smoke towards the ceiling.

'I'd agree with you, except you don't have the full picture. You don't know why I killed Tynaliev, or how much money's at stake. More than you've ever dreamt of.'

'Suppose you tell me, as we've got time on our hands?' Aliyev said. Not a suggestion, an order.

'My tea?' I asked. 'It's a long story, and talking's a thirsty business.'

I sat back and smiled, content to wait. The longer we waited, the longer I carried on breathing.

'Zakir,' Aliyev called, and the ugliest and scariest of the bodyguards came over. Aliyev told him to make tea, and Zakir obeyed, giving me a scowl that told me he'd rather be tearing my arms off. I made certain to give him an insincere smile as he slopped my cup down in front of me, watched him stomp back to his colleagues. If the killing started, Zakir would be the first one I'd have to take out.

I sipped at my tea: no sugar, no surprise there. A boiled sock would have tasted better.

'I'm waiting, Inspector,' Aliyev said, irritation plain in his voice. 'Delayed anticipation is a much-overrated virtue.'

'You know I've done some things for Tynaliev that weren't exactly part of my official duties,' I said. 'Things that could get him into big trouble and me into a shallow grave.'

Aliyev stayed silent, gestured for me to continue.

'We were like the USA and the old USSR; we both had weapons of mutually assured destruction, even if the minister was far and away the more powerful of the two of us.'

I took another sip of tea, wondering how plausible the story I'd planned would sound.

'Tynaliev wasn't a poor man. You have to be very stupid or very honest not to make a fortune in this country if you've got contacts and influence, a power base to back you up. But you know how it is with some people. More than enough is never enough, they always need – no, want – more. Money, sex, power, whatever.'

'And the minister wanted what he didn't already have?'

'Tynaliev was a millionaire, several times over. He knew the secrets of the great and the powerful. He was a very big fish in a pretty small pond. But he wanted to be respected. By the oligarch billionaires who plundered Mother Russia. By the men in power in the Kremlin. A house off Chui Prospekt and a dacha near Talas were never going to be enough for him.'

I stubbed out my cigarette, shook the pack to make sure I had refills close to hand. I looked over at Zakir and his colleagues, huddled around a TV with the sound turned low. I lowered my voice to little more than a whisper.

'Where was his luxury London apartment near Harrods? His Upper East Side townhouse? His Malibu beach house? We might be the most landlocked country in the world, but that doesn't stop a man wanting a superyacht, complete with helicopter pad and topless blonde models lounging on the deck.'

Aliyev looked around, gave a rueful smile. Perhaps he had once craved such toys, only to find himself in a cellar miles from anywhere remotely civilised.

'He believed they would grant him the respect he craved. His vanity wouldn't let him believe that no matter how much he spent, he would never have *kulturny*; for the people he admired, he would always be that thug from some godforsaken shithole at the furthest end of the former Union.'

Aliyev threw back his vodka, reached for the glass he'd poured for me.

'You'd think he'd know better,' he said, raising the glass in a mock-toast. 'And now all his money and power are useless. Unless he's discovered a way of spending it in hell.'

He downed the vodka, wincing as the alcohol burnt his throat.

'But you still haven't told me how he planned to acquire all this immense wealth. Or why you killed him. So I think your story is only half-told, Inspector. And it's that half that's stopping me ensuring you end up like my predecessor, Maksat. On a slab waiting for Kenesh Usupov's scalpel to unpick your secrets.'

It was time to come clean. Any more dancing around and I'd waltz right into a grave. I finished my tea, cleared my throat, ready to sing.

And that was when Zakir came over, his face a curious mix of triumph and worry.

'*Pakhan*, the news on the TV? Tynaliev? The minister this *gopnik* shot? They say he's alive, seriously wounded but expected to recover, undergoing surgery with the reporters waiting outside the hospital.'

Zakir turned to me, and the hatred in his eyes was unmistakable.

'You *pizda*, you useless piece of shit, you couldn't even kill him.'

And to prove his point, he spat in my face.

Chapter 14

The warm phlegm dribbled down my cheek, thick, sticky as glue. I wiped my face with my sleeve, looked up at Zakir, gave the forgiving smile I knew he would hate. I kept my voice level, unconcerned.

'Look at my face, Zakir. Remember it, memorise every feature, every crease and wrinkle. Because it's the last face you'll see before your world goes dark. And I'll be looking down the barrel of a gun, smiling, just like now.'

Zakir raised his fists, ready to rearrange my face, but his boss held up a restraining hand.

'Go sit down,' he said. There was nothing but steel in his voice.

Zakir scowled at me, drew his forefinger across his throat, walked away. I know myself how hard it can be to follow orders, but sometimes you have no choice.

'You have a talent for pissing people off,' Aliyev said, 'and Zakir doesn't forget insults. Of course, you might not live long enough for him to do something about it.'

I shrugged; there comes a point where the threats start to cancel each other out, and you start to wonder how to turn shit to your advantage.

*

We spent the next two days like moles, emerging only at night to grab ten minutes of clean air before returning to our cellar. I wondered if it might not become our tomb, depending on who was hunting us. Aliyev had forbidden anyone to smoke, knowing how far the smell can carry on the air, so most of us were bad-tempered in our withdrawal, looking for any excuse to argue or fight. The news continued to carry the latest reports on Tynaliev's condition, and the less in danger he appeared, the more in danger I became.

Aliyev and I were the only ones interested in showers, so the smell of Kyrgyz thug grew heavier, sickly sweet as rotting fruit. Aliyev had decided to wait to question me further until we were certain Tynaliev would live. Now my future seemed so short, I just lay on my bunk and thought about my past.

My dreams were broken and confused, as if the unfamiliar surroundings prevented me from diving fully into sleep. I relived the mercy killing of my wife, Chinara, as she lay in the hospital bed, cancer chewing the meat off her bones. The pillow placed over her face, the final upraised hand, whether in protest or waving a farewell approval and benediction, I would never know. I would jerk awake at that point, heart hammering, hands clammy, wonder why I never dreamt of the happy times we had together. Guilt binds you with heavy chains and there's no key to the padlock.

The nights were difficult but the days were harder. Tell nothing but the truth, you don't have to worry about remembering the lies you told. If you're doing all you can to keep as many cards as close to your chest as you can, knowing a single slip-up could put you in your grave, the strain becomes enormous. Aliyev was the sharpest interrogator I'd ever come across: a large part of his rise to the underworld throne must have depended upon it. Every few moments, he'd track back to a question he'd asked earlier, to see if I gave the same answers, if the pieces still slotted together. When I'd questioned suspects in the past, it was to find out whether they were guilty or not. Aliyev wasn't interested in such moral judgements, he just wanted as clear an idea of the big picture as possible, on which to base his strategy and tactics. Right or wrong, good or bad, was never part of his equation.

We kept returning to the central questions: how did Tynaliev intend to become rich; why did I try to kill him?

The answer to the first question was obvious, I told him. Heroin, smuggled across the Tadjik border from Afghanistan, then shipped on to Russia to feed the veins of almost two million 'antisocial elements'. It's become harder to get heroin out of Afghanistan and into the lucrative markets in the West via Pakistan, so now it's a case of go east, young man. The Tadjik borders are as porous as muslin; the mountains make it almost impossible to police. And there's usually someone to turn a blind eye as the mule trains go past in return for a few engraved pictures of Benjamin Franklin. Life might be cheap in our part of Central Asia, but that doesn't make living any less expensive.

By the afternoon of the first day's relentless questioning, my nerves were frayed to the point where I could almost admit to anything, simply to sit back and smoke a cigarette down to the filter in one long majestic drag. Hell, I'd even smoke a *papirosh* cobbled together from roadside tobacco and the sports page of *Achyk Sayasat*. But it would be the final cigarette of the condemned man, and I wasn't quite ready to face my execution yet.

'What made Tynaliev think he could get away with trying to cut into our operation?' Aliyev asked, giving me the kind of look that said we both understood the world doesn't work like that.

'He didn't get round to explaining that to me,' I replied. 'He might have wanted me to work for him, but that doesn't mean he was going to share his plan with me.'

'He must have given you some idea what he wanted you to do? His tame policeman, used to obeying orders, doing as you were told.'

I simply shook my head, knowing any answer would be a lie.

'Didn't he realise that if he tried to move into our territory, we would have sent someone to eliminate him? Someone with a better aim than yours?'

My head was pounding, the dull burn you get when all you want is caffeine, nicotine and the chance to close your eyes.

'He wasn't too specific,' I said, as if having a truth reluctantly dragged out of me. 'I'd be some kind of liaison, with the Afghans, or maybe the Tadjiks. I knew I'd never get my old job back, and I need to put *samsi* on the table like everyone else.'

'You wanted to go back to Murder Squad? Back to dealing with all that shit?'

'It's what I do,' I said, with as much dignity as I could manage in a dank cellar surrounded by hoods. I didn't tell him I've always believed either everyone has a right to justice, to a final peace, or no one does. Chinara always used to tell me it was my Achilles heel.

'We handle the import, the distribution, the export. It's a Circle of Brothers operation, and there wouldn't have been room for newcomers, not even ones with an office in the White House, all fancy wood panelling and a view over Panfilov Park.'

I shrugged.

'So who was he buying from, and how was he going to move it?'

'Above my need-to-know level,' I said.

At a nod from his boss, Zakir stood and walked towards us, cracking his knuckles.

'I'm not sure the inspector is being entirely open with us,' Aliyev said. 'You may have to give him a little encouragement.'

Chapter 15

The open-handed slap Zakir gave me could have been heard in Kazakhstan. I used my tongue to check for loose or missing teeth, found everything more or less intact, shook the stars out of my eyes.

'Nothing more you want to tell me?'

I carried on shaking my head.

Zakir clenched a boulder-sized fist in front of my face, but Aliyev held up a restraining hand. I knew it was time for me to talk.

'You make a good living keeping heroin out of Kyrgyzstan,' I said, 'and the authorities turn enough of a blind eye for you to make a fortune from the Russkies. I dare say a few *som* changes hands in the process as well. But so far, you've seen yourselves as working to keep the country clean.'

Aliyev shrugged. 'I've never thought of myself as an influence for good, but if people choose to think that and let me make money, why should I disagree?'

'Tynaliev wanted in on the operation, a chance to suck on the Russian tit. He knew he couldn't take any of your slice, not without blood. But when your only child has been murdered, your mistresses cost a fortune and your wife only contacts you when the credit cards are due, why not take a chance?'

'I'm all for entrepreneurship. But I have very sensitive feet; my toes don't like being trodden on.'

'The way Russia is now, you could expand your market several times over. All that stops you is getting supplies into the country, right?'

'The Russians are getting more prosperous, or poorer,' he agreed. 'Either way, we can shift the powder.'

'Tynaliev wanted to open up the market, but without threatening you or your supplies,' I said. We'd reached the crunch point, and both of us knew it.

'How, exactly?'

'Afghanistan's not the only place in the world that grows poppies,' I said. 'And there's more than one route into the Russian market. And other markets as well.'

'Go on.'

'I already told you Tynaliev didn't confide in me; I was just a useful fool as far as he was concerned.'

I patted my pockets, brought out my cigarettes. As I lit up and felt the nicotine hit, I felt like I'd won a victory, however small.

'Right now, you feed the Russian market with heroin from Afghanistan, brought into Osh and sent abroad. Because you keep the bulk of that shit out of the hands of the addicts in our country, you have a fair amount of freedom to do what you do. You control the supply so no one else splits your monopoly, right?'

Aliyev gestured for me to continue.

'Imagine if the drugs were sourced from somewhere else,

brought into here. From Laos and Thailand through Myanmar. It would be a fresh source that you couldn't control.'

'Why would Tynaliev bring smack into the country? This isn't a big market, there's not much money, and big risks attached. A difficult supply route with the chance of getting busted all the time.'

Aliyev sat back, shrugged.

'Tynaliev was a bastard but I don't believe he'd want to fuck over his own people like that. Remember, he's survived two revolutions, he knows what the Kyrgyz are capable of when they finally rise up.'

I nodded agreement. There are graves out in Ata-Beyit to testify to what happens when people reach the conclusion enough is enough, together with a lot of stolen money and backhanders safe in foreign banks, and former politicians safe in exile.

'Suppose you get the Golden Triangle heroin into this country, but you don't want to sell it here?' I said, flicking my ash onto the floor. I could tell Aliyev saw the bigger picture.

'China.'

'Sure,' I agreed. 'Ship it over the mountains to Urumchi and then filter it out. The Chinese already know the Triangle powder is better quality. And there are a lot more addicts there, with a lot more money.'

The Chinese authorities aren't noted for their softly-softly approach to addiction, and when it comes to suppliers, the most you can hope for is a bullet in the brain. Which makes the business much more risky, and therefore much more lucrative.

'Tynaliev must know such a move would put him on a Beijing death list,' Aliyev said. 'Surely easier for him to just stick to robbing his own people?'

I stubbed out my cigarette, considered lighting another, decided against it.

'Not if he lays the blame for smuggling the drugs into China onto someone else,' I said.

'That someone else being?'

'You.'

Chapter 16

We sat there in silence for several minutes. I'd baited the hook; all I had to do was see if the shark would take it or pull me into the water. The last thing I expected Aliyev to do was change the subject.

'I'm afraid you still haven't told me who was responsible for the bomb at Derevyashka,' he said, and I thought I could detect the slightest hint of uncertainty in his voice. 'Clear that little incident up to my satisfaction, and I'll make sure you die with the absolute minimum of pain.'

'No need to be hasty,' I said, trying to inject a note of confidence but being betrayed by a dry mouth. 'I admit, I haven't told you everything. Tynaliev didn't tell me much more, but I can still put two and two together.'

'Once a detective, always a detective, eh?'

'You're right, Tynaliev couldn't have built up an organisation from scratch. You'd have wiped it into the dirt before it got too powerful to threaten you. So he had to have reached out for a partner, a potential rival to you.'

Aliyev stared at me, his face impassive, as if I'd just passed on a truly uninteresting piece of information.

'Whoever he was talking to would have been the ones that tried to kill you with the bomb in Derevyashka,' I continued.

'Cut off your enemy's head straight away and you need no longer fear him. Then, while your forces try to regroup and secure a new leader, he seizes power. Getting rid of me at the same time would have been a bonus, drawing a line under past issues.'

I sat back, pleased with my analysis.

'You don't need to be an inspector to work that out,' he said. 'Even an idiot could put that scenario together. You don't have any idea who he might have decided to go into partnership with?'

'The obvious answer would be an Uzbek team,' I said, 'trying to get in on the Russia trade, and hit out at you. After all, Osh is pretty much an Uzbek city in all but name, and that's where the Tadjiks bring the drugs.'

I didn't need to explain there's always been tension between the Kyrgyz and the Uzbeks, and it sometimes erupts into mob violence, leaving bodies and burnt-out houses in its wake. Stalin knew 'divide and rule' was the best policy for keeping a grip on somewhere as vast as the Soviet Union, so he drew the country borders to set Kyrgyz and Uzbeks at each other's throat. Smart move, and one both sides have paid in blood and death ever since.

Aliyev nodded but didn't look completely convinced.

'The old *pakhan* hated Uzbeks worse than poison. And Kazakhs, Tadjiks, Chinese and Russians, now I come to think of it. So he refused to have Uzbek partners. Me? I believe there's more money to be made out of peace than out of war. I negotiated an agreement with the big men in Tashkent. We leave each other's markets alone, nobody dies and everyone goes to the bank.'

I nodded my understanding: there's nothing profitable in killing each other when there's a whole world out there ready to be plundered, bled dry.

Then Aliyev almost caught me out, with one of the unexpected changes of subject in which he was clearly expert.

'You're an ex-cop, kicked out of the force, wanted on charges. Why would Tynaliev let you within a hundred kilometres of any scheme he was setting up?'

I knew I only had a few seconds to answer, or everything was going tits-up. I pretended to look puzzled, gave Aliyev my best innocent look.

'It's obvious, isn't it?'

'Enlighten me.'

'Tynaliev was going to need protection, right? From you, from whoever he was involved with if things went wrong. So he put about the story I'd been fired, told the security forces to work with me as if I were undercover. That way, his arse was covered if I put a foot wrong. And there was one other reason he chose me.'

I paused, pointed to my cigarettes. Aliyev shook his head.

'The minister might have beaten the shit out of suspects down in Sverdlovsky basement, given a few dentists some extra work, had doctors sew a few stitches. And he probably killed my old boss with his bare hands, revenge for organising the murder of his daughter Yekaterina. But he's never had to kill someone who was about to kill him. Look them in the eye, pull the trigger first, watch the hope and the life go out of their face. And I have. There's a world of difference in using your fists and boots on some poor sod tied to a chair in a cellar, and looking down the barrel of a Makarov.'

Aliyev didn't look entirely convinced, but shrugged and gestured to me to keep going.

'So you were best of friends, comrades together in the crusade to get rich? So why did you shoot him?'

I knew my life hinged on the answer. And fortunately, I was granted a little time to think of a convincing lie.

Because that was when the hand grenade exploded in the house above us.

Chapter 17

The entire room shook, as if the building itself was being swept away by an avalanche. The harsh overhead lights flickered for a couple of seconds, and then we were swamped with total blackness until the emergency batteries kicked in a moment later. One of the men cried out, his voice driven by terror rather than surprise. The air was thick with dust, acrid and dry in my throat, and I could feel my eyes beginning to sting.

Like most Kyrgyz, I've felt the after-shock of the earthquakes that hit our country every so often, escaping from the intolerable pressures hiding deep below the mountains. But knowing this tremor was man-made, deliberate, made it feel malevolent, its sole purpose to terrify and then obliterate.

Shouts of confusion and fear bounced off the concrete walls, until Aliyev gestured to his men to remain silent. Whoever was standing above us had clearly come prepared; I could hear pickaxes biting into the packed earth concealing the cellar. The noise changed as steel rang upon the steel of the trapdoor entrance. The heavy bolts on the underside of the door would hold for a long time, but that wasn't what concerned me. A high-speed drill could gnaw its way through the metal in minutes, creating holes through which gas could be

pumped, either to force us to surrender, or to kill us. Knock-
out gas, maybe the sort that killed so many children during
the school siege in Beslan, an agonising death, hands tearing at your throat, struggling not to breathe, failing, choking,
dying.

Along with his men, Aliyev was staring up at the trapdoor,
its outlines obscured by the clouds of dust and dirt raining
down from the ceiling. I seized the moment to pocket my
phone, make my way towards the back of the cellar and the
bedrooms. I knew there would be an escape route; you don't
survive long in the world of the Circle of Brothers without
preparing for every eventuality. A hand on my shoulder spun
me round: Aliyev.

'Come with me, Inspector.'

I let him lead the way, into the furthest of the rooms. A
metal-framed bunk bed stood against the far wall, and I
watched as Aliyev pulled it towards himself. A low and narrow hole broke through the concrete, barely wide enough for
either of us to squirm through on our bellies. A rancid stink
of damp earth and rotten wood belched out at us, but Aliyev
jerked his thumb towards the hole.

'Get going, we haven't much time,' he whispered, dropping
to his hands and knees.

'What about the others?'

I knew they would be standing away from the trapdoor,
waiting for it to swing open, for a tornado of bullets to spray
the room.

'If there's no one here when whoever it is breaks through,

they'll know we've escaped. This way, just you and me, we have an advantage, and maybe even a chance.'

He jerked his head back at the main room, shrugged.

'Expendable. Cannon fodder. I can get a hundred of their sort tomorrow.'

He must have seen the expression of disgust on my face, gave a smile that never reached his eyes.

'If you want to change places with any of them, Inspector, and go down fighting . . . No? I thought not.'

Aliyev pushed me towards the hole in the wall and I clambered through. He followed me, using a length of rope to pull the bunk beds back into place, switching on a torch he'd kept inside the entrance for when a day like this would happen. Then he kicked at a piece of wood supporting part of the ceiling, and I watched as a fall of earth blocked the entrance. No one would be joining us in our escape.

I took the torch from his outstretched hand, directed the weak beam of light down into the blackness. Tree roots emerged from the earth walls and ceiling, like misshapen hands waiting to clutch at us as we crawled past. I felt a familiar panic rise up in my throat, threatening to drown me: I've always thought the most terrible thing in the world would be to be buried alive.

I half-cried out as something scuttled over my feet. Unbidden, impossible to ignore, I thought of vipers, rats, scorpions, all the creatures that lie hidden in the dark and the shadows, waiting to strike, to bite and tear, then to feed. Including humans.

91

I forced myself to control my breathing, to not think about the weight of earth pressing down upon us. The roof of the tunnel seemed to get lower, until I could feel stones and clods of earth scraping against my back. I was still on my hands and knees, my muscles protesting against the unfamiliar strain.

'How much further?' I whispered, as if a loud voice would cause the roof to collapse and bury us.

'Maybe another ten minutes until we reach the treeline,' Aliyev said, his voice subdued, gasping between each word. I wondered if he shared my phobias, if the stink of damp earth and vegetation reminded him of death and oblivion as well.

I pushed those thoughts away, tried to focus on our immediate future. I had no way of knowing where the tunnel would emerge, if we were crawling towards capture or something as final as a bullet in the head. I ignored the scrapes and cuts my hands were accumulating, forced myself on, counting down from a thousand, willing myself to keep going.

It wasn't as if I had a choice.

Chapter 18

I sensed rather than felt the roof begin to rise above us, even as the tunnel became an upward crawl. My face was slick with sweat, not all of it from the effort of crawling. I'd had more than enough of being trapped in dark enclosed spaces with the weight of the world above, waiting for the roof to cave in and bury me alive.

'We should be able to stand up in a minute,' Aliyev said. 'The tunnel widens into a chamber: look for the ladder against the far end.'

I reached above my head, sensed cold damp air on my face, slowly started to climb to my feet. In the torch's dim glow, I could see the metal rungs of the ladder, welcome after an eternity since escaping the cellar. I reached for one of the rungs and slowly pulled myself upright. My knees, elbows and shoulders all shrieked at the effort, but I bit the inside of my mouth to ensure my silence. I didn't know what was waiting for us up in the open.

Nor, I was certain, did Aliyev.

'Any idea who attacked us?' he whispered, his breath hot against my cheek.

'Run through the list of your enemies, it must be long enough,' I said. 'Maybe the crew that bombed the bar?'

'Or Tynaliev's men looking to make you pay for what you did to their boss?' he suggested. 'But how would they know where to find us?'

I rubbed thumb and forefinger together. Money is the usual reason. There's always someone who will sell you out if the price is right, no matter how much they protest their loyalty. It's the ones who say they'll die for you who are the ones happy to let you die first.

'Here, take this.'

Aliyev reached into an alcove behind the ladder and handed me a Makarov. I checked it was loaded, a bullet in the chamber. Aliyev did the same with his gun, reached for the ladder.

'I go left, you go right,' he whispered. I nodded. No percentage in presenting a single target.

'Try not to shoot anyone,' he added. I hadn't figured Aliyev as a pacifist, until I realised he was more concerned about giving away our location than sparing the lives of whoever might be above our heads.

'I'll go first,' he said, starting to climb. The better cover must be to the left, that's why he'd picked it. And going first, he had a better chance of surprising whoever might be up there. I'd be in the perfect place and time for someone to recover and target the tunnel exit as I emerged.

I thought about shooting Aliyev, persuading the people on the surface I'd arrested him, shot him while he was trying to escape. But I had no way of knowing if our attackers were police, or if they'd riddle us with bullets first, then interrogate our corpses. And, ministers apart, I don't believe in shooting anyone in the back.

I followed Aliyev up the ladder, the bare metal greasy and damp, trying to ignore the dirt and dust falling onto my upturned face. It was an awkward climb, one-handed. Tucking the Makarov into my belt would make climbing easier but could prove a fatal delay once we were outside.

The flashlight showed a steel trapdoor, a single bolt smeared in grease so it could be opened with the minimum amount of noise. Aliyev looked down at me and raised a finger to his lips. From below, his face looked grotesque, distorted with hate or fear. He slid the bolt back, jaw tense with effort. The trapdoor swung down across from the ladder. Smart to have the trapdoor swing that way; less chance of being observed. Aliyev was more cautious, more dangerous, than I'd given him credit for. He moved quickly up the remaining rungs, swung himself over the edge, disappeared.

I took a deep breath, tried to move as swiftly and silently as he had, emerged like some clumsy mole into the light.

I'd lost track of time down in the cellar, and I was surprised to realise it was dusk, the light fading behind the trees. I rolled away from the hole until I came up against the rough edge of a tree trunk, hunted around for any sign of danger, tensed my finger on the Makarov's trigger.

The escape tunnel's exit had been carefully planned; we were in a small clearing surrounded by thick brush and mature trees. It was a good site from which to assess the threat that had made us use the tunnel in the first place; more smart planning by Aliyev.

The shadows were lengthening and I calculated we had about an hour to wait before it would probably be dark enough to move on. No moon, which was a bonus. The air was bitter, and I shivered, not sure whether from the cold or shock. Either way, I wasn't happy about spending the night outside, surrounded by people who wanted to kill us.

Aliyev patted the air downwards; stay still, keep calm. We couldn't have been more than a couple of hundred metres from the safe house but the silence seemed absolute. I thought I caught a whiff of cordite on the air, decided it was my imagination. The shooting over, I was certain everyone in the cellar would be dead. All we had to do was evade their killers. Child's play to a tough guy like me.

We lay there for several minutes, until we heard a car start up in the distance, listened to the engine retreat until we could no longer hear it. If anyone had set a trap to flush out any survivors, this would be the time to spring it.

The night crept in on tiptoe, but we continued to lie still. My shoulder started to cramp, the muscles biting into my neck, and I struggled to hold back a cough. The need for a piss was growing urgent as well. I looked over at Aliyev, but the dark had camouflaged him so completely I couldn't read his expression.

I was about to whisper to him, to try to catch his attention, when I heard it, so faint at first I wondered if my imagination was playing tricks. But no: someone was walking towards us, cautiously, placing each foot with care, waiting a few seconds between steps before carrying on.

Whoever had attacked us must have found the tunnel and was now hunting for the exit. I took a tighter grip on the Makarov and wished I had a hunting knife. To use the gun would bring twenty kinds of shit down on our heads, and I was pretty certain neither of us could outshoot a semi-automatic.

A torch beam stabbed out through the dark, pointing down, showing grass and the first of the autumn's fallen leaves. I watched the light edge nearer to the tunnel exit. The footsteps stopped, and I could sense the man's legs almost within my reach, the sour smell of his sweat mixed with cheap tobacco, rancid on the night air.

The beam flicked over to my right, as if suddenly alerted by a suspicious sound, found Aliyev's face. I didn't know if the man had been left alone to guard the site, but I knew we couldn't risk him raising a warning. I grabbed at his ankles, grasped the thick leather of army boots and pulled backwards with all my strength.

As the man fell to his knees, Aliyev pulled him forward, slamming his head hard against the metal edge of the tunnel, once, twice. I heard the sullen crack of bone, felt the man's feet jerk and convulse out of my hands, as if suddenly electrocuted, then lie motionless.

'You've killed him,' I whispered. It wasn't a question.

Aliyev simply nodded, reached for the torch, its beam lighting up the nearby bushes.

'You had a better solution? Help me turn him over.'

The dead man wore a mix of grey-green fatigues, the sort soldiers of fortune and wannabe mercenaries wear all over Central Asia. No name tag, no suggestion he was part of any military unit. Aliyev shone the light at the man's face. Broken teeth from the fall, blood dark in the torchlight smearing his lips and smudging his face.

See enough bodies and they turn into pieces of some giant puzzle, where you rearrange them over and over in your mind, trying to find a pattern, a reason, the bigger picture. None of it makes any sense, but you keep trying. Not to find a god in charge of the universe, but simply to assure yourself lives have a significance that murder takes away.

Some people believe the dead look like they're merely asleep. The body lies with all the energy that drove it evaporated, a lightning strike dissipated into the ground. Nothing left but empty flesh, hopes discarded, ambition washed away, love and anger, pain and joy no longer even memories.

As we dragged the body into the cover of the bushes, it was the face that interested me, beyond the staring eyes and the rictus of pain.

No doubt about it: I wasn't looking at a Russian or Kyrgyz hitman. The body at my feet was unmistakably Han Chinese.

Chapter 19

We didn't have time to work out what this new surprise meant. No telling if he was alone, or if one of his colleagues would come in search of him, suspicious of his silence. But I had no idea how we could get away; the last thing we needed was to blunder into a group of armed men hunting us down.

'With any luck, they'll think he stumbled when he found the tunnel, fell forward, brained himself. No proof we were here,' Aliyev said, rising to his feet, holding out a hand to help me up. My knees protested but I knew we had to get moving.

I didn't mention the patches of crushed grass, the open tunnel, the two deep gashes on the man's forehead. A crime scene officer would piece the whole thing together in a couple of minutes. There are advantages to being a detective, but I couldn't see how they would help me right then.

'You've got a car stashed somewhere?' I asked as we pushed through the bushes.

'Only one road near here; a simple roadblock would snare us,' Aliyev answered, and snapped his open hand shut into a fist, to press the point home.

'So we walk back to Bishkek?'

'If you haven't already realised, I always have a backup plan to the backup plan. But no talking until we're clear. Tread as if you're not a flatfooted policeman. And keep your gun ready.'

We walked in silence, single file, Aliyev leading the way. He didn't bother holding the branches back for me so I kept my head down to avoid being lashed across the face. After about twenty minutes pushing our way through the wood, I could hear the sound of running water, getting louder as we approached, until we stood on the banks of a narrow and rapid river, gurgling and dancing past water-smoothed rocks. Dim starlight gave them the look of sleeping creatures, bodies half-submerged in the constant flow.

'I suppose you've got a motorboat moored nearby,' I said.

'Too noisy, too easily tracked and that means too easily ambushed,' Aliyev replied, casting round to get his bearings before scrambling down to the riverbank. 'And you look like you could use a little exercise.'

He reached beneath a low-lying tree whose branches hung out over the water. A rope trailed from the lowest branch and I watched as Aliyev hauled on the line. After a moment, a package broke the surface of the water, and I helped pull it out. Aliyev stripped off the waterproof cover and laid the contents by the edge of the river.

'A dinghy,' he said. 'I assume you know how to paddle.'

I shrugged. Living in the world's most landlocked country hasn't made my countrymen keen mariners, and I was no exception. But I could see the dinghy's advantages: silent, disposable and untraceable.

'I'll learn,' I said.

Aliyev gave me a dubious look, but he had no option but to take me along. Leave me there and who knew who would find me, kill me and end his chances of finding out what Tynaliev had planned for his takeover.

'We'll be here all night inflating that,' I said.

Aliyev gave me another look, this time of despair at my stupidity.

'Self-inflating,' was all he said, tugging at a cord. I watched as the dull synthetic rubber blob transformed into a craft big enough for both of us. We pushed it into the water, and I scrambled into the front as ordered. Aliyev wouldn't want an ex-cop with a loaded Makarov sitting behind him.

We used the small paddles to push ourselves out into the current; the water was running fast enough to make the paddles necessary only for steering.

'Is this the Chui?' I asked, genuinely curious, turning round to stare at the *pakhan*. In reply, Aliyev put his finger to his lips.

'Sound carries a long way over water,' he muttered, and I lapsed back into silence.

For the next three hours, we floated down the river, not using the paddles for fear of attracting attention, unless we had to steer clear of rocks or overhanging trees. The adrenalin which had fired me throughout our escape had been spent, and I ached in every muscle and joint. The soft-throated murmur of the river almost had me drifting away into sleep.

I remembered my first professional encounter with the Ala-Archa, the river that rises in the mountains, fed by glacier and snow melt, then ploughs its way through Bishkek in a wild spring tumult that becomes a dry rocky bed in late summer. A woman's body had been spotted, wedged between two boulders down where the water was channelled between concrete culverts. As the junior officer, I was the one elected to wade in and tie a recovery rope around her body. I waded in quickly up to my thighs, spring water brutally cold against my skin. My colleagues yelled crude jokes as I took the woman's naked body in my arms, slipped the rope over her head, past her breasts and around her waist. It was the first corpse I'd ever recovered from a river, and her unthinking embrace filled me with a kind of sorrow I've never quite been able to lay aside.

Once she was on dry land, I could inspect the damage caused by her passage down the river. Large slices of skin and flesh filleted and torn away by sharp rocks, bruising from the constant punches of the water as it cascaded down towards its final drowning in the Chui river. Her left eye was missing, gouged out, but her other eye stared up at the sky with a look of faint surprise.

It's almost impossible to tell how someone has died, or been murdered, if they've spent enough time in the water, unless the marks are evident. But the stab wounds in her stomach told their own story. I knew we'd question her husband, her brother, her father, maybe a lover. We'd observe the shock, hear the denials, finally bear witness to a confession. Murder is rarely glamorous or mysterious; usually it's as mundane as the lives of the people it devours. And to someone like Aliyev, it's merely part of business. As I suppose it is to me.

The first signs of dawn were beginning to dance upon the water, a smudge of faint light here and here, and it was staring into these that I saw the face below me, submerged and indistinct, deep in the water.

Chapter 20

At first I thought it was simply a trick of the reflections on the water's surface, a false portrait created by the swirling and weaving of the current. But the face grew nearer, a swimmer rising up through the water towards the air, body half-distinct. As I watched, the features grew clearer, sharper, and I was staring at the face of my dead wife, Chinara.

Her hair wove and swam around her face, as if it were alive, as if she were alive, rising to break the surface, the way she used to when we would dive into Lake Issyk-Kul, over and over, until we would clamber out onto the shore, and drink water-chilled vodka, eat fruit, share kisses.

I wanted to stretch out my hand, grasp her wrist, help her scramble into the dinghy, brush the tendrils of wet hair back from her face. But Chinara remained tantalisingly just out of reach, her eyes staring up at me, a smile on her face, the smile that broke my heart every time I remembered it. And just as my delight at seeing her was overwhelmed by the knowledge I was dreaming, her expression changed to one of anger.

She pointed to the back of the dinghy, to where Aliyev sat. Then she pointed her finger at me, mimicking a gun, pretended to fire. A warning or an instruction, I didn't know which.

Her final smile showed her sorrow at leaving me, her eyes never straying from my face. I watched, helpless, as she sank back and was lost into the dark. And it was then I woke back into a world that no longer held the woman I once loved.

We floated down the river until the sky began to lighten in the east, and it was no longer safe to be on the water. I scrambled over the side, gasping as the water's icy bite gnawed at my legs. I dragged the dinghy the last metre or so into the bank, stretched my hand out to help Aliyev, remembered he could walk perfectly well.

He slashed the side of the dinghy to deflate it and we watched it slowly settle into the water. With any luck, it wouldn't be found until we were long gone, with no reason to connect it to us.

'Now what?'

'We walk.'

Two hours later, the sun was up, a thin mist rolling across the farmland in front of us. There wasn't any sign of civilisation ahead, and I wondered if Aliyev had any idea of where we were going.

'There's a road about three kilometres ahead. I've arranged a pickup from there, made the call while you were asleep,' he said.

An hour or so later, we reached a narrow track that gave every appearance of being abandoned.

'Now we wait,' he said, and gave a rare smile, coloured by a gold filling towards the back of his mouth. I found it reassuring that the *pakhan* had endured Kyrgyz dentistry along with the rest of us. No expensive private dental work in Moscow for him. A man of the people, as long as the people are also criminals. I sat down with my back resting against a tree, trying to ignore the chill seeping into my legs and sodden feet.

I must have dozed off again for a few minutes when Aliyev woke me. For a few seconds I wondered where I was, then remembered my strange nocturnal cruise along the Chui.

'Time to go, Inspector.'

'You're taking me with you?'

'Of course,' Aliyev said, his grin hardly reassuring. 'You're much too important to leave behind.'

The waiting truck was held together by rust and some army-green paint. An exhaust pipe gave out an occasional tubercular cough followed by a cloud of blue smoke. I gave Aliyev a look of surprise.

'What dim-witted rural *ment* is going to stop a broken-down shitheap like this?' he said. 'Everyone knows a *pakhan* wouldn't travel anywhere in anything less than a Mercedes.'

He led the way towards the truck, with me walking off to one side, keenly aware of the rifle aimed at us from the half-open passenger window. I didn't want to get in the line of fire if this turned out to be a bid for a new leader for the Brothers. I could tell Aliyev had the same thought, as he let his gun swing seemingly nonchalant by his side, eyes alert to a possible ambush.

He only relaxed when he saw the driver and his passenger,

recognised them as loyal men. Or possibly his feet hurt as much as mine did.

'You're riding in the back, I'm afraid, Inspector,' Aliyev said. 'Don't worry, there are enough holes in the sides to see you get lots of fresh air. And the boys will have cleaned out most of the goat and sheep shit.'

I opened the back door, took a deep breath. The boys could have done a better job, but I didn't have much choice. I climbed in, heard the bolts scrape shut behind me. Thin shafts of light streamed in through bullet holes on one side of the truck. I picked the least dirty part of the floor and sat down on the bare metal.

Chapter 21

I managed to doze off, in spite of the unyielding floor and the constant buffeting from the unmade road. When I woke, the noise of traffic outside and the comparative smoothness of the road told me we were back in Bishkek. I assumed we were going to yet another of Aliyev's safe houses – in another life, he would have made a great property developer. Finally, we ground to a lurching halt and a fist hammered on the back door. The hinges screamed and the light poured in; I wondered if it would be accompanied by a spattering of bullets.

'Out.'

A gruff voice I didn't recognise, so I pulled myself to my feet, lurched to the door, lowered myself onto the ground. We were in an enclosed courtyard, with high brick walls and solid metal gates. The two-storey house was nothing special to look at, but all the windows had steel shutters, and the front door looked capable of withstanding anything short of a shell from a T-42 tank.

Half a dozen men stood nearby, hands close to their weapons, watching for the first signs of threat. Aliyev shrugged at the look on my face.

'They don't know you, Inspector. You'll understand trusting a police officer doesn't come naturally to them.'

'These days, it doesn't come naturally to me either,' I said.

'I'm sure the penalties for failing to kill a state minister are much lighter than if you'd actually succeeded,' Aliyev said. 'Perhaps better marksmen in the firing squad?'

We both knew if Tynaliev ever caught up with me, I'd want to die a long time before he finally obliged.

'What have I got to lose?' I shrugged. 'Whoever kills me, they can only do it to me once.'

'It's how they do it that counts,' Aliyev said, and I sensed the shark's fin break out of the water, circling in search of prey.

'Something to eat?' he said. 'Then perhaps we resume our chat? I find your insights illuminating. Like reading the mind across the other side of the chessboard.'

Except you're not the one facing checkmate, I thought.

We walked towards the house, the door swinging open as we grew near.

'I made a few calls on the way here,' Aliyev said, gesturing for me to enter before him. 'You'll be surprised to hear we weren't the only survivors of last night's troubles. I'm not sure how they managed to get away, but it should be enlightening to find out.'

The hall was as gloomy as I'd expected, brown-painted walls, pairs of outdoor shoes and felt slippers scattered in one corner. A large mirror hung slightly askew on one wall, the backing silver tarnished and chipped away in places. A diagonal crack split my refection in half, obliterating my left eye.

'Not the Hyatt Regency, I'm afraid, but at least it's above ground,' Aliyev said with an almost-sincere apologetic smile.

'No one trying to kill us either,' I said.

'Give it time.'

That wasn't the most comforting comment I'd ever heard, but the house looked impregnable enough. The only question was who would come looking for us. The police and Tynaliev's security team? The attackers at the last safe house? Aliyev's rivals in the mob? Quicker and easier to compile a list of people who didn't want us dead. But at least I'd made it into the inner circle, the first small step towards what I had to do.

As I stood in the hall, avoiding the accusing stare from my reflection in the mirror, I heard footsteps on the wooden staircase at the far end of the room.

Then all questions of who might want to see me dead at some point in the future faded away. Because I knew the man who stood in front of us, fists clenched at his sides, was very keen to see me dead there and then.

'*Privyet*, Zakir,' I said. 'Good to see you escaped too. You couldn't make me a cup of tea by any chance, could you?'

Chapter 22

For a second Zakir looked confused, almost childlike, as he tried to work out what lay behind my simple request. Then, as the full force of my insult hit him and he snarled with rage, my boot connected with the side of his kneecap. Hard. His bellow of anger morphed into a howl of pain as he stumbled against the wall.

When it comes to fighting, whoever gets in the first, unexpected blow almost always wins. Do it like you mean it and it usually takes just one. You don't bother waiting around to discuss exactly what's troubling them; strike first.

'You're quicker off the mark than I'd taken you for,' Aliyev said.

'Being impetuous will be the death of me,' I said, and it was only partly a joke.

Zakir was helped out of the room, hurling me a glare that promised a slow and agonising death at some future meeting.

'Don't worry, he'll be able to play football in a couple of days,' I said. 'If I'd really been impetuous, I'd have shattered his kneecap, then kicked his head from between his shoulders.'

'That's the problem when you hire people with muscles, not

brains,' Aliyev said. 'By the time they've geared up for action, anyone with quick wits has already removed the problem.'

He stared at me, the sort of look you give when you're trying to assess just how great a threat someone might be. When he finally spoke, his words came as much of a shock to me as my toecap had come to Zakir.

'You've ended your career in law enforcement. Conclusively, I would have said. How would you feel about coming to work for me?'

When I finally spoke, I was as cautious as I'd ever been with Tynaliev at his most threatening.

'I'm not good at taking orders. You know what happened to my last boss. I can be rash, impulsive.'

'I prefer to describe it as decisive,' Aliyev said. 'Assessing the situation, making a decision, considering the consequences, carrying it out.'

Praise of a sort, at least if you live without any sense of loyalty or decency, and if your code of ethics is as basic as 'feed on the weak'.

'I wanted to ask you,' Aliyev continued, 'what made you shoot the minister? You'd worked for him long enough without pulling the trigger. Tired of being his puppet?'

His casual tone was deceptive, but I'd had the ride among the sheep shit in the truck to work out an answer. Now I was about to find out if it was credible.

'Have you ever considered suicide, *pakhan*?' I asked. The question took Aliyev aback, but he shook his head.

'If I'm going to die from a bullet – and I almost certainly

am – I want it to be from someone else's gun, not mine,' Aliyev said.

'Tynaliev wanted me involved in his crazy scheme, act as his go-between, his bodyguard, his patsy and his fall guy. I figured that gave me a career expectancy where I wouldn't need to buy new shoes. I'd done a few things for the minister but they didn't come with a guarantee of getting killed. But turning Tynaliev down wasn't going to be a live and let live option either, not with what I knew of his plans. Killing him and going on the run seemed my best option. My only option.'

Aliyev nodded, as if what I'd said made sense, rather than the bullshit I knew it was.

'Still a pretty big call, Inspector.'

'I think it's time we dropped my old job title, don't you?' I suggested.

'I'll keep it if you don't mind,' Aliyev said. 'It will remind me of who you were, and, of course, to never underestimate you.'

I shrugged, as if I didn't give a fuck one way or another. The past wasn't going to complain. It was time to turn Aliyev's attention away from me, give him something else to feel paranoid about.

'Don't you think . . .' I started, then paused.

Aliyev raised an eyebrow. 'Think what?'

I did my best to seem reluctant to speak.

'We escaped the attack on the safe house. Now Zakir and I are never going to be best friends, but isn't it a little surprising he managed to escape? Considering the amount of lead flying around?'

I let the barb sink in for a moment, knew Aliyev would consider possible scenarios.

'Did anyone else survive? I haven't seen anyone.'

'I dare say Zakir can explain,' Aliyev said, a flicker of doubt crossing his face.

'I'm sure you're right,' I agreed, 'but all the same . . .'

'You'll find clean clothes upstairs in your room,' Aliyev said. 'Third door on the right. You might want to wash off the sheep shit as well. And now, if you'll excuse me, Inspector?'

Once Aliyev left the room, I'd done my best to set Zakir up for a beating, at the very least, but I couldn't bring myself to feel any remorse. He made a lousy cup of tea.

Chapter 23

I showered, changed into the army fatigues laid out for me, and lay down in the narrow bed to rest my eyes for a few moments. Resting them took rather longer, because my watch said I'd slept for five hours. I sat up, uncertain for a few seconds as to where I was. Then it came back to me: in the lion's den.

I didn't have an escape route; all I could do was wait and react to whatever happened. I wondered about food, decided hunger was preferable to nausea. And while I was putting on my shoes, the screaming started.

If you've ever heard an animal caught in a trap, that shriek of pain and fear, you'll know how primal and terrifying it sounds. What made it worse was I could hear human sobs, a man's voice begging to die.

I took the stairs two at a time, not because I wanted to join in, but because I wondered if it would be me doing the screaming next time.

I traced the noise to the kitchen, pushed open the door, entered into hell. Zakir knelt by the stove, pinned down by two bodyguards. Aliyev, wearing an oven glove on one hand, was heating a metal spoon in the flame from one of the front gas burners.

He turned and stared at me, gave a welcoming smile.

'Did we wake you, Inspector? You're just in time to help me prise the truth out of our friend.'

I looked down at Zakir, his face swollen, bloodied, burnt almost beyond recognition. My stomach lurched as I stared into the empty socket of his left eye, realised the piece of flesh stuck to the spoon in Aliyev's hand had once been how Zakir saw the world.

'Don't worry, Inspector,' Aliyev said, as if reading my thoughts. 'He still has the other eye. For the moment. And he's never been one for watching television anyway.'

I felt the vomit spill out of my throat, burning and unstoppable. I stumbled over to the sink, emptied my stomach, long, shaking, shuddering heaves that left me weak and disoriented.

'I'm surprised, Inspector,' Aliyev continued. 'Surely Sverdlovsky basement hardened you to minor upsets such as this? I thought you might like to join in; after all, you could have died in the safe house along with my other men. Revenge doesn't always have to be served cold.'

Aliyev held up the spoon to the light, brought it closer to his face, as if to check the heat of the red-hot metal. With a casual, almost careless flick of his wrist, he lightly brushed the spoon across Zakir's cheek. The howl that followed was empty of any hope, simply begging for a swift end. Zakir's cheek blossomed with the red of a burn.

'For fuck's sake, Aliyev,' I said.

'I want to find out how this piece of shit got out alive. It also sets a good example to the others, reminds them how I reward disloyalty.'

Aliyev stared at me, then dipped the spoon back into the flame.

'You're in *vorovskoi mir* now, the thieves' world. And I'm *vor v zakone*, the boss. Which means it's my duty to uphold our rules, just as you upheld those of the world you once belonged in.'

Aliyev brought the spoon close to his mouth, spat. Saliva hissed and bubbled on the metal the way flesh sticks and burns.

'But you don't belong there any more, not after shooting your boss,' he said. 'You're in my world now.'

I kept my face impassive. Nothing could help Zakir now.

Aliyev waved away the men holding Zakir, who fell to the floor, barely conscious as I watched a puddle of blood spread beneath his head.

'Our friend tells me he simply pretended to be dead, lay among the bodies of his comrades, waited until the attackers had gone. Then he made his way to the road, caught a ride, turned up here just before you and I arrived.'

Aliyev gave the semi-conscious bundle at his feet a nudge with his toe before tossing the spoon into the half-full sink. A hint of steam rose from the water then the spoon was just a kitchen utensil once more. That's the frightening thing about torture; how quickly it reverts to normality. Not just for the instruments, but for the torturers as well.

'For all we know, this house might be surrounded by men

Zakir led here. And there's no tunnel for us to scramble through. So if we're going to end up fighting, I need to know whose side you're on, Inspector.'

Aliyev reached over to the next counter, picked up the Makarov lying there, handed it to me.

'For a start, finish off this piece of rubbish,' he said, pointing down at Zakir.

Chapter 24

I've been a serving police officer for too long to have any illusions about the criminals I come into contact with. But I can live with myself knowing I've fired my gun in self-defence; otherwise it would have been me lying on the left-hand side in the traditional yurt, the man's side, waiting for the men to wrap my body and carry me down to the burying place.

I could even argue that shooting Tynaliev was a case of getting in my retaliation first. But killing Zakir would mean overstepping the line I've always drawn for myself. It would make me a criminal, perhaps worse than a criminal, a man who betrayed everything he'd ever thought important and honourable. I didn't know if I could live with myself if I pulled the trigger, watched the begging in Zakir's one remaining eye fade into indifference.

'You want him dead,' I said, 'you do it. Or maybe you don't have the stones. I think you're worried about his face appearing on the pillow next to you before you go to sleep.'

I paused, considering the matter, gestured at the guards in the room.

'You'll really win their respect, won't you? The *pakhan* who can't kill. Big man. Until the next big man comes along.'

Aliyev swung the gun in my direction, and I imagined the bullet's bite as it gnawed its way deep into my guts.

'You're betting your life I won't kill you?' he asked. 'Remind me never to play cards with you. It would be too easy to win.'

I took the gun from Aliyev's hand, pointed it at Zakir's head. I didn't take my eyes off Aliyev's face.

'This is how a man does it,' I said, in a harsh, brutal voice I hardly recognised, and pulled the trigger as Zakir gave out a last anguished howl.

The gun dry-fired, as I'd gambled it would, the dull click somehow filling the room. Aliyev was far too smart, far too cautious, to give a fully loaded gun to anyone he didn't trust, and so far I fell hard into that category. I handed the gun back, shrugged, refusing to look at Zakir and see the misplaced hope in his face.

'Misfire,' I said, not wanting Aliyev to think I'd guessed his bluff all along.

'I'm sure you're right, Inspector,' he said, taking a magazine out of his pocket, loading the gun, pulling the trigger.

The back of Zakir's head took flight across the room, followed by a crimson spray and grey gobbets of brain. The stink of his shit where he'd messed himself was suddenly stronger. I could taste the tang of fresh blood in my mouth, wondered if it was his, realised I'd bitten the inside of my cheek.

'Perhaps you should stick to shooting ministers of state,' Aliyev said, waving a head at the others to clean up the mass that had once been a man.

'I wasn't even very good at that,' I said, forcing a grin onto my face.

'Different people, different skills,' Aliyev said. 'Zakir was a stone killer, a one-man death sentence, but, let's face it, not as smart, not as cunning, as you. And these days, winning is all about brains. That's why they're mopping his up off the floor, and you and I are still talking. Betrayal? Disloyalty? You've seen where that gets you in my world.'

'Do you end all your job interviews like that?'

Aliyev spread his hands, palm upward, the universal image of a man misunderstood.

'I need people who can think, then act. Just one or the other is no use to me.'

I simply nodded; I didn't tell him that when you've handled hundreds of guns for thousands of times over a couple of decades, you can tell at once if the weapon is loaded or not. It's knowledge you keep to yourself, just in case it comes in handy sometime.

Aliyev ordered coffee, had someone bring me tea, asked if I wanted sugar or a spoonful of jam. Maybe this was also part of the recruitment process. Better than boot camp, at any rate.

I had been wondering when the 'if I only had the manpower, I could rule the world' speech would kick in. Every major criminal I've ever sent to Penitentiary One has been convinced he'd been caught because of the failings of others. I was pretty certain Aliyev, however smart and resourceful, would share this basic flaw.

No doubt the man was persuasive. His vision and plan stretched far beyond the latest sports car, lavish meals that never ended with a bill, and a procession of beautiful woman who demanded everything expensive they could think of when their mouths weren't otherwise engaged.

He talked of extending his markets, of importing new drugs for people who wanted to get high but didn't want to go within a hundred metres of heroin. He spoke of extending the old tried and tested methods – bribery, intimidation, murder – to include social media, news manipulation, innovative delivery routes. And all the time, it came back to the familiar lament: where can I find people who understand and want to be part of the new order, the world according to Aliyev?

'Men like Zakir and the others are fine when it comes to waving a fist full of *som* or a fistful of fist in front of some minor border guard. But where's the nuance, the subtlety? I want an operation that moves without ever disturbing the surface of the waters, you understand?'

I nodded. I did understand. A shark, invisible, moving towards its prey until the final seconds before the strike and the killing. The instant when you know everything is about to end. I remembered the poem Usupov had found on the dead girl once he'd stripped her of her secrets, her hopes, her identity. *Tiptoes past kisses still sweet but fading.* Life once you start using your veins as a dartboard? Or when you decide to betray yourself and all you've worked for?

I could still see the pallor of her skin, count the bites of the syringe, smell the moment of her death. I knew about the children that would never be hers, the home of which she would be so proud, of the husband who stayed loyal.

Either the dead all count, or none of them do.

A philosophy by which I've tried to live so far. Maybe one which was going to kill me.

Chapter 25

Finally I'd endured enough of the master plan, decided it was time to drag reality back into the picture.

'I'm flattered you're telling me all this. But right now, don't you think we should find out who set out to blow us into scraps of meat at Derevyashka? And whose storm troopers attacked the safe house? Imported mercenaries or problems with your Chinese suppliers?'

Aliyev nodded, slammed his open hand down hard on the table. One of the guards looked over, saw no immediate danger, turned round to stare blank-faced into the unfathomable future.

'That's exactly what I'm talking about. Someone who understands the big picture and the details that need to be dealt with.'

Aliyev gave the smile I was getting used to, the one that never considered reaching his eyes.

'Handing you over to the authorities gets me a lot of concessions. And the minister's interest in seeing you wouldn't be held back by being in a hospital bed.'

I nodded. Better to shoot myself, get it out of the way, than reach the same conclusion after a few hours or days dark with pain.

'You're not worried Zakir might have betrayed this location as well?' I asked, genuinely curious.

'He didn't tell anyone about the underground safe house,' Aliyev said, his nonchalance surprising me.

'But you still blew his brains out.'

Aliyev shrugged.

'Loyalty will only take a man so far, then he starts remembering the humiliation, the begging in front of his comrades. Then because the pain isn't there to remind him he's weak, he gets ideas above his station.'

'So you shot him?'

'What would you have done? Waited until he pressed a gun barrel into the back of your neck?'

I said nothing. Aliyev shook his head.

'Your scruples hold you back, our survival drives us forward. You want the sunlight and the mountains, but we live in the dark, in the shadows.'

He rubbed at one of the streaks of blood on the floor with his shoe.

'Zakir was a piece of shit anyway,' he said, dismissing a man's life the casual way you stub out a half-smoked cigarette.

We spent the next four days cooped up in the house, while Aliyev questioned me about every aspect of the police force. What I'd learnt, what corners could safely be cut, what was a no-go area that would pull down the wrath of the law upon his head. To my surprise, he didn't seem interested in which police officers would be willing to look the other way, or make a quick phone call to warn of future trouble. Perhaps he'd already bought everyone worth knowing.

I'd once watched Leonid Yurtaev, the first Kyrgyz grand master, play a series of games in a chess tournament; the way Aliyev thought reminded me of Yurtaev's approach. Always aggressive, ready to smash forward, confident he could see ahead more clearly than his enemies, thanks to his deeper knowledge and understanding. If it ever came to the endgame between Aliyev and myself, he would sweep the board clean.

Every night I would crawl into my bed exhausted, wondering if I'd made a fatal mistake, a flaw in my defence that would conclude the game with a midnight opening of the door, the bark of a shotgun. It didn't make for a restful night's sleep.

Then one morning, as I stood naked by the window, staring out at the high brick wall, wondering what was taking place in the world beyond, I heard the door open. I didn't turn round, concentrated on what looked like the first snow clouds of early autumn race across an ice-blue sky.

'I've seen more muscles on a chair.'

Aliyev. Perhaps I wasn't going to be executed after all.

'Brains beat brawn. Your words, not mine,' I said, still gazing out at the sky.

'Get dressed, ten minutes for *chai* and *khleb*, then we're out of here.'

I heard the door shut behind me, let out the breath I'd been holding in without even knowing it. Once outside the high walls, my chances of surviving – even escaping – might improve.

The bread was stale, the tea tasteless; whatever Aliyev spent his millions on, elegant dining wasn't one of his weaknesses.

'Time to move on,' he announced, dropping a single cube of sugar into his cup. I helped myself to my customary three.

'You've heard something?' I asked. 'A police raid?'

'The police aren't my only enemies,' Aliyev said, giving the twisted smile that somehow made him seem more human, more likeable. 'But I don't believe in waiting until anyone makes a move on me before I react. One step ahead for preference, two for advantage, three to make sure I win.'

Very different from the old *pakhan*, I thought, an attitude that might even see Aliyev climb into his grave as an old man, grandchildren gathered around.

'So where are we going?' I asked.

'Rule Number Two. Know everything, tell nothing until it suits you.' Aliyev gave me an interrogative stare. 'Right now, you don't need to know. And why is it so important to you anyway?'

I tried to make my tone flippant.

'I just wanted to make sure I packed the right clothes. No point in taking a swimsuit to the mountains, is there?'

'Don't worry, you'll find everything there you need,' he said.

Breakfast over, Aliyev led the way outside. A battered *marshrutka*, one of the minibuses used by everyone as cheap transport around the city, was waiting for us, exhaust giving the depressing cough of a dying chain smoker.

'Stylish,' I said.

'Safe,' Aliyev replied, as the side door squealed in protest. 'You'd rather be dead sitting in leather seats?'

'I'd rather be somewhere warm, preferably several thousand kilometres away.'

'Interesting,' Aliyev said, beckoning me into the darkness of the vehicle. 'That's exactly what I have in mind for you.'

Chapter 26

Aliyev's bodyguards clambered into the *marshrutka*, and the driver placed a worn sign announcing this was the 188 to Tungush on the outskirts of the city.

'We're going there?' I asked, only to get a withering look from Aliyev.

'I always tell my enemies where I'm heading,' he said. 'It makes it easier for them to kill me.'

I shrugged, concentrated on staring out of the grime-encrusted window. No need for tinted glass here, not with several seasons of dust and mud to shield us.

The sky was still clear, with the mountains rising up to meet it on the horizon, but I could sense the possibility of snow later on, even this early in the autumn. Like most Kyrgyz, I'm constantly aware of the weather. We watch it with all the attention of a farmer or a goatherd, people whose livelihood depends on it. Get it wrong, and you face inconvenience, delays, problems. Get it badly wrong and you could find yourself in serious, even fatal, trouble. Weather in Central Asia isn't the mild-mannered polite affair you find in lots of countries. We joke we spend six months of the year outdoors in the heat of summer, the other six months trying not to freeze to death. Like most of our jokes, it's not really a joke at all.

I didn't know if Aliyev had a fleet of Ferraris tucked away somewhere in a villa on the North Shore, but he certainly knew how to travel around Bishkek with a complete lack of style. The engine of the *marshrutka* had advanced lung cancer, the tyres were smoother than an adolescent's first shave, and the seats had endured generations of overweight *babushki* planting their over-wide arses on them. I settled back and tried to relax, treating the bouncing around as a form of rough massage therapy.

Eight of us had clambered into the bus, sprawling across uncomfortable seats, staring out of the windows or demonstrating cool by trying to nap. We were headed out of the city up into the mountains. The air turned colder as we climbed, the clouds beginning to darken and gather like mourners at a funeral. I felt a chill the *marshrutka*'s heating failed to combat; perhaps it was saving its strength for the return journey.

The scenery was familiar; we were on our way to Issyk-Ata, the old Soviet-period sanatorium still used by the locals for the hot springs and cold baths. I'd been there once before, to solve the murder of a prominent member of the *nomenklatura* found floating face-down one Sunday morning in a hot springs pool with his bathing trunks around his knees, a wrist-thick mountain ash branch inserted into his backside.

My enquiries gave me a number of leads, but all the suspects I questioned had rock-solid alibis, their wives testifying that their husbands were not only indoors on Saturday night, but inside them as well. I never solved the case, and the inquest decided the deceased had 'accidentally impaled himself while diving into the pool while drunk'. No mention of the three empty vodka bottles and a hundred cigarette butts at the scene of the 'accident'. A warning for us all.

The wheezing from the engine grew more laboured as we climbed up towards the Issyk-Ata Gorge. Finally, with the *marshrutka* on the point of collapse, we pulled into an empty gravelled car park. The main building of the sanatorium was visible through the trees at the end of an overgrown and winding path. The upraised arm of Lenin pointed through a gap in the trees, the statue reaching out to snatch a cloud. After independence, no one dared to pull down the statues of the Great Leader just in case the Soviets came back, but it was decided to move them to rather less prominent sites, just in case the Soviets didn't return. Having stared at Vladimir Ilyich's embalmed corpse, his face candlewax yellow, in its mausoleum outside the walls of the Kremlin, I didn't think he looked too upset.

'You spoil us, *pakhan*,' I said, as brightly as I could manage, looking at the tree-lined gloom shrouding the path. It looked bad, but I knew the buildings would be worse.

Soviet architecture was designed with the best of intentions and the minimum of skill and materials. I knew what to expect: broken steps made of rotting concrete, corridors painted murk-green up to waist height, then mottled cream up towards stained ceilings. Only half the light fittings would contain a bulb, and only half of those would be working, giving a thirty-watt attempt at illumination. The smell of cabbage overlaid with disinfectant. Unwashed windows with cracks repaired with thick brown tape, light blue paint covering more of the glass than the frame. Only the best for the people, as Lenin and then Stalin and then Khrushchev had decreed. And this was a place where people came to get well.

We made an odd-looking party as we traipsed up the path, avoiding the worst of the mud, bodyguards leading the way and bringing up the rear, with Aliyev and me firmly secured in the middle.

Before independence, you might have thought we were members of the Politburo, come all the way from Moscow to see just how well the Great Soviet Experiment was working. Now, we looked exactly what we were – a bunch of thugs on our way to a hideout or a shootout.

'You promised me somewhere warm,' I complained. 'This doesn't look like it, unless you're planning to torch the place.'

Aliyev gave one of the shrugs that were beginning to annoy me.

It had begun to drizzle, the rain pushing its way through the mist clinging to the tops of the trees, then waiting until I was underneath before beginning its final descent.

Finally we paused in front of the main building, drab as all the others but with double doors that gaped open. A note taped to the left-hand door proclaimed opening hours, next to a handwritten scrawl saying the complex was closed 'for a week, due to a prior booking'. I couldn't help noticing we were two hours earlier than the scheduled time; on the other hand, the place looked as if we'd arrived forty years too late.

Aliyev saw the look on my face.

'Relax, Inspector, we're expected. I made a couple of calls before we left Bishkek. And round here, I'm not just anyone, you know?'

He waited for the guards to check the entrance, ushered me in with a sweep of his hand. The hallway wasn't as bad as I'd feared; if anything, it was worse. There were patches on the wall, where the portraits of previous dignitaries had hung until they fell from favour, took the long one-way trip to Siberia or the short ride to the Lubyanka. Naturally, as they vanished, so did their portraits. Long streaks of damp and mould created a surreal mural of swirling patterns and stains. The air smelt of rotting wood, mouse shit and more than a hint of despair. Offhand, the only place I could imagine being less healthy for someone requiring treatment would be at the bottom of a plague pit.

'The Hyatt Regency was fully booked?' I asked.

'The Hyatt is where my predecessor would have chosen for a meeting like this,' he said, 'and that's why there's a marble slab in Ala-Archa Cemetery with his ugly old mug engraved on it, and his ugly old body rotting away underneath. His epitaph should read "Predictable". I've no wish to join him until my own face is just as old and just as ugly. So this place suits my purposes, Inspector. My apologies if you're accustomed to better surroundings. I always thought you were that rare creature, an honest policeman. I'd hate to discover I was wrong.'

I couldn't think of a smart answer to that, decided to hold my tongue, wait to see what surprises were on their way for me.

'Kenesh? Kairat?'

Aliyev waved towards a door at the end of the hallway, his guards already halfway there, guns drawn and held down by their side, reluctance to be first in the line of fire clear in their faces and their cautious approach. I expected a hail of bullets as they opened the door, but heard only silence.

By the time they reported the place was empty, with no sign of an armed reception party, the cold mountain air had started to gnaw at my bones. I watched my breath turn white, felt my feet ache from the cold. Judging by the state of the floorboards, stamping my feet to keep them warm might earn me a quick trip to the cellar.

'Perhaps we could wait in the *marshrutka*?' I suggested.

'Smart,' Aliyev said. 'That way we can be grouped together as a sitting target for whoever drives up the road. You might as well make yourself comfortable; we have a little time to wait before our meeting.'

He didn't volunteer who we were going to meet, or at what time. Either he'd tell me when he was ready, or he wouldn't. I wondered why he'd brought me along. A sacrificial offering perhaps, or a sign of his good faith. Backed by the AK-47 assault rifles two of his men were carrying.

I tried not to think of piping hot *chai*, raspberry jam stirred into it for sweetness. Even the thin blanket in my room back at the safe house held a sudden delicious promise. The way the temperature was dropping as the afternoon wore on, if a bullet didn't kill me, pneumonia would.

The next four hours passed in a delirium of boredom. I tried to spot faces in the stains on the wall, counted the number of missing window panes, wondered whether my watch had died.

Aliyev gave a nod of dismissal, and four of the guards left the room, Kalashnikovs slung over their shoulders like a refugee army on the march. The remaining two guards took up position by the windows looking out onto the path.

'Can I ask who we'll be meeting? I don't want any nasty surprises, like coming face to face with an armed man I sent to Penitentiary One for a ten stretch.'

Aliyev gave me another of those pretending-to-be-human smiles.

'Don't worry, Inspector, none of our guests have ever seen the inside of a Kyrgyz prison. Or prison anywhere, for that matter.'

I supposed that was reassuring, and it did suggest the people we were about to meet were both foreign and professional.

'Maybe an idea not to call me Inspector,' I suggested. 'We don't want your guests to get the wrong idea.'

'These people wouldn't give a fuck one way or the other. And they already know exactly who you are. Shooting a minister earns you a certain notoriety; you mustn't be modest.'

'Why am I here at all?'

A not unreasonable request, I thought, but Aliyev wasn't to be drawn.

'In good time, when the moment is ripe. I've got big plans, and they do include you.'

'At least tell me when they're due to arrive. I don't want to spend the night here.'

Aliyev looked at his watch, perhaps as keen to return to his bed as I was to mine.

'Another few minutes before they land,' he said.

'They're not driving?'

Aliyev shook his head.

'Time is money. And our guests are short of one and possess plenty of the other.'

It was then I heard the unmistakable clatter of a helicopter. Whoever they were, money was never going to be a problem.

Chapter 27

I don't care for helicopters. When I'm in one, I have to concentrate through sheer willpower on keeping the thing from tumbling from the sky and smashing into some mountainside. The winds are unpredictable in the Tien Shan, especially in the autumn. Sudden unexpected gusts sweep the loose snow from the peaks, hurling it into the air, reducing visibility to zero in seconds. And it's at that moment the mountains are transformed into giant, jagged and razor-edged teeth, ready to bite down in anger at the temerity of anyone foolish enough to intrude on their territory.

I still had no idea who I was going to meet, but I knew they must be reckless. That didn't do much for my confidence. The rotor blades grew louder, dropped in pitch as they slowed down, finally stopped.

In the sudden silence, my stomach rumbled, and I wondered why Aliyev hadn't brought food. Either the meeting was going to be a short one, or no one would be leaving alive, so why bother?

I watched the two guards in the room as they checked their Kalashnikovs, flicked the safety catches into the 'fire' position, positioned themselves at opposite sides of the room slightly in front of us, to command a complete field of fire. Ex-military, had to be, maybe lured out of the forces by dollars or the adrenalin of danger. There's a perverse comfort in knowing the men with weapons are trained not to panic and spray the room and everyone in it with sudden death. I only hoped our visitors would be as well-behaved.

We waited in silence, alert for the sound of boots on the gravel path outside. I moved to behind the wooden table, ready to topple it onto its side for shelter in case whoever walked through the door came in shooting.

'Aliyev?'

A voice from outside, shouting from a safe distance. I glanced over at Aliyev, saw him nod to the guards. The one nearest the door pulled back the bolt, let the ill-fitting wood swing open. The guard peered outside, seemed satisfied with what he saw, beckoned Aliyev to join him.

In the doorway, Aliyev cupped his hands, made sure anyone outside could see he wasn't carrying.

'I've got two guards with me. And the inspector. Please join us. With two of your men, obviously.'

I moved to one side, so I could look beyond Aliyev in the doorway. At first, I saw no one, then a patch of green detached itself from the larch trees opposite, became recognisable as a man wearing camo. Two more figures emerged, both similarly armed as Aliyev's men, pointing the business end of their Kalashnikovs in a vague direction not too far from us.

As the man moved closer, I could see he wasn't Russian, not even Kyrgyz. He had the dark colouring and flat cheeks of the Chinese who live over the other side of the mountains near

Urumchi, skin weathered and baked by the desert. Uyghur maybe, or Dungan, with a dash of Han Chinese thrown in for good measure. Thick black hair swept back from his forehead gave him a powerful, confident look, a man used to giving orders and having them obeyed.

I watched him approach, until he stood a couple of metres away from the entrance, his men flanking him, their eyes watchful, cautious.

'Yusup,' Aliyev said, holding out his right hand in greeting. Yusup raised his right arm in response, and even from where I stood, I could see three of the fingers on his hand were missing. He said nothing, but nodded his response to the greeting.

'We've always got along in the past, Yusup,' Aliyev said, his hands palm upwards, a peaceful gesture. 'You've had your business interests, we've had ours, and where they've coincided, we've reached an agreement, divided the territories up.'

Aliyev stepped outside the building, the wind catching at his hair, his jacket open to show he was unarmed. I followed him, the guards close behind. When Aliyev spoke, his voice was mild, conciliatory.

'Neither of us wants a war. Dead bodies draw the attention of governments, yours and mine, and I imagine your prisons are every bit as brutal as ours. If any of us even succeed in making it as far as a cell, that is.'

Yusup continued to remain silent, but nodded his assent.

'We know you need our trade routes to get to the Russians, the ones not already dosing themselves on home *krokodil*, that is. And we permit that, for a price, and up to a point. But now you've started to shift the "serial killer" into this country, and it's got to stop.'

Without turning round, Aliyev must have guessed at the puzzled look on my face.

'Carfentanil, Inspector. Hundreds if not thousands times more potent than heroin. Known in the USA as "serial killer". For once, that's an understatement.'

I thought back to the dead girl I'd found in her decrepit apartment, saw her body being turned into stewing steak, wondered if the man standing before us was her source, her executioner.

My fists tightened in anger, nails digging half-moons into my palms, and I knew I would enjoy beating him to death. Slowly, making each blow count, painful but not fatal. Cheekbones splintered, the ribcage torn apart like a tree struck by lightning, teeth scattered on the ground, dripping with blood.

You're never going to stop people damaging themselves, with booze, nicotine, sex, drugs. But some things go beyond tolerance if you witness them yourself. I've always prided myself on self-control, even in the face of the horrors I've witnessed, so this visceral unexpected rage left me gasping. As a policeman, it would have been my duty to arrest him. As a human being, I thought the best thing to do was to put him in the ground.

'We both supply drugs, Aliyev, you don't have a moral high ground to preach from,' Yusup said.

'I don't supply "serial killer",' Aliyev answered. 'And I don't supply drugs to my people.'

'Which is why they come to me,' Yusup said. 'Or they buy once your product has reached Moscow, which naturally jacks up the price. So to feed themselves, they cut it so the next junkie down the line has to take more. Which costs more. So they steal, rob, mug . . . you know the story.'

Aliyev smiled.

'As far as I'm concerned, the Russkies can shoot up with whatever they want. There's no love lost between us. If they're stupid enough to give me roubles to help them kill themselves, I won't sit on my hands and shake my head. Of course, I sell. But not here.'

He paused, cupped his hands, blew into them for warmth, looked up at the sky, at the clouds starting to gather and shroud the mountains.

'Anyway, the market here isn't big enough to make the risks worthwhile. Especially if someone decides to trample on my turf.'

Commercial interest and self-preservation disguised as patriotism. I hated it, and I was trapped in it. For the first time I was grateful Chinara was dead and buried: my wife would have been ashamed of me.

A sudden breeze grew in strength and threatened to become a gale, scuttling along the treeline, pulling down leaves and sending them spiralling up into the air. I could taste the electricity in the air, smell the sharp, fresh scent of the ozone promising rain that would turn to snow up in the mountains. Issyk-Ata didn't strike me as the sort of place you'd want to weather out a storm overnight.

'I won't sell them carfentanil either. One lethal and all too easy shot, you've lost a customer, so the money turns to a trickle. When you don't have enough money for everyone to dip their beak, people get confused, nervous. They decide you're weak, ready to be overthrown, and the safety catches on their guns are released. And after that, the first shot starts war.'

I've heard some clever arguments for legalising drugs before, maybe even been half convinced by some of them. Personal freedom, the need to end organised crime, even the idea that a medicated country is a peaceful one. I'd heard the same arguments about vodka when I was a rookie officer out on the streets.

I've seen just how peaceful people are when they've finished a bottle of the good stuff, never mind the home-made *samogon*. I've taken some of them to the emergency unit at the hospital on Krivonosova, taken others to sober up in one of the cells in Sverdlovsky station. Then there were the ones I'd had sent over to the morgue, men killed with an unlucky punch, women beaten for refusing sex, children battered for crying too loudly or too long.

Let people have the stuff that stuns elephants and kills humans with a single grain? Not a chance.

Yusup stamped his feet, the cold clearly working its way into his shoes. Aliyev looked down at his own boots, then at Yusup.

'You should have come prepared,' he said. 'I wouldn't want you to catch cold. It's amazing how quickly a cold can turn nasty. Even fatal.'

The threat was not lost on Yusup, judging by the way he narrowed his eyes, pulled his coat collar up.

'I'm sure you have men beyond the treeline, guns trained on the back of my head.'

Aliyev shrugged, noncommittal.

'And, of course, you know I have a couple of snipers with you in their sights.'

Aliyev showed no surprise.

'I'd expect nothing less from you.'

'So it's stalemate?' Yusup said.

'Let's call it a draw. Here's the deal. You ship whatever you want to Russia. To pass through Kyrgyzstan, you pay the usual tariff. In dollars, not product. And not to a bank here. Somewhere secluded, peaceful and very, very private. Preferably warm as well.'

Even as Yusup nodded, Aliyev held up a forefinger in warning.

'It arrives, it passes through in transit, it leaves. And not a gram of that shit falls out and lands here. Not in Osh, not in Bishkek, not on the road over the mountains. If it does, then our agreement is over.'

I watched Yusup's face as he considered Aliyev's words. He looked ahead, impassive. At that moment, if someone could have carved a series of giant faces into a mountaintop, like the ones in America at Mount Rushmore, Yusup would have been the ideal model. He ran the hand with the full complement of fingers through his hair, looking more than ever like an Asian version of Brezhnev.

Our breath gusted on the cold air as we stood in silence.

'I'll be in touch.'

And with that, Yusup strode away down the path, his bodyguards walking backwards, keeping us covered with their guns.

As they reached the cover of the trees, Yusup turned and shouted something, but the wind snatched his words away. And then he and his men were gone.

We waited until Aliyev's men emerged, guns ready in case Yusup was considering a surprise attack. Before they reached us, I turned to Aliyev, saw implacable anger stamped across his face as if he'd been branded.

'What did Yusup shout?' I asked.

For a moment, Aliyev stared at the forest, his eyes black and unblinking. Then he turned to me.

'Condolences, that's what Yusup shouted,' he said, his voice flat and unemotional. 'Condolences.'

He didn't explain why.

Chapter 28

'Where are we going now?' I asked, the wind from the mountains gnawing at me. I could have sworn I felt the first snowflakes of winter tremble across my face. Aliyev ignored me, staring out towards where Yusup's helicopter had landed. I repeated my question. Finally he turned to me, looked at me almost puzzled, as if wondering who I was, or from where I had appeared.

'Back to the city, of course,' he said. 'No point in staying here any longer.'

I started to make my way towards the *marshrutka*, but Aliyev put his hand on my sleeve to stop me.

'In a couple of moments,' he said. 'Indulge me, Inspector.'

As if hearing his words, the noise of the helicopter engine starting up filled the air, the whine of the rotors rising as they picked up speed. I returned to his side; he was the man with the guns, after all.

'It looks like he's leaving,' I said, suspicious of our delay.

'And if he's waiting until we're on a narrow, winding road with no turn-offs, where we can't drive fast, and he decides to spray us with machine-gun fire from the air, you'll be happy, Inspector?'

The possibility hadn't occurred to me; once again I understood why Aliyev had become *pakhan*.

'I anticipate scenarios, then neutralise them before they happen.'

I lit a cigarette, relishing the instant of warmth against my face, dragging the hot smoke deep into my lungs, pluming the smoke to dissolve in the air. The sun was setting, leaves on the trees falling faster now, as the wind picked up momentum. I had no reason to think of Chinara, but suddenly a memory of her grave overlooking the valley below and the mountains beyond came into my head. I hoped she was at peace; it's all I've ever wanted for the dead, to lie quiet in their graves. And if they don't? I may not believe in redemption, but I do believe in revenge.

I wiped my eyes dry, damp from the evening mist or the tobacco smoke blowing back into my face. Not tears; they're wasted on the dead.

We could hear the rotor blades of the helicopter, and after a few seconds, it came into sight, moving slowly as the pilot gained cruising height. I guessed their plan was to skim the treetops, fly to their prearranged landing spot, transfer Yusup and his men to a less conspicuous form of transport to take them back across the mountains and over the border.

The pilot dipped the helicopter nose slightly, a mocking tribute to those left on the ground, turned away from the sanatorium towards the hills.

Then the air shimmered for a brief second as the helicopter was transformed by a spasm of fire.

It hovered in the air for a few seconds, as if uncertain it had been hit, the rotor blades stuttering and dancing erratically. I could see flames devouring the cockpit, saw a figure on fire plunge towards the ground, arms raised in a parody of flight. The body – I hoped it was a body – bounced across the tops of a couple of trees taller than their neighbours, then fell from sight.

The helicopter gave a couple of feeble half-turns, as if gravity and death were now its masters. I watched as it dragged a trail of black oily smoke behind it, then fell to the hillside, cutting branches aside as it fell. I waited for the big movie explosion, but nothing happened. Perhaps in real life it never does.

I turned and looked at Aliyev.

'You set this up?' I said, finding the courage to ask.

'Not at all. If we'd reached an agreement, then he'd be on his way to home, warmth, in time to read a bedside story to his children. He didn't know one of my men served in Afghanistan, did two tours and became an expert with plastic explosive. The Taliban weren't the only ones who set traps, you know. Easy enough to plant a few grams when the pilot isn't looking, even easier to detonate when the time is right.'

'Is that all you've got to say?' I asked, throwing my cigarette to the earth. Aliyev ground it out with the toe of his boot, mashing it into the fallen leaves. I looked around. The smoke from the explosion was already thinning out into tendrils and strands drifting across the setting sun. I could smell petrol, fumes, the smell of autumn about to give up the ghost and transform into winter. The first few drops of rain began to fall.

'Well, at least we know the people who bombed Derevyashka and blew our safe house cover won't be bothering us any more,' Aliyev said as he headed for the *marshrutka*. 'And naturally I'll send my condolences.'

Chapter 29

We rode back to Bishkek in a silence punctuated only by the coughs, splutters and general wheezing of the *marshrutka* engine. After the guards had checked the grounds and house were clear, we sat in the kitchen to get warm. Aliyev made tea and handed me a glass.

Finally, he spoke.

'You've nothing to say about what happened up at the sanatorium?'

I stared at the ceiling for a moment, picturing the smoke drifting up from the trees and across towards the mountains. I remembered the smell of the burning, wondered if any of it was human flesh, dismissed the thought.

'I hate helicopters,' I said. 'Always have.'

Aliyev looked at me, as if examining an unusual and rare botanical specimen.

'That's a very pragmatic attitude, Inspector, particularly for a man with a reputation as a white knight.'

I shrugged; when you're on the run, noble gestures become too great a risk. And I couldn't help wondering if all the police work I'd done, all the crimes I'd solved, all the villains I'd put behind the walls of Penitentiary One, if it had all been pointless. Perhaps all it had led to was drinking tea with the biggest villain in Kyrgyzstan.

'I didn't take any pleasure in eliminating Yusup,' Aliyev explained, his voice thick with fake sincerity. 'He would have done the same to me in different circumstances. When you're in a business like ours, you have to do harsh things.'

He drained his glass, poured himself another half, pushed the sugar in my direction.

'No woman to take care of us, you see,' and there was an almost apologetic tone in his voice, as if being on either side of the law excludes you from normal family life. 'You have no family, I believe, Inspector?'

I shook my head.

'I know about your wife,' Aliyev said. 'A tragedy. And if you'd been working for me . . .'

'Yes?'

'We would have flown her to Moscow. Or Geneva. Wherever the best treatment was to be found. We look after our own, you see.'

I knew Chinara would never have accepted treatment paid for by drug addiction, prostitution, blackmail and corruption, even if it cost her her life. I debated telling Aliyev, decided there was no point. Chinara was dead and buried, and the sun had rarely shone for me since.

I thought about Saltanat, the woman I was half in love with, wondered if she was back in Uzbekistan or somewhere in the field, her cross-hairs already trained on eliminating an enemy of the state. Perhaps I was on her hit list, if Tynaliev's influence stretched as far as Tashkent.

I wondered about Otabek, the small boy Saltanat and I had rescued from the clutches of a wealthy foreign paedophile, the man I'd later assassinated knowing the only justice he would ever have to face would be when he walked with the dead. Saltanat had taken Otabek away with her, hoping to mend his mind, and I wondered whether he was still mute, suspicious of the adult world, afraid of the horrors that stalked it.

'It can't be easy, losing someone to such a terrible disease,' Aliyev said, and I wanted to punch his sympathy back down his throat until the hypocrisy and pointlessness of it choked him.

But most of all, I knew my anger and resentment and disgust were all aimed at one person, the man who stood every morning with a razor in his hand and avoided staring into his eyes in my mirror.

Using a pillow to end Chinara's final suffering, I'd spared her some small amount of pain. The world at large would call it a mercy killing. In the deepest caves of my heart, I could call it nothing else but murder.

'You're offering me condolences now?' I asked.

'You're not the only person who's lost someone,' Aliyev said, a surprisingly gentle tone in his voice. 'Maybe I'll tell you about it one day.'

I didn't reply, stood up.

'Sit down.'

I remained standing, and I saw the attention of the guard in the room suddenly switch to high alert.

'Sit down. Please.'

I couldn't see an alternative that wouldn't get me shot, so I did as he asked.

'You need to get out of the country.'

A statement, not a question, and one with which I could only agree.

'You don't have any money, any hidden savings, unless you're not the policeman I take you for.'

It's all very well being told you're an honest cop, but honeyed words did nothing to get me out of the shit I was in.

'Your former colleagues will shoot you down on sight, and if you survive, then the minister will pick your bones clean.'

I nodded.

'So really, the only choice you have is to work for me.'

Aliyev saw the self-disgust in my face, took a cigarette, sparked it and inhaled.

'Don't worry, I'm not suggesting you become a hitman. One simple job and you're done, with enough money to stay out of trouble as long as you stay out of Kyrgyzstan. Interested?'

'I'd like to hear more.'

'Of course, but first let me ask you something. You're not afraid of flying, are you?' he asked, and I could hear the concern in his voice. 'You have flown before?'

'Sure,' I said, 'I just hate—'

'I know,' Aliyev interrupted, 'helicopters. I'm not surprised, after what you've seen today. But you don't have a problem with regular flying?'

'No.'

'Good. Because you're going to be doing a lot of it.'

Chapter 30

Nothing prepares you for the sheer scale and noise of Bang-kok. People in a raging hurry wherever you go, swarming like ants along the pavements, faces taut and stressed, as if a moment lost meant an opportunity missed. The scent of exotic spicy foods hanging in the thick moist air that drapes itself like a wet blanket around your face. Endless streams of cars beyond counting, drivers hammering on their horns as if the din could make the gridlocked traffic creep forward even a few metres. The high-pitched scream and blare of thousands of vehicles bounced off the glass-sided towers clinging to the roadside. I was overwhelmed by the energy, the ferocious never-ending pace of the city. I felt helpless, a swimmer strug-gling against a current dragging me inexorably to a waterfall whose journey ended on jagged rocks. I was a long way from Bishkek.

I'd watched the green fields turn to endless rows of build-ings from the aircraft window, leaning over in the business-class seat Aliyev had provided.

'Thailand isn't like Kyrgyzstan,' he'd said. 'Here, we keep our heads down. But in Asia, you need to put yourself about a bit. The best hotels, fine restaurants, a limousine service at your call twenty-four hours a day. You'll be representing me:

that means they have to believe you're important, a big man in my organisation. No backpacker hostel on Khao San Road and a one-week Rabbit Travelcard for the Skytrain. Who knows, Inspector, once you get a taste of luxury, you might even get to like it.'

I decided not to fight it. And as Aliyev pointed out to me, flying business means you stand out from the crowd of tourists, and being in full sight was the best disguise I could have. One of the guards had taken my measurements, came back a few hours later with a couple of suits, shirts, shoes, and an elegant leather case to put them in. They were the smartest, most expensive clothes I'd ever worn, and I could almost forget the blood and tears staining them.

I'd flown to Bangkok from Tashkent, since heading to Manas Airport would have meant my sure arrest. Aliyev could have fixed me up with a new passport, but I knew my face would be in front of every immigration official, ticket counter clerk and security guard at the airport. A change of name and nationality wouldn't help.

I'd been smuggled into Uzbekistan in the middle of the night, thrown like a sack of potatoes into the boot of a Moskvitch that had never seen better days. The car had once boasted a suspension and efficient brakes, but those glory days were nothing but a memory. There were a few tense moments as we stopped at a checkpoint, and I had to hold the boot closed, but after a brief exchange of words (and maybe a quick gift of dollars), we were on our way again. I suspected I could probably have ridden across the border on a white stallion, dressed as a ballet dancer from the Bolshoi Ballet, given Ali-yev's connections, but I think the Moskvitch catered to his sense of drama and intrigue. As well as reminding me who was boss.

Twenty kilometres and several bruises later, I was hauled out of the boot and given the back seat to sit on. I wasn't sure which was more uncomfortable.

Checking in at Islam Karimov International Airport wasn't a problem. I used my own passport, expecting my name wouldn't have been circulated outside Kyrgyzstan. One of the good things about not getting on well with your neighbours: they're never too anxious to help you catch your domestic criminals.

I had a couple of hours to get through before my flight, so I wandered into the business class lounge, hid behind a news-paper for an hour, and made a free local phone call, got an answerphone, left a message. Then a charming stewardess told us we had ten minutes to get to the boarding gate, only six hundred metres away.

Once on board, I watched out of the window as we taxied to the runway, expecting a jeep full of soldiers to come racing up to stop the flight, haul me off, and hand me over to a Kyr-gyz welcoming party, but we took off without incident. The six-hour flight was certainly the most luxurious I'd ever been on, with wide seats and good food. The seat turned into a bed, but even if it hadn't been the middle of the day, I had too much on my mind to let me sleep.

Aliyev had given me a thorough briefing on who I was to

meet, what I was to say, what I could offer, what compromises I couldn't make. I was surprised he'd chosen me to make the approach, but his logic was supremely easy to follow.

'The people you're going to meet are naturally cautious, suspicious of new faces. But when I tell them I'm sending the man whose balls are so big he shot the Minister for State Security in the back – well, that kind of reputation can't be bought, only earned. And I've made sure they know all about it.'

I'm not sure if high praise from a notorious criminal boss counts in your favour in most social circles, but if it meant I wouldn't be found face-down in a rice paddy, I was willing to accept it.

I was fast-tracked through immigration, and walked to the courtesy vehicle pickup. The airport was enormous, but still felt packed with thousands of people milling around. I was already starting to feel claustrophobic, missing the emptiness and silence of the mountains. But I had a job to do, and I'd never see the Tien Shan again if I didn't succeed. Perhaps I wouldn't see anything ever again.

I saw a long black town car was parked by the kerb, dwarfed by the driver who stood in front of it holding a sign with my name on it. In Cyrillic, no less, which impressed me. Clearly, I was meeting people who paid attention to every detail. It's strangely comforting to see your name printed in letters you can read; God knows what I would have done with the beautiful but incomprehensible Thai alphabet.

The nearer I got to the car, the bigger the driver looked, until I realised I was standing next to a man well over two metres tall, and broad to match. An immaculate black suit, not a chauffeur's uniform, would have made him look like a highly successful businessman, except I'd already spotted the bulge under his arm. My guess was a Glock Parabellum, and I wondered how I was going to manage without a weapon of my own.

The driver stared at me as I approached, or so I thought, his eyes hidden behind black sunglasses. Finally, I stood in front of him. No reaction, impassive. I think I was meant to be impressed, maybe even a little scared. I reached up and removed the glasses, and as he reacted, I slid my other hand into his jacket, lifted his gun partway out of the holster. His reaction was a half-second too slow, and he froze as I pulled at the gun.

'If I pull the trigger now, my guess is I'll hit a lung, maybe go through a kidney or the liver as well. You need less practice at looking scary, more time on the range.'

I let the pistol slide back into place, tucked the glasses into his pocket.

'I'm Borubaev, and before I get in any car, I like to know where I'm going and who's driving it.'

The driver glared, and began to lumber towards his seat. I simply stood there, my bag on the ground, my arms folded. Finally, he got the message, reached inside the car, released the boot lid, walked round to pick up my bag and stow it away.

After a moment, he reached for the rear door handle, but as he did so, I stepped forward, opened it myself, slid inside. Always keep men like that uncertain what you'll do next, whether you'll smile and ask after their children or start throwing punches and pulling triggers. It means they'll be alert, which is never a bad thing in a bodyguard.

'The hotel, sir?' he finally said, and I nodded.

Against Aliyev's advice, I'd had him book a small boutique hotel on Langsuan just up from Lumpini Park. It didn't look like the sort of place where a successful international criminal would stay, and that suited me just fine. Big luxury hotels have lots of security men, CCTV cameras and staff who can spot when someone's not quite right. It's also all too easy for someone to find out what room you're staying in, knock at the door, then put a bullet through the spyhole when it goes dark as you look out.

Langsuan isn't a long street, at least not by Bangkok standards, with the park at one end and Chit Lom Skytrain station at the other. The road is one-way, so it's easy to shake off anyone in a car or riding a motorcycle, and with only one entrance, the hotel seemed as secure as anywhere.

We rode the expressway into the city centre to avoid the worst of the traffic jams, stopping only to pay the tolls at regular intervals. The manic jumble of Bangkok revealed luxury tower blocks jostling up against rundown houses, shops with garish neon signs, stalls with a couple of chairs selling street food. I felt tired after the flight, but alive in a way I hadn't felt for a long time, as if some of the city's energy had transferred itself to me.

I reached for the wooden box lying on the seat beside me, opened it, recognised the black metal of a Makarov. Thoughtful of someone to provide me with a gun I'd carried for most of my career. Maybe they didn't want me to shoot my toe off by mistake.

The car windows were tinted, so I checked the gun was loaded, knowing no one outside could see what I was doing. Two spare magazines, more than I needed. That many bullets, you're either facing an army or about to wind up dead. I put the gun in my jacket pocket: it would spoil the line of the suit, but bullet holes would ruin it.

The gun meant I could finally relax, wonder where I was going to meet Aliyev's friends, whoever they were. Perhaps I even allowed myself to smile.

Chapter 31

I was feeling distinctly less confident by the time we'd reached Langsuan and spotted the discreet sign for the Luxx XL Hotel, pointing down a narrow drive between two buildings. I found the scale of Bangkok intimidating, as well as the sheer foreignness that surrounded me. It's not easy being out of your depth when there are eight million people all around you who know exactly what they're doing. But I knew I had to carry on with Aliyev's mission – if Tynaliev ever found out where I was, I'd be looking at an unmarked grave face-up from the inside.

Tyres crunching on gravel, the car pulled into a small walled courtyard with an elaborate shrine in the far corner. What I know about Buddhism could be written on the head of a prayer wheel, but that didn't mean I didn't appreciate the colourful flowers and garlands draped around an image of the Buddha. Two massive plain wooden doors, maybe four metres high, were set back from the courtyard; the entrance to the hotel.

True to stereotype, I waited for the driver to open my door, then followed him into the reception area. A very pretty Thai girl placed her hands together and bowed her head to me, long liquorice-black hair spilling down over her shoulders. I didn't know whether I was expected to return the greeting *wai*, so I simply nodded as the driver set my bag down beside me.

'I pick you up, four hours, meeting,' he said, his broken Thai-inflected English almost as bad as my English. I nodded, and handed the receptionist a credit card, another gift from Aliyev. She examined my passport, then the card, gave a slightly puzzled look.

'You speak Russian?' I asked, and she held up her thumb and forefinger.

'A few words. For work,' she said, in a low husky voice.

'Corporate card. My company.'

She nodded her understanding, processed the payment, before handing the card back to me. I looked once more at the name. Bolshoi Vor. Big Thief. Aliyev's idea of a joke, obviously.

She handed me one of those plastic cards with a built-in chip to activate the lock of my room. The sort of place I usually stayed at used the old-fashioned metal key, attached to a piece of wood the size of a brick, to make sure you didn't accidentally forget to hand it in at reception when you left. I was moving up in the world.

I don't normally like using lifts – too easy for someone waiting with a gun to shoot you as the doors open – but I figured this once would be OK. I'd check out the stairs on the way back down, explain to the receptionist I didn't like cramped spaces.

The lift doors opened onto a whitewashed corridor with doors on either side. I found room 404, pressed the card against the lock, watched the light change, pushed open the door.

My room was clean, simple, furnished in what fashionable Europeans call minimalist and we Kyrgyz call empty. Wooden floors and white walls, a bed, a desk, a chair, a phone, and a bewildering array of light switches. A bathroom with a sliding wood and glass partition dividing it from the main room, the point of which escaped me. Floor to ceiling sliding glass doors with a narrow balcony outside, shaded by a tree with thick olive-green leaves.

The fierce shower pummelled every inch of me and managed to rinse some of the tiredness out of my body. Afterwards I lay down on the bed and shut my eyes for five minutes. Three hours later, the phone woke me, the soft-voiced receptionist informing me my driver had returned.

I took my time shaving and dressing, headed down to the lobby. My friend the driver was talking on his mobile, which he switched off when he saw me. I didn't tell him I could lip read he was speaking Russian.

'I'm impressed,' I said, in my thickest Kyrgyz accent, 'you must have a friend.'

I wondered if he'd been chosen for his language skills; his driving certainly wasn't impressive. The driver shrugged, to show he didn't understand me, then pointed at the door. My suit may have been the most expensive piece of clothing I'd ever worn, but I still got the obligatory pat-down. I didn't mind; it meant I was meeting someone important. I hadn't flown four thousand kilometres to go sightseeing.

The traffic was even more congested, but finally we crept up a major road which ran beneath the shadow of the Skytrain.

'Sukhumvit,' the driver explained, and I nodded as if I understood. He drove for the rest of the journey in silence, until we pulled off the main road into a side street. I looked out of the car window at a parade of Thai women in shorts, denim miniskirts, cropped T-shirts and high-heeled shoes. One of Bangkok's red light districts, flashing neon lights, taxi and scooter horns blaring, rock music pounding out of the bars. A huge spaghetti-tangle of wires, electric cables, telephone lines and God knows what else drooped across the road or ran across the tops of head-high walls. There was a sense of expectation in the air, the feeling anything could happen tonight, every event could turn into an adventure or a disaster.

A sign high above the entrance to a courtyard on our left read 'Nana Plaza: The World's Biggest Adult Playground'. The pavements were crowded with a procession of middle-aged, balding and overweight Western men hunting for their next bedmate or simply staring at the spectacle. Nana Plaza's reputation for anything-goes sex had clearly spread far and wide. Dressed in faded singlets, oversized shorts and colourful trainers, the men all wore the roadmap of their lives on their faces, tired, cynical, hoping for a distraction from the failure of their lives.

The car pulled over to the side of the road, and the driver pointed to a bar opposite called the Lurch Inn. The bar frontage was open to the street, and the stools which gave a view of the passing street trade were all occupied. For the price of a Tiger beer, a man could stare at as many Asian prostitutes for as long as he wanted, until it was time to buy another bottle. A lot of the customers were already drunk, shouting insults at their friends, their arms draped over the shoulders or circling the slim waists of girls young enough to be their daughters.

I'd seen prostitutes before – show me a cop who hasn't – but never on such an industrial scale. Even above the music, I could hear the high-pitched chatter of women. Maybe the laughter was real, maybe not. We all have to earn a living, and I certainly wasn't looking down from any moral high ground.

I looked over at the driver, shrugged what now? He pointed again at the bar, mimed drinking, said, 'Wait.' He obviously wasn't going to get out of the driver's seat and open the door for me.

The car pulled away, sleek and expensively anonymous, as I stood there, looking out across the road at the hotel car park opposite, where the freelance street meat smoked, chatted, or tried to make eye contact with every passing male. Every now and then, a man would stop, a quick discussion would follow on price, preferences, location, and the two of them would get in a taxi or walk down the street.

The girls were all tiny, exotic and very young, but knew how to use a knee or a stiletto heel. It's a tough life, and even tougher if you're not prepared for trouble.

I stared at the crowd for a couple more moments, pushed my way past the hectic street-food stalls cooking fish, shrimp, satay and an array of unidentifiable things. Once I was on the pavement, I walked up a few steps into the bar. Not for the first time in my so-called career, I was on my own, with no one to cover my back.

At once I was pounced on by a middle-aged woman, clearly in charge of maximising the volume of alcohol the bar sold. She took in my suit, placed me as a possible high-roller, and showed me to a small table far enough from the band to make thinking possible. Three girls in matching outfits that looked like school uniforms hovered nearby, ready to take my order.

'Whisky? Bottle? Walker Red?' the manageress asked, her smile revealing crooked white teeth with just a hint of scarlet lipstick smeared here and there. I shook my head, knowing the quickest way to get rid of her was to not spend thousands of *baht*. I didn't know if that would work with the schoolgirls. I've seen vultures up in the mountains looking less predatory.

I ordered a Tiger, watched her send one of the schoolgirls for my beer, then stalk off in search of more profitable prey. The beer arrived with a menu the size of a telephone directory. I flicked through the laminated pages, sticky with spilt beer and food. I didn't know how long I would have to wait, or who I was supposed to be meeting. I'd already been warned about the fiery nature of Thai food, so I pointed at a steak, watched the waitress scurry off in search of a cow.

The meal arrived quickly. One bite told me the cow had spent a lot of its adult life hanging around bars, getting into fights and generally being tough. After a couple of mouthfuls, I pushed the plate away.

'One more Tiger?'

I looked at the untouched bottle in front of me, shook my head. The waitress touched the side of the bottle, shook her head.

'Too much warm,' she said, implying only an idiot would drink warm beer. I thought only an idiot would drink in the Lurch Inn at all.

I looked at the unruly collection of misfits, drunks and lecherous tourists, decided to wait another ten minutes, then leave. Nine minutes later, I sent a text to Saltanat, paid the bill, saw my driver pushing his way through the crowd towards me. He beckoned to me and I followed. It wasn't as if I had a choice.

Chapter 32

To my surprise, we didn't go back into the main street, but pushed further back into the bar, past the pool table and bandstand, then out through the back door. We were in a large courtyard with open-air bars in the centre and around the sides. Stairs on either side led up to two horseshoe-shaped galleries, with more bars. Dozens of women, many wearing only underwear with a numbered badge pinned to their bra straps, stood gossiping and eating, clearly on a break from working inside the bars. Everywhere the air was filled with the smells of cooking, stale beer, cigarette smoke, the promise of whatever kind of sex turned you on.

We climbed up the stairs to the top floor, walked along past strangely tall and slim women. The driver nodded at them, shrugged.

'*Kathoey*. Ladyboy.'

I've always had a certain amount of sympathy for gay people in Bishkek. It's a conservative city, and obviously feminine men run the risk of being attacked, beaten up, even raped or murdered. It usually wasn't difficult to find the attackers; the nearest bar was where they would end up with a bottle of vodka, celebrating their bravery in attacking some man who'd done them no harm.

Bangkok was a different world. I did what I suppose most tourists in a red light district do, and stared. They all looked beautiful to me, and I wondered what happened when someone took a 'girl' back to his hotel room and got a surprise. Perhaps no one really cared, that sex was either a matter of personal preference or a way to make money.

I did my best to ignore the blown kisses, admiring whistles and the tugging at my arm as a girl wearing a scarlet dress slit to her hip tried to drag me into her bar. I noticed they all stayed away from my companion; either they knew he wasn't interested or they'd spotted the gun.

We came to a bar that looked derelict; no neon, no curtained door, no girls grabbing customers, insisting they come watch the show. The driver pushed at a glass door covered over with old newspapers, and we entered.

The room smelt of mould, dust and abandonment, with just a lingering hint of sex on the damp air. A stage formed the centrepiece of the room, with metal poles at regular intervals for the girls to dance around. A few dusty mirrors hung on the walls, some engraved with beer signs. Empty bottles, cigarette butts and the remnants of used tissues littered the floor.

The driver led me to the inner door, pushed it open, jerked his thumb for me to enter. The room I found myself in stood in complete contrast to the squalor on the other side of the door. Discreet lighting highlighted the stylish conference table, the black leather chairs, the massive flat-screen TV where a constantly changing parade of exchange rates and share prices scrolled upwards. The man at the head of the table stood up, gave me a hands-pressed-together *wai* visible enough to suggest welcome, minimal enough to show he didn't give a damn for my approval.

'Please, Mr Borubaev, take a seat, make yourself comfortable before we start. Whisky? Or perhaps you prefer vodka?'

His Russian was flawless, educated, much better than my thick accent. I shook my head and sat down. The man was Thai, perhaps in his early forties, immaculately dressed in the kind of suit I'd only ever seen in the windows of high-end stores in Dubai. As he moved, the colours of the material seemed to change, from a deep blue to a grey-silver. The watch on his wrist was the thickness of a ten-*som* piece, his cufflinks the fluorescent crimson of Burmese rubies. I was in the presence of serious money, someone who wasn't afraid to display the fact. Dark hair swept back from a face that could have been lifted from a centuries-old temple, black eyes that pierced yet gave nothing away. He could have been an army general out of uniform, a leading politician, a high-ranking policeman. He looked invulnerable, supremely confident, in absolute mastery of himself and his power.

'My name is Quang,' he said, patting himself lightly on the chest. I bowed my head, acknowledging the courtesy shown in telling me his name.

'It means "good reputation, brilliant",' Quang said, in a matter-of-fact tone that told me he wasn't boasting. He paused then said, 'I understand your name – Akyl – means the same?'

'Not brilliant,' I replied, 'merely clever.'

I didn't add that the Boru part of my family name means

wolf. I'd been known to my former colleagues back in Sverdlovsky station as 'the clever wolf' because I would solve a murder by stalking, biting and never letting go until I'd brought my prey down. I didn't want Quang to get any ideas I might be dangerous to him or his people.

To him, I was simply a renegade mid-level foreign cop, a useful idiot, a glorified messenger boy sent to broker negotiations, agree a deal, or wind up floating face-down in the Chao Praya river. I was very happy for him to think that. If death were to come and attack me, it wouldn't really matter to me who administered the *coup de grâce*, the man sitting in front of me or Aliyev back in Bishkek. Dead is dead; anyone who investigates homicides will tell you it's a simple truth. Sometimes I even believe it myself. The only issue is how long it takes and how much it hurts beforehand.

I hadn't noticed the elderly man sitting in a dark corner, massively overweight, wearing a torn plain black T-shirt and shorts. His feet were bare, and a pair of sandals rested beside his chair. He hadn't spoken and we hadn't been introduced, but I knew he must be important. In South-East Asia, the person who doesn't speak is often the one who makes the major decisions once a meeting is over. But I knew any discussion like that would take place without me present.

'You managed to rest on the flight?'

'It was very comfortable,' I said, wondered how long it had been since I'd last told the simple truth.

'I was surprised you didn't want to stay at one of Bangkok's luxurious hotels.'

I nodded my understanding at his puzzlement, did my best to explain.

'The Royal Thai Police have a well-known reputation for extreme thoroughness,' I said, choosing my words carefully, 'and your prisons have a worldwide reputation as well. I'd rather stay somewhere simple, just a tourist here to see the sights, try the food, maybe even sample a little of the local nightlife.'

I winked, did my best to appear dazzled by all the smooth brown flesh I'd seen on display outside, and it must have been a pretty accurate impression, as Quang smiled his understanding of a man's needs.

'You've never been to Bangkok before?'

I shook my head.

'It is the centre of the world, Mr Borubaev. Art, culture, history, business, love, despair: you find it all here. Then, once you've exhausted all those possibilities, there is always the opportunity for pleasure.'

Quang must have pressed a button under the table, because the door behind me opened.

'You must be tired, and indeed, you shouldn't spend your first night here talking business. My driver can help you find a suitable companion for the evening. More if you require variety. Whatever your tastes prefer, my organisation will be delighted for you to indulge yourself. And, of course, I'm pleased to meet you.'

Quang and the older man both stood up, preparing to leave. At the door, Quang turned and looked at me, his gaze quizzical, slightly mocking.

'When we next meet, Mr Borubaev, it would greatly improve our mutual trust and advance our talks if you came unarmed.'

As they walked out of the door, the driver seized my arms, forcing them behind my back. I thought no one had seen me liberate my steak knife in the bar, but as it fell from my sleeve onto the table, I realised just how closely I'd been watched.

The driver released my arms, took away the knife. Perhaps he was going to return it to the kitchen. I hoped so: I didn't want to get the schoolgirls into trouble.

'I know you understand Russian,' I said, 'so if you don't mind, I'll make my own selection for a bedfellow. Maybe even go home alone.'

The driver simply grunted, shrugged, gestured at the door. A few minutes later, we were back inside the Lurch Inn, and I was inspecting the merchandise while the merchandise cast their eyes over me.

Small barely budding breasts, breasts that highlighted a plastic surgeon's skills, flat stomachs, long, lean legs. Women whose hard faces suggested they were *kathoey*, ladyboys, eyes drowning in mascara and desire. Tiny women in lace under-wear, promising everything, revealing nothing.

Suddenly the idea of a woman in my bed became erotic. The thought that I could lose myself in a stranger's body and not have to explain anything, to forget my dead wife, not have to justify being on the run was immensely appealing.

I looked around the bar, saw a woman drinking a whisky and ice in a long glass, smoking one of those long slim white cigarettes that feature in porn movies at the start of a seduction. She was beautiful enough, disdainful enough, to pick and choose and charge the earth. I wasn't the only man in the room watching her. Every male was eyeing her, wondering if he had the courage to approach.

With a brave face, and the knowledge I had a lot of Aliyev's money in my wallet, I walked over. She stubbed out her cigarette, fished out another from the pack and turned to wait for me to provide a light.

She put her hand on mine, ostensibly to steady it, but the electric spark was as unmistakable as the flame of my lighter. The thin, red silk blouse, the tight white jeans, the strappy shoes with impossibly high heels, all suggested she normally played for pay at much higher rates than she was going to find in Nana Plaza. Long ice-blonde hair was tied back from her face and hung down her back, the way Chinara often wore her hair. A quick wave of guilt hit me at the memory, but high cheekbones, jet eyes and a generous mouth swept my past away like a tsunami.

'You speak Russian?' I asked, in case anyone was listening.

'*Malenky*,' she replied. Little.

'*Ty ochen' krasivaya*,' I said, as if stumbling over even a simple sentence like 'You're very beautiful.'

If she understood, she showed no signs of being flattered. She tapped the ash from her cigarette onto the bar floor, pushed her drink away and prepared to stand up. I lightly touched her arm, and she looked at me as if I had some unpleasant skin affliction.

'Five thousand *baht*?' I said, trying to sound as if it was my final offer. She looked annoyed, held up the fingers of both hands. Ten thousand. Expensive. But I decided that if I was going to die in the next few days, it would be with the satisfaction of having slept with a truly beautiful woman.

She considered, nodded, waved at a cruising taxi as we walked out. My driver pointed to his car, keen to make sure I got back to my hotel safely. But the woman shook her head. Climb into the back of a limousine with tinted windows and who knows who or what's waiting for you inside.

As the taxi pulled away to get back on to Sukhumvit, I could almost swear the driver smiled his approval at my choice of bed companion.

The taxi swung over potholes, through red lights, with the car horn on full auto. I stared at the woman's profile, the ever-changing lights of the shops we passed adding mystery to her features.

As the taxi pulled into Langsuan, she turned to me, looked at my face with an unreadable expression, and finally spoke, in a voice as rich and sensuous as honey poured over ice cream.

'Well, Akyl, what shit have I got to get you out of now?'

Chapter 33

Back in my room, Saltanat sat on the bed to unfasten her heels, then take off the long blonde wig, revealing ink-black hair. Utterly different from the last time I'd seen her, but still beautiful, unattainable in spite of having been infrequent lovers.

'Nothing to drink, I suppose, Akyl,' she said. It wasn't a question, so I didn't bother to shake my head. 'Don't you ever get bored with facing reality head-on, twenty-four hours a day?' I smiled, didn't speak. The brutal fact was Saltanat had not only seen as much violence and death as I had, she'd caused a fair proportion of it as well. Working for the Uzbek security services as a 'troubleshooter' (their discreet name for an assassin), you don't spend your days at a desk sharpening pencils, unless you're planning to push them into someone's ear.

'So are you going to tell me what this is all about? Why you've dragged me here, made me dress up like a thousand-rouble hooker on Nevsky Prospekt?'

'I thought we could have a kind of pre-event honeymoon?' I said. 'You know, lie on a deserted beach, the sun warm and sensuous on our bodies, that sort of thing.'

'Bangkok has deserted beaches?'

'The travel agent lied,' I said, pleased when she rewarded me with a slight smile. 'But now you are here . . .'

I plucked up the courage to reach for her, stroke her face, even feel the contours of her head, so subtly different with her new haircut. I felt dizzy with the scent of her perfume, the nearness of her, the way we seemed always to come together, then drive ourselves apart. We've both killed people; perhaps that gives a strange sideways view of the world, or relationships, of the amount of guilt an individual can carry.

We moved closer together, held each other without kissing, her head resting on my chest. I felt strangely lacking in desire, feeling content the gap she always left in my life when she departed was narrowed, however temporarily. She took my face in her hands, kissed me, close-mouthed, ran her fingers along my cheek.

'Shave. Or that's the only kiss you'll be getting tonight.'

When I came back from the bathroom, drying my face with trembling hands, Saltanat was already in bed, her clothes lying on the floor.

'Come here,' she said. I did as I was told . . .

It's a movie cliché that afterwards a couple lie in bed and smoke a cigarette. So we did.

'I didn't think you'd come when I called you from Tashkent,' I said, and I wondered if she heard the hint of sorrow, of self-pity, in my voice.

'Texting me to meet you in the bar was pretty smart. A pain in the arse to sit there, rejecting the propositions I got. Five thousand *baht*, you offered me? I turned down twenty and a weekend in Chiang Mai to end up here in bed with you.'

'I hope it was worth it.'

'Don't flatter yourself.'

But she smiled as she said it, and that made all the difference. I took water from the fridge, poured two glasses, gave one to her. Ignoring the sign on the wall forbidding smoking, she lit a cigarette, sent a jet trail of smoke at the ceiling.

'We can go out for a drink if you like,' I said. 'I don't know the area but I'm sure we can hunt down a bar.'

'You're supposed to be making passionate love all night long to me, remember?' Saltanat sat up in bed, pouted, said, 'Me love you long time, too much,' in a high-pitched imitation-Thai voice.

'How long can you stay?'

Saltanat gave a noncommittal shrug, tipped ash into her half-empty water glass.

'You mean in bed or in Bangkok?'

Her voice was serious, professional, the emotionless tones I remembered from our first encounter. But still desirable.

'Both would be great,' I said, but Saltanat put a finger to her lips to silence me.

'I'm here on official state business, and I don't mind seeing you, maybe even helping you with whatever trouble you're in,' she said, 'but that doesn't mean I want to get killed on your behalf. Kyrgyzstan was bad. Our time in Dubai was worse. I have a feeling Bangkok may be worst of all.'

'You heard about Tynaliev being shot?' I asked.

'Of course. That's why I'm here. You probably know he didn't die?'

I nodded.

'And you know who shot him?' I asked in return. Now it was her turn to nod, her face even more serious than usual, her body suddenly coiled, tense.

'Tynaliev would be pretty unlamented throughout Central Asia if he'd died,' Saltanat said, 'but he didn't. And from his luxury private room at the Hyatt Regency, an entire floor swamped by his bodyguards, he sent a message out to his counterparts, his rivals in Tashkent, Almaty, Dushanbe.'

'Let me guess,' I said. 'The tricky bastard said "Providence has spared me, but my would-be assassin is still at large. This attack says any of us is vulnerable. My friends, this time it was me. Next time, his bullet could be for you. We must deal with him so that no one emulates his folly."'

Saltanat said, 'Actually, that's a rather more logical and restrained way of putting it. His actual words were, "Gut the bastard and deliver his head and balls."'

A dark suspicion began to slither into my mind.

'The word went out, together with mention of a reward for my head. And that's why you're here. To hunt me down. And kill me.'

Just like the first time we met, back in Bishkek as I tried to hunt down the killer of Yekaterina Tynalieva and avoid her father's rage.

Saltanat's eyes never left my face, as she reached for her bag.

I felt numb, beyond shock, betrayal written across my face like a blow. I couldn't move, thought about throwing the glass in my hand at her, couldn't raise my arms. I felt my balls tighten with fear.

Saltanat's hand emerged, holding a gun no longer than my middle finger. I stared at its black mouth, knowing that if it spoke, its voice would be the last thing I'd hear.

'Turn around, Akyl. Please.'

'Can't bear to look at my face?'

'Just do it,' she said. Was there a note of sorrow in her voice? I couldn't tell.

'I've always said I wanted to be buried next to Chinara. Up in the mountains, overlooking the valley,' I said. 'But that isn't going to happen, is it?'

I looked at the cheap mass-produced painting on the wall, showing an old lady in a floating market boat selling noodles. Garish, banal, but the colours hit me with a fierce intensity. Hardly the most profound vision of a dying man. But perhaps the best I deserved or could hope for.

And thinking that, I shut my eyes, tensed my shoulders, prepared to die.

Chapter 34

The explosion filled the room, but it was the blast of a voice, not a gun.

'Don't be such a fucking idiot, Akyl, I'm not going to shoot you. Although I probably should. But that doesn't mean I trust you either. I need to know what's going on, and standing naked at gunpoint usually encourages people to speak freely.'

I decided turning around too quickly wasn't the smartest idea I've ever had. Better to answer her questions, and let her deal with Quang, Aliyev and Tynaliev, in no particular order.

'First of all, why did you try to kill Tynaliev? I know he was a shit, but he owed you.'

'Owned me, more like,' I said. 'And I knew that one night, lying awake at four in the morning, he'd decide I knew too much about him, I might be a threat to his wealth and his position. And an hour later, someone would drag me out of my apartment and into a secluded field to watch the dawn for the last time.'

'Then how was it you didn't kill him before he could kill you? Point-blank in the back, I heard. Twice. That Yarygin of yours, it's not a gun, it's a cannon. I'm surprised they didn't find pieces of his liver halfway across China.'

'I used an old Makarov, not mine, obviously,' I said, reproach clear in my voice. 'What can you expect with a piece of shit like that? The amount of vodka Tynaliev drank every day, I was only surprised the bullets didn't ricochet off his liver and hit me.'

'If you'd succeeded in offing him, his successor would prob-ably have had you promoted,' Saltanat said. 'As it is, you're in up to your neck. I would never have thought you'd move over to the dark side.'

'I didn't move, I was pushed,' I said, irritated. 'And is it all right if I turn around now? Talking to a wall gets boring pretty quickly.'

'Put the glass in your hand down first. And move as if you're treading on very thin ice. Which, of course, you are.'

Finally, I turned around, pleased to see the gun in her hand wasn't pointing so resolutely at my heart.

'Why don't we get dressed and I'll explain it all to you?' I suggested.

'Sure,' she said. 'Pick up your clothes and go shower.'

Half through the bathroom door, Saltanat called out to me, 'Akyl, you need to lose a couple of kilos. Too many expensive meals with your gangster friends.'

That reminded me I hadn't eaten proper food since I'd landed, and maybe the thought of sudden death and then reprieve straight after sex had given me a surprising appetite.

'Maybe we can go out and eat something?' I suggested, and closed the bathroom door.

But when I came out, Saltanat was gone.

Chapter 35

The corridor was empty, of course, and Saltanat was too sharp an operator to have not planned more than one escape route well in advance. The deep-voiced receptionist wouldn't remember the woman who'd arrived with me, or which direction she'd taken.

I went back into my room, the sharp, almost acrid smell of sex and perfume still riding on the air, felt my stomach turn inside out. A combination of fear, adrenalin, survival and the knowledge that trained killers from every Central Asian country had become bounty hunters racked my body, and I knelt before the toilet vomiting them all out of my system as best I could.

When it was clear I had nothing left to bring up, I stumbled to the shower, stood under scalding hot water, turned it to ice-cold. But the sweat of fear still stuck to my body.

Towelling myself dry, wishing I'd never given up drinking vodka, I noticed a cheap black mobile phone lying on my pillow. Left by Saltanat, obviously, an untraceable pay-as-you-go burner to which only she had the number. I checked the directory; there was only one number stored in the memory.

The phone vibrated in my hand, and a message ran across the screen. It read, 'Need to talk more.'

I wasn't sure if my heart could cope with another conversation like the one we'd just had, but I typed 'Where? When?' and sent the text. I waited for a few minutes without a reply. I wanted somewhere secure to hide the phone in case Quang or his friends came by, found nowhere. Tired to the marrow of my bones, I said fuck it, slid the phone into my jacket pocket. The best hiding place is in open view. Except when it isn't. Time to put the bed to less active use.

The driver picked me up early the next morning. Before leaving, I'd hidden the mobile on a high ledge on the balcony of my room. A thorough search would find it, of course, but there's only so much you can do in foreign territory. Foreign it certainly was; I hadn't worked out yet whether it was hostile.

Instead of returning to Nana Plaza we drove for an hour until the city sprawl began to give way to the occasional patch of green. Finally, we pulled up outside two massive bronze gates set in a high wall topped by broken glass. I was uncomfortably reminded of the villa of Morton Graves, the foreign paedophile I'd killed back in Bishkek. He'd kept his victims in the cellar, where he filmed all kinds of horrors before killing the small boys and girls. I wondered if I was entering a death zone of my own.

The gates opened, we drove through, and they swung shut behind us. There wasn't going to be an easy way out of here if things turned tense.

I got out of the car and looked around. Another courtyard, but a world away from the one at Nana Plaza. Immaculate areas of lawn, with a narrow stream meandering from one boulder to another, crossed by Japanese-style wooden bridges. A larger lake had stepping stones fashioned from white marble, laid out to resemble nature rather than any human design. One perimeter wall had a water feature set into it, running at irregular intervals to give a pleasing melodic effect. I wasn't just looking at money and lots of it; I was admiring taste and style.

The villa itself was a single storey, with a veranda running around each side. The walls were wood-slatted to give a sense of tradition, although I was sure reinforced steel lay behind them. As I stared, Quang appeared from the right-hand side, accompanied by the overweight elderly man I'd seen the day before. Quang gave a *wai* of welcome, which I returned.

'I thought you might like to begin our discussions in rather more elegant surroundings, Mr Borubaev.'

His use of Mister rather than Inspector was unsettling, as if I'd been demoted in importance, although I was surely no longer a member of the Bishkek Murder Squad, or indeed, the police force. It was a ploy to show our relative status, and despite myself, I could see it worked.

The driver frisked me, with particular emphasis on the sleeve of my suit, as if I imagined I could hide a steak knife there twice. I was glad I'd hidden the mobile; I suspected Quang would not approve of me carrying it. Straightening my jacket, I followed Quang and the old man into the villa.

I'd heard about the Jim Thompson House in central Bangkok, had even promised myself a visit if I could manage it. Quang's house contained sculptures of inscrutable heads staring out with empty eyes, ornate carved wooden traditional furniture, even exquisite silk drapes and wall hangings. I had no doubt everything was of the highest quality and immensely valuable, like living in one's own private museum. After all, what was the point of being Thailand's most successful drugs overlord if you couldn't spend your money on the best in life?

'First, may I offer you some breakfast?' Quang asked. 'We have a local speciality, *joke*, a jasmine rice congee, although my chef has omitted the marinated pork out of respect for you.'

I didn't explain I wasn't a Muslim; I figured the less Quang knew about me, the fewer flaws he could find in my story when he sat down to pick it apart.

I shook my head, thanked him for his hospitality, asked for tea.

'I know you are a very important and busy man, Khun Quang, and I don't wish to take up any more of your valuable time than I have to.'

'As you wish, let us begin,' Quang said, gesturing towards a beautiful rosewood conference table that cost more than my apartment in Bishkek. As we sat down, a servant entered, pouring each of us a cup of tea and a glass of water. Quang smelt the aroma of the tea with an appreciative smile.

'Lapsang souchong, from Fujian in China. You're familiar with it?'

I shook my head: in Kyrgyzstan we're more used to iced tea from Lipton, or fermented mare's milk.

'A weakness of mine, I'm afraid, and rather expensive. But then, the best usually is, don't you find?'

The tea tasted of pencil shavings.

'As you know, I have no faith that modern communications cannot be intercepted. What man invents, man can decipher. I never conduct business online, by telephone or any other means that can be recorded, copied, or used against me.'

He took a sip of his tea, nodded approval.

'The reputation of your superior, Mr Kanybek, precedes him, although we have never met. He does not wish to visit Bangkok, and I – forgive me – don't find your northern cold and snow to my taste.'

'I understand,' I said, noting the use of 'superior' to put both Aliyev and myself in our respective places.

'He knows that to contact me at all requires a whole series of cut-outs and go-betweens,' Quang continued, 'and even then I will only discuss matters that may compromise me on a face-to-face basis.'

'*Pakhan* Kanybek shares your sentiments,' I replied. 'He believes the snow leopard stays alive from the hunters by remaining out of their sight. That's why I have been sent here, to act as his personal emissary, pouring his words into your ear.'

Quang listened intently, while the old man sat nearby on a sofa, apparently asleep.

'We both share similar retail interests, although we serve different markets,' I began.

'Heroin,' Quang interrupted. I paused, uncertain how to continue.

'Don't worry,' he continued, 'this house is entirely secure, scanned every day for listening devices in every room. The windows are vibration-free, so sound waves from conversations cannot be intercepted. My staff are all absolutely loyal, knowing as they do that any lapse on their part would result in the torture and death of their entire family, immediate and extended. And needless to say, I have certain financial arrangements in place with senior police officials and army officers. Please continue.'

'The one market that causes you some problems is the former Soviet Union,' I said. 'You supply large quantities of extremely high-grade heroin, and your shipping and distribution networks are the finest in the world. But the very quality of your product causes problems in our market.'

'Please go on,' Quang said.

'Quite simply, the addicts in our market are poor and indiscriminate about the drugs they take. You will have heard of *krokodil*, I'm sure?'

Quang nodded, and the old man turned to look at me, before shutting his eyes and resuming his slumbers.

'Easy to make, no smuggling or transportation costs, essentially home-made so no need to generate a profit margin except to make enough to sell to pay for the ingredients. And more to the point, it's fatal in a very short period of time. The customers who use *krokodil* die off even quicker than they can be replaced, or weaned away onto purer, safer drugs.'

'As you say, that's your market, not mine.'

'A major problem of the Afghan trade is that it's become harder to reach the more lucrative markets. A greater clampdown by the West, drones watching smuggling convoys headed west, political pressure backed by promises of aid or bribes to wipe out the poppy fields.'

Quang said nothing, simply templed his fingers together, stared at me.

'It's easier to send shipments east, transport them through Tajikistan and from there to Osh, my country's second city. The mountains are spattered with unofficial paths, littered with border guards who can earn a year's money by going for a piss behind the border hut at the right time.'

Quang shrugged.

'And?'

'The worldwide market is expanding,' I said. 'Look at the way opium production has tripled in the Golden Triangle in the last decade. But prices haven't dropped significantly.'

'I know all this, Mr Borubaev,' Quang said, impatience clear in his voice. 'I'm waiting to hear your proposal. As you said earlier, I'm a busy man.'

'Injecting addicts die sooner or later, usually sooner. An overdose, an unusually pure shot or a bag cut with brick dust, baby laxative or whatever boosts the street dealer's profits. So you're relying on future addicts, the ones who are still sniffing glue or getting drunk on cheap beer, before they graduate to the hard stuff.'

Quang didn't bother to hide looking at his watch. I knew it was time for me to cut to the chase.

'What we would like is for you to agree to exit our markets, and allow us to take over your distribution chain.'

As I'd expected, Quang was too intelligent to be angered by

this suggestion. He merely raised an eyebrow and waited for me to continue.

'By leaving the marketplace to us, we get a monopoly that allows us to set prices and quantities, to stabilise the market, to maximise profits. We can make more money per gram, per kilo, per tonne than you can because our network costs are lower.'

I paused, took a sip of water. No matter how often I'd rehearsed the arguments with Aliyev, I still felt my nervousness would scupper any agreement, and a bullet in my brain would be my pay-off.

'Where we in Kyrgyzstan benefit is that we're a transit country. The Fergana Valley is one of the most fertile areas of Central Asia. We ship thousands of tonnes of produce all around the region, to the point where the authorities know they can only seize a tiny amount of what we transport. Every shipment from Thailand is scrutinised, regarded with suspicion.

'With us, the volume is so overwhelming the authorities don't have a chance. Try to find a kilo of heroin in a truck loaded up with three tonnes of apples, or nuts, or onions, or cabbages. You have to open every bag, and even then, if you find something, who can you arrest? The driver, who swears blind he knows nothing, and probably doesn't?'

'Your points are very clear, if I may say so, but I'm still waiting to hear how pulling out of a market benefits my organisation, however low the profits, however great the risk or inconvenience of doing business.'

It was time for me to pull the rabbit out of the hat with a grand flourish, a bow, and hope I wasn't booed off stage.

'I've already pointed out what we both know – injecting users aren't a long-term proposition on an individual basis. And the demographic is an aging one as well. We can help you reach a younger consumer, one who doesn't want oblivion or death. And that's what we'd like to offer you in exchange.'

Quang studied me for an endless moment, and then gave the slightest hint of a nod and a smile.

'It all sounds very promising, Mr . . . forgive, I should say Inspector, should I not?'

'I think I'm almost certainly a plain, run-of-the-mill mister, thank you. But I appreciate your remembering.'

Quang tapped twice on the table, and the servant from earlier reappeared, so swiftly I assumed he'd been hovering, lurking outside the door.

'I look forward to hearing the rest of your proposition. But I'd be remiss if I didn't suggest lunch, a chance to gather our thoughts, refresh our bodies. You are, after all, an honoured guest.'

Quang nodded at the servant, who scurried away as silently as he'd arrived. Turning back to me, Quang stood up.

'Lunch? In an hour? Perhaps you'd care to rest until then?'

I got the impression nobody refused an invitation from Quang, so I simply nodded.

Chapter 36

I'd been shown into a guest bedroom by Quang himself. The room was spartan in contrast to the meeting room, but the bed was a welcome sight. The adrenalin my speech had ridden on was beginning to fade, and I thought perhaps thirty minutes' rest would revitalise me.

'Our climate can be rather wearing for people unaccustomed to it,' Quang had said before leaving the room, 'especially from your part of the world. Please take some time to relax.'

I unlaced my shoes, took off my jacket, lay down on the bed. An air-conditioning unit ruffled my hair, and tiredness hit me like a club. Even as my eyes began to close, I heard the door open and close behind me. I turned around, half expecting a summons back to the conference table, but what I saw was completely unexpected.

A young Thai woman in some type of kimono was carrying a tray filled with small cut-glass bottles. As I stared at her, she placed the tray on the bedside table, unstoppering the bottles, so the scent of perfumed oils filled the air. Long thin fingers with beautifully manicured and red-painted nails began to undo my shirt, while a shy smile revealed small white teeth.

I began to rise up, to protest, but a hand pressed me back against the mattress.

'From Khun Quang. Only for most honoured guest. My name Achura.'

Her voice was soft, clear enough without the sing-song Thai accent so that even with my basic English I could understand her meaning.

I put my hands to stop her, protested I was honoured but didn't need a massage, but that didn't deter her. I told myself Thai massages were said to be the finest in the world, with several temples containing schools to learn the art. Quang would certainly employ only the most skilful practitioners. And I would have been lying if the idea of having a beautiful stranger stroke my skin didn't have a certain erotic frisson.

The thought of Saltanat's opinion made me reluctant, but then I considered she and I had never made promises to each other, that she was a free agent in these things just as much as I. It's very easy to be noble when temptation isn't a few inches away, gazing at you with enormous dark-brown eyes, framed with gold and silver eyeshadow and tinted lashes that set off high cheekbones and honey-shaded skin.

Finally I removed my shirt, rolled onto my stomach, felt the delicious coolness of the oils poured onto my back. My body heat released their perfume: jasmine, rosemary, herbs I couldn't identify, all mingling together into a musk soaking into my skin.

Achura's hands pressed into the muscles around my neck and shoulders, surprisingly strong, kneading out any tension placed there by the stress of my trip. I shut my eyes, let my thoughts drift away into pure sensation.

The fingers on my back pressed hard then soft, hard then soft, in an unending circular movement. I could understand why people became devotees, swore by its power to provide tranquillity and harmony with the world.

I was drifting off into a state of total relaxation when I felt the hands tap me on the top of my head, a sign the massage had ended. I opened my eyes to find Achura already stoppering the glass bottles, her movements precise and delicate. I watched as she bowed and exited the room, leaving only the perfume of the oils like a fading memory.

A thought struck me and I looked up at the ceiling. The camera was almost impossible to spot, if I hadn't been looking for it; I wondered if Quang filmed all of his guests, perhaps as a bargaining tool or even for blackmail. I sat up, struggled back into my shirt, thankful I hadn't been tempted into doing something foolish.

In an earlier case, in Dubai, I'd been drugged and photographed with a woman, both of us naked, posed to look as if we were hard at it. Saltanat had seen through that particular set-up, although I didn't fancy my chances of appeasing her a second time. It's never a good idea to cheat on a trained assassin. Thankfully, that was one bridge I didn't have to cross. But first of all, I had to deal with Quang.

Chapter 37

I returned to the conference room, the table now hidden by an extravagant display of Thai food, most of the dishes unknown to me. Quang was already seated at the head of the table.

'I trust your massage was satisfactory, Mr Borubaev?' he asked, his face absolutely straight. I wondered if Quang had set me up with the *kathoey* to see my reaction.

'I can honestly say it was a completely new and unique experience for me,' I replied, with previously unknown diplomacy.

'I devote an hour every day to a massage, even with my schedule. It's so important to keep the body and spirit in harmony, don't you think, denying the senses nothing, experiencing new sensations to prevent one's psychological palate becoming jaded.'

I wasn't sure what any of that meant, or if it meant anything at all, so I simply smiled and nodded. No point in falling out when there were millions at stake.

'I feel relaxed in a way I never have before, and any repetition would only dilute the pleasure I felt,' I said, trying to make the point it wasn't going to happen again.

'Very wise,' Quang said. 'You have something of the Confucian philosopher in you. Many foreigners quite misunderstand the place of *kathoeys* like Achura in Thai culture.'

I nodded, knowing I would go down in Quang's estimation if he decided I was simply an ignorant *farang*.

'Many foreign people assume the third gender is merely a vehicle for sex, for breaking taboos that exist in their country. Of course, sex can play a role in their life – doesn't it in everyone's? But they can be charming, artistic, highly talented, the chosen companions of many influential and respected people. I hope you will learn our culture is an ancient one, whose secrets aren't always open and on the surface.'

Quang smiled, gestured towards the table.

'But excuse my manners, talking away while you must be hungry. Please, join me at the table.'

We ate for the next hour, tastes and textures that I'd never encountered before, all exquisitely presented. Fresh spicy shrimp noodle salad ('Flown from my private farm near Chiang Mai'), green eggplant curry ('The lemongrass adds a certain piquancy that highlights and contrasts the sweetness of the vegetables, don't you think?'), steamed fish with lime and garlic ('Barramundi, line-caught naturally') and dozens more, most of which I couldn't identify.

Finally, my mouth scorched as if a miniature blowtorch had been at my tongue, we moved away from the table and sat down.

'You said before lunch that the traditional injecting addict population is unstable? And you have a means of recruiting a younger market?'

'You have obviously heard of spice, Khun Quang?'

Quang nodded. 'Synthetic cannabis. Expensive and difficult for us to produce here.'

'Exactly. Thailand is essentially an agricultural nation, and to synthesise spice in the volume to make it financially viable requires skilled chemists, high-tech labs and a regular reliable supply of ingredients.'

Quang frowned. 'But my understanding is that there is virtually no quality control over the spice sold in European and American markets. Tea leaves or grass cuttings, natural ingredients but coated in synthetic chemicals to create hallucinogens. But the problem is no one knows the strength of the spice they're buying, whether it will get them high or kill them. Lots of possible side-effects – paranoia, psychosis and so on. That's why it's known as the zombie drug.'

'Which is where we come in,' I said. 'We can ensure you get a regular, ingredient-approved product that will appeal to the young demographic in Thailand. People who want to get high but who don't want to find themselves in a psychiatric ward or a morgue drawer. Safe spice, in other words; a weekend in another galaxy and a relaxed return to earth.'

Quang took another sip of tea. His face gave nothing away, no anger, no interest, no disbelief. We Kyrgyz pride ourselves on being stony-faced but Quang was in an entirely different league.

'How do you propose to do that?'

I paused; this was where the whole plan might fall apart, and I'd be lucky to get back to Bishkek.

'Yours is a primarily agricultural economy, and you've got a relatively large population in a relatively small space. I don't just mean Bangkok, but the country as a whole. Setting up spice labs, hiring chemists, getting reliable ingredients; it all takes time and money, and there's always the danger the local police show too great an interest, then you've lost your investment and your credibility on the street.'

The elderly man was awake now, listening intently to what I said.

'Go on,' Quang said, his face impassive, but I sensed he was sniffing the bait, inspecting the hook.

'Central Asia is vast, as you know, and so is Russia. There are eleven different time zones in Russia alone. So you can manufacture spice a long, long way from anywhere that might attract attention. As a whole, Russia is barely populated, about nine people per square kilometre. Which means there are vast tracts of land where you can travel for hours and not see a soul. Ideal for a spice factory.'

I took a sip of water, cleared my suddenly dry throat.

'There's no problem getting the necessary chemicals, either through the porous borders to the east or the industrial ports and entry points to the west. Highly trained chemists happy to work for something less than the pittance paid by the state.'

I watched Quang nod his understanding.

'Spice sells for a lot more per gram than heroin. No use trying to sell it in Russia. People are making their own *krokodil* because they can't afford anything else. But Thailand has a more affluent population, as well as a huge number of foreign tourists. The way things are at the moment, we can't sell it, and you can't get it.'

Quang gestured around the room, at the museum-quality works of art.

'What makes you think I need any more money, Mr Borubaev? You'll agree this is hardly the home of a poor man.'

'It's not about wealth, it's about business, about dominating a market opportunity. If you don't supply spice, eventually someone else will. And every *baht*, dollar or euro that goes into their pockets is one less to go into yours. Eventually they'll buy the influence and power you currently have, turn it against you, and sooner or later, the walls of your villa won't be high enough to protect you. If you don't lead the market, your competitors will steamroller you.'

I paused, wondering if I'd said too much, gone too far. I didn't think Quang would take offence at my blunt speaking, but I hoped I'd presented my case without causing him to lose face.

'Yours is a very interesting analysis, not without merits,' Quang said, 'but you still haven't told me exactly what it is you propose between our two organisations.'

'Think of it as a trade agreement. You leave the heroin business in Russia to us, a monopoly so we can control supply, prices, quality. In return, we'll manufacture spice for you, to an agreed volume and quality, then ship it to Thailand, all at a major discount, a price you couldn't possibly match if you were to manufacture it yourself. We take the risk, we do the hard work, the manufacture and the transport, and you have a superior product that gives you much more profit per gram.'

Quang was silent for several moments, his only movement to raise his cup to his lips, taking minute sips.

'There is one other issue,' I said. '*Yaa baa*. Methampheta-mine. We know it's used a great deal here in Thailand, to give people energy, the ability to work harder and longer. It's extremely profitable for you. But that income may be coming to an end.'

'How so?' Quang asked, looking puzzled.

'We know your government is seriously considering legal-ising *yaa baa*, controlling the quality, guaranteeing purity. And that's a huge slice of your business gone at the stamp of a government seal.'

'You're very well informed,' Quang said. 'You are in contact with your colleague?'

I noticed Quang had demoted Aliyev from the status of superior to that of colleague: perhaps he had decided dealing with me would be preferable. Or that by rejecting the pro-posal, perhaps even killing me, he would be sending a message to Aliyev to stay clear.

'Obviously, I want to discuss this matter with my advisors,' Quang continued. 'They will have questions to ask regarding their particular roles. And naturally, we need to know the mechanics of the operation, how you bring the spice into the country, for example.'

'Whoever heard of anyone smuggling drugs into Thai-land?' I said. 'We're used to moving quantities across borders, but you will, of course, appreciate that the exact specifics are our concern. The more people know our methods, the easier it is to get caught.'

For the first time, Quang smiled, and his normally austere

face took on a sudden charm. 'If you wish to keep a secret, tell it to only one other person, then kill them?'

'Something like that,' I agreed. 'Even better if you don't tell anyone.'

'How long do you intend to stay in Bangkok, Mr Borubaev?'

'Only a few days, until I hear of your decision,' I said.

'And then? Back to Kyrgyzstan? My understanding is you would not be welcomed with open arms by your former colleagues.'

Quang knew about me being on the run. It made me easier to manipulate. He must have known a cell or a bullet were all that would be waiting for me back home.

'You might find Bangkok a congenial place to settle, somewhere to base your part in the operation. Unless you have a passion for snow and ice, that is.'

I knew Quang was thinking of me as a potential hostage, someone to punish and make an example of if things went wrong. He overestimated my importance to Aliyev and the Circle of Brothers. A cell in Bishkek would come courtesy of my former colleagues, a bullet courtesy of my new ones.

'I gather you've already enjoyed some of the pleasures my city has to offer,' Quang said. 'Apparently you have excellent taste.'

I smiled as if to suggest a liking for commitment-free paid-for sex. I thought of Saltanat, wondered where she was, if I would be able to contact her. A familiar sense of hope for our future together was, as usual, replaced by the despair of knowing it would never happen.

'I hope to take further samples,' I said. 'My country is considerably more conservative in such matters.'

'Please make yourself comfortable while I organise your transport to your hotel. More tea?'

I shook my head, and Quang left the room. I wandered over to the far wall, where one sculpture had caught my eye when I first arrived. A sandstone bas-relief, an elaborately clothed slender and beautiful woman was shown in a highly stylised dance position, the grace and sinuous poise of her figure captured in a moment of ecstasy. The surface of the stone was weathered although the details of the sculpture were still clear, and I imagined it had once been part of a temple. I couldn't hazard a guess at its age, but it was a thing of beauty.

'You have such things in your country?'

I turned round; the elderly man was standing staring at me, amused at my interest in the bas-relief. His accent was so strong, I wondered if I had misheard, then shook my head, wondering how to explain that a nomadic people didn't have the skills or interest to spend time carving stone.

'Twelfth century, Cambodian, from the temple complex at Angkor Wat. An *apsara*, a celestial dancer, a female spirit of the clouds and water, you like it?'

I nodded, raising one hand to stroke the dancer's cheek.

'I brought it here myself, many years ago, just as the Khmer Rouge were being driven out. I had to kill four men to do it. One with a rope around his throat. Two with a dagger. And the last one, I used my hands. And the *apsara* has danced here for me ever since.'

I looked down at the old man's hands with a new respect. They were large, raw-knuckled, capable of inflicting immense pain. I had the feeling he may have lost some of his speed but none of his power and ruthlessness. Quang's father, perhaps? I didn't think we would ever have enough trust to confide personal matters to each other.

The elderly man cracked his knuckles with the sound of snapping chopsticks, gave a gap-toothed smile, settled back down in his chair. He folded his hands across his huge belly, appearing to go back into a deep sleep.

Suddenly the room felt more like a prison or a dungeon than an elegant home of taste and luxury. The celestial dancer had been courted and won with blood, and everything else in the room was tainted by the hopeless misery and addiction that had paid for it. I felt the food I'd eaten rise in my throat, wondered if I was about to vomit. Suddenly I hated everything I had become, everything Chinara would have despised.

'You're pale; are you feeling faint?'

Quang had returned, was standing by my side, looking solicitous.

'It's nothing. The long flight, very little sleep last night, and, as you say, the climate is very different to the one I'm used to.'

'I hope our lunch hasn't disagreed with you. Just simple peasant food, I'm afraid, not what you're used to.'

I thought of the bowls of rice greasy with mutton fat I'd been served in yurts all over Kyrgyzstan, and decided Quang had no idea what simple peasant food was.

'It was delicious,' I assured him, watching his superior smile.

'Your driver is waiting for you outside the main gate. You'll forgive me if I don't walk out with you. Spy drones, satellite cameras looking down, perhaps even a sniper waiting to pin his cross-hairs to my forehead. I rarely leave here; last night was an exception I made for you. I'm sure you agree, caution adds years to your life. All the same, I do sometimes feel as if I'm in a prison.'

Not like any prison I've ever been in, I thought, and shook his hand. Something about him had reminded me of Aliyev for quite some time, and I finally realised what it was. Neither man seemed capable of understanding the suffering of others, of realising their involvement in its cause. I had to leave before my face betrayed me. Some of the most evil people I've encountered in my work – and I use the word 'evil' very care-fully indeed – have been almost telepathically sensitive to the moods and thoughts of other people, as if their senses were finely tuned to pick up the merest hint of betrayal. Of course, there are also the things of which they seem completely unaware, like pity, compassion and, of course, love.

And some of us are aware of the dead who watch us from the shadows, hoping to see how we avenge them so they can sleep.

Dead is dead.

Except when it's not.

Chapter 38

On the drive back to my hotel, I wondered how successful my pitch to Quang had been. Nothing concrete had been decided; Quang was obviously as cautious as Aliyev in his business dealings. But I felt certain we would reach some kind of agreement. The possible legalisation of *yaa baa* would have a major impact upon his profits and, by extension, on his ability to control law enforcement, the army, rival suppliers. That worked in our favour. On the other hand, removing access to the Russian market might seem like the first step in a takeover bid, which could only lead to war.

The journey back took for ever, not just because I was impatient to contact Saltanat, but because we'd hit rush-hour traffic. I now realised traffic jams in Bangkok lasted around the clock, but this one seemed particularly slow. I even wondered about getting out and walking, but the thought of the heat and humidity made an air-conditioned limousine with leather seats my preferred option.

Finally, we turned into Langsuan and back to the hotel. It was already getting dark, and I could see flocks of birds rising up and spiralling to find somewhere to roost in Lumpini Park. The idea that wildlife could survive, even thrive, in such an urban chaos was oddly reassuring.

Back in my room, I retrieved the burner from its hiding place and switched it on. A single message, 'Asia Books, Landmark Hotel, 20.00.' Saltanat was nothing if not concise. I didn't know whether she intended for us to meet there, but I only had an hour to get there. In reception, I spoke to the husky-voiced *kathoey* receptionist (I was beginning to recognise the telltale signs) who told me it was about three quarters of an hour away on Sukhumvit, if I was willing to walk. A taxi? Who knows, this time of night? The receptionist gave a sweet smile, apologising for being unable to be more helpful, told me I couldn't miss the Landmark. Just follow the Skytrain overhead. I gave my thanks, pushed through the oversized doors and out into the night.

I wondered about getting a tuk-tuk, one of the three-wheeled motorbikes with seating and a roof attached that hurtle through the city, decided I'd had enough excitement for one day.

I strolled up Langsuan past the luxury condominium blocks and building sites towards Chit Lom BTS station. I looked at the concrete stairs climbing up to the platform, saw the crowds heading towards the trains, and chose walking as preferable to being squashed to death.

It was a very pleasant walk, if you took away the incessant roar and blare of traffic, the fumes hanging in the air, the humidity visible under the streetlights, and the countless people who in their hurry to be somewhere decided to walk through me. It was a relief to find myself at the Landmark, which I discovered was just around the corner from Nana

Plaza. From low life to the high life in just a few steps; maybe that was part of the charm of Bangkok.

This was the sort of hotel where Quang thought I should be staying, with a spacious terrace proclaiming 'Al Fresco Dining'. It was populated by the kind of people who've never gone hungry or cold. I could drink a very expensive cup of coffee, nibble at an even more expensive piece of cake, or simply enjoy the air conditioning. I wandered around in the aimless fashion that anyone following me would expect of someone sightseeing with nothing particular in mind. I looked at tourist souvenirs, studied restaurant menus discreetly positioned by the dining area, looked for the toilet, came out drying my hands.

I arrived at the Asia Books shop a little after eight. One thing I've learned is never to arrive exactly on the hour or the half-hour. Nothing spells rendezvous more clearly than that; six minutes past the hour is just a random time. Simple tradecraft, but you'd be amazed at the number of people who don't use it.

I smiled sweetly at the assistant who scurried over, shook my head to show I didn't need any help, and started to browse the big books of photographs of Thailand. I'd been there for maybe ten minutes when I felt the burner in my pocket vibrate. I pretended to stumble, looking down at my shoe as if I'd tripped over my lace, then knelt down behind a large display of self-help books and checked the burner. The last time I'd been in a bookshop, I'd shot and killed a man. That doesn't say much for literature as a civilising influence.

The screen message simply said 'John Burdett. Bangkok 8'. I deleted the message and stood up. I didn't know anyone called Burdett, and I had no idea where Bangkok 8 was. But I wandered around the store until I came to the fiction section, and there, under B, were half a dozen copies of the book. I picked up a copy at random, flicked through, replaced it. *Bangkok 8* seemed nothing out of the ordinary, but as I leafed through the third book, I found a small strip of paper, the kind you tear off the edge of a newspaper to use as a bookmark. Someone had written 623. Saltanat made it a rule never to leave an obvious trail; it was part of how she'd stayed alive for so long.

I put the book back on the shelf, screwed up the paper and dropped it to the floor. Probably a room number. Maybe when all this was over, I could rejoin the police and work my way up the ranks to detective.

I spent a few more minutes thumbing through a photographic history of Angkor Wat, the sort of book that takes two hands to hold and a deep wallet to buy. Some of the pictures showed where statues, sculptures and carvings had been cut away from the temple walls, and I wondered if one of them showed the spot where Quang's bas-relief had been hacked away.

The assistant hovered by me, hoping to snatch my credit card and ring up a purchase before I could change my mind, but I simply shook my head and replaced the book.

Outside the store, I saw a row of lifts, walked over, looked at the destination board. The Rib Room and Bar Steakhouse sounded ideal, not that I was particularly hungry after lunch. Maybe a drink or two first.

The lift was empty when I arrived, so I pressed for the thirty-first floor. When the doors opened and a group of well-fed diners entered, I exited, making sure to press the button for the sixth floor on the way down. The lift hadn't stopped on the journey up, so anyone on the ground floor who had been watching me would assume I'd gone to eat, drink and stare aimlessly out of the plate-glass windows. I was pretty sure I would have an hour or so to remain out of sight, so I looked for the stairwell, started to make my way down.

I prefer stairs to lifts any time; it's harder to be surprised by a gun or a knife. However, walking down twenty-five flights of stairs is not my idea of light exercise, particularly when the stairwell doesn't have air conditioning, and I hoped Saltanat would have a fridge full of cold water when I reached room 623.

I knocked on the door and waited. I could see the glow of lights in the room through the peephole. The door swung open, just a little, and I knew Saltanat was standing to one side, gun in hand, ready to shoot at the first sign of anything wrong. I didn't know how she'd acquired a firearm, but she wouldn't have had any trouble, or have any problems using it either.

I pushed the door open a little further, didn't step in right away. Caution keeps you breathing, even air as polluted as Bangkok's.

'Thanks for the book recommendation,' I said, 'but my English isn't up to it. Perhaps when it comes out in Russian.'

'Shut the door,' was all she said.

I watched as she put the gun away behind a newspaper on the table. In movies, people hide guns under pillows, but in real life that's clumsy, and when fractions of a second count, possibly fatal.

I shut the door, put on the chain, operated the deadlock and one of those horseshoe-shaped hasps that hotel guests believe keep intruders out. They don't; you just have to be determined and not care if you make a bit of noise.

As always, a first glimpse of Saltanat was enough to deprive me of breath, let alone sense. The elegant hooker outfit of the night before had been abandoned in favour of jeans and a crisp white blouse. No make-up, hair tied back in a chignon, I couldn't imagine anyone looking more elegant, more poised. I suspected she didn't see me in quite the same worshipping light.

'I've made a few enquiries, Akyl, while you've been out playing footsie with one of the biggest criminals in the Far East.'

I didn't bother to ask how she knew where I'd been; in fact I'd expected nothing less.

'What in the name of God possessed you to shoot Tynaliev?' she asked.

'Because I knew he was going to shoot me,' I said. 'And I'd rather be on the run than in a grave.'

'How do you know he was going to kill you?'

'Lenin didn't announce he was going to have the tsar and his family lined up against a wall. Stalin didn't tell Trotsky he was sending him an ice-axe,' I said, starting to feel rather heated. You can only spend so much time defending yourself before it begins to irritate. 'You think Tynaliev was going to say "Thank you for all your help in the past, Akyl, time to kiss the world goodbye"?'

Saltanat surprised me by making an appeasing gesture.

'Calm down, Akyl, I know you had reason to worry because of how much you knew, and how paranoid the minister could be. But working for the Circle of Brothers? You must have had a good reason, a better reason than "I'll get him before he gets me".'

I crossed over to the fridge, took out a bottle of water, looked over at Saltanat. She pointed at the bedside table where I could see a half-drunk glass of red wine sitting there.

'When you called me from Tashkent and asked – no, begged – me to come and meet you here, you said you'd explain. Well, I'm here. And I'm still waiting for your explanation. I've got a flight to Tashkent booked for tomorrow morning. And without some pretty convincing answers, I'll be on it. And you won't be seeing me again.'

'It's complicated,' I said, trying to keep self-pity out of my voice.

Saltanat crossed over to the bed, picked up her wine, took the smallest of sips and stared out of the window.

'Things are always complicated for people like us, doing what we do,' she said, and I sensed compassion in her voice. I could only hope it wasn't pity. 'You asked me to come and help you, and I came.' She was still staring out of the window, never turning to face me. 'I came because I wanted to help. You're in the worst trouble of your life, and there's no way you could haul yourself out of the swamp on your own.'

I could feel my heart beating as if suffering repeated body blows. My mouth was dry, my hands trembling.

'And I had a reason of my own,' she said, her voice flat, expressionless. 'I'm pregnant.'

Chapter 39

I sat down heavily, opened and closed my mouth a couple of times. There are moments in your life when the road suddenly veers at a right angle to the expected direction. This looked like being one of those.

'Is it—' I started to say, but Saltanat forestalled me.

'Yes, it's yours,' she said, with an edge to her voice that told me to tread very warily indeed. 'You'd prefer a boy?'

'Either is great,' I said, in spite of knowing girls have a harder passage through life, whether they're in Kyrgyzstan or Uzbekistan, Bishkek or Tashkent.

'You're angry?' Saltanat asked. 'I know it's something that neither of us talked about, even considered. Well, I didn't at any rate.'

She picked up her wine glass, watched as I stood up and took the glass out of her hand.

'That stops, as of now,' I said. 'And the cigarettes.'

'I take it you don't want me to get rid of it?' Saltanat asked, staring at me and my new-found assertiveness. I shook my head. I'd never told her about Chinara's abortion, how it had eaten at me ever since.

'I've never felt particularly maternal,' she continued, 'and you've always struck me as being too self-involved to play the role of happy Pappa.'

She must have seen the look on my face, because her tone altered.

'The job I'm in, the situation you're in, you think we'd make the best possible parents? Especially in a shit-filled world like this?'

I said nothing; I couldn't speak. I was thinking of the time Chinara got pregnant, not long after we were married, and we'd both decided the time wasn't right to have a child. I remembered going with her to the clinic, seeing the brave smile that stopped before reaching her eyes and the thumbs-up she gave me, dressed in the ill-fitting surgical gown they gave her as they took her away to kill our child.

'It's a shock, that's all,' I said. 'As you said, not something we were planning.'

I remembered lying next to Chinara in bed two nights later, after an evening of forced smiles, avoiding each other's eyes. Then the silent sobs moving her shoulders, the mattress shaking to mourn the passing of our child the way it had shaken when we created it. I felt helpless, impotent in the face of the blow reality had dealt us. We survived, because that's what love does; we'd said we could always have another when the time was right. And then the cancer stepped in, took away all Chinara's time, right or not.

'What do you want to do?' I said, thinking this would probably be my last chance to father a child, even if it was almost certain I wouldn't be alive to watch it grow up. I've always lived my life trying to avenge the dead, but I've always shied away from admitting I've killed an innocent victim as well.

'Don't you mean, what are *we* going to do?' Saltanat said.

A lot of my countrymen, and Saltanat's too for all I know, would say it's a woman's decision, it's her body, as long as it's not a boy. We bride-steal a girl, marry her, get her pregnant then head off to Moscow for a life of a little more money and no responsibility. And none of that money finds its way back to the city or the villages. After that, the divorce, a shrug of the shoulders, it's all in the past now, life, it can't be helped, just the way it is. Until the next time.

'I mean, you're the mother, you're carrying it in your body for the next few months. I'm not even sure how many days I've got left, before Tynaliev or Aliyev or Quang decide to finish me. I can't make a sensible decision about a child I'm never going to see. The most I can hope for is that if it's a boy, you call him Akyl.'

Saltanat sat down beside me, took my hand.

'I didn't come to Bangkok to pressure you into a shotgun wedding,' she said, 'but you'd better not meet my brothers unless I have a ring on my right hand. I came here to try to help you, not because I'm pregnant but because I know you love me, and I appear to be stuck with you.'

She smiled, that enigmatic haunting smile, and I thought how lucky I was to know her, how unworthy to deserve her. Saltanat might be a trained killer, but she's my trained killer. And a selfish part of me knew that if anyone could get me out of the mess I was in, it would be her.

'I've got your back when you next go to see Quang. You won't spot me, but I'll be there.'

I nodded. You don't need an army when you've got the best on your side.

'And now you'd better go,' she said. 'If someone followed you here, they might decide it's time to see if you've finished eating. Or if you're getting blind drunk and liable to cause trouble.'

I nodded, stood up, tried to kiss her. But she pushed me away, pointed to the door.

'Next time. Go,' she said, and then I was in the corridor, getting ready to climb up to the top floor. I reached the Rib Room, washed my face in the bathroom, sat at the bar, ordered an orange juice. I was halfway through the glass, lamenting the absence of freshly squeezed oranges in Bishkek, when the driver appeared in the doorway, obviously looking for me.

I looked over at him, as if trying to focus after a few vodkas, recognised him, smiled, waved.

'*Tovarich,*' I slurred. 'A drink for you?'

The driver simply shook his head, took my arm, a band of steel tight against my bicep.

I finished the juice in a single gulp, winced as if it were three-quarters vodka, smiled at the bartender, left several thousand *baht* on the bar top.

'That should cover all the drinks,' I said, and got up off the stool, swaying slightly as I did so. The bartender was discreet enough, or greedy enough, not to raise any objection, and we made our way to the lift.

Once inside, I straightened my jacket, surveyed myself in the mirror.

'How did you know I was here?' I asked, innocent curiosity in my voice.

'Mr Quang has a lot of friends, who like to keep him informed,' was the neutral answer. I was pretty sure no one had spotted my detour to the sixth floor, but I guessed I'd know soon enough.

A parking valet brought the limousine around and I clambered into the back, making sure I caught my foot on the door edge as I did so. Maybe I was overdoing it, but then the driver had probably had experience of drunken Russians before.

'Now we go to a club, yes?' I suggested, tapping the side of my nose.

The driver said nothing, but steered in the direction of my hotel, which suited me just fine. I needed time to plan ahead for my next meeting with Quang, to work out how to keep Aliyev happy, how to avoid the wrath of Tynaliev, and, most importantly, what I was going to do about Saltanat.

At the hotel, I gave a stiff and formal nod to the driver, before making my way unsteadily to the doors.

'Seven tomorrow morning,' was all the driver said. I assumed that was when I'd been summoned back to thrash out a deal with Quang. After that, I'd just have to trust to luck and what natural cunning I possessed. But sleep was a long time in arriving, coming as it did complete with dreams of pain and death.

Chapter 40

In the morning, sober, I felt as rough as if I'd necked a bottle of *samogon* the night before, a headache drumming at the back of my eyeballs like a miniature metronome. Lack of sleep and fear will do that for you. All night long, I'd dreamt of a gun barrel pressed against my forehead, or watching helpless as a faceless interrogator brought a red-hot iron closer and closer to my face. It was almost a relief to wake up.

My watch said six thirty so I made myself a cup of vile coffee, grabbed a shower, found clean clothes in the wardrobe and put on my suit, which now smelt of spilt beer, cigarette smoke and sweat.

I wondered where Saltanat was, if I'd get to see her before I left Thailand. Maybe she simply wanted to make sure I left on my own two feet and not in a box, before getting to work on the job she'd been sent to do. I was stranded in the dark myself, without a clue or a plan. And although that was nothing new, I wondered if my luck was wearing very thin.

The air outside was hot and humid, wrapping itself around my face like an old wet blanket, but my mind felt as if I was walking on a frozen lake, each foot wondering if this was going to be the step that plunged me forward through the ice. The driver was waiting for me, his usual silent self, without even a grunt as greeting. I clambered into the back of the car, sat back, closed my eyes.

I loosened my tie, undid the top button of my shirt, then felt something in my jacket pocket. Slowly, so as not to arouse the driver's attention, I checked the shape, and realised I'd forgotten to hide the burner. I knew there was no way I could allow it to be found when I was searched before seeing Quang. It would set off all his alarm bells, and any deal we might have made would immediately be cancelled, along with my breath.

The regular Bangkok morning traffic meant we were crawling down Sukhumvit at glacier speed, and I waited until I could see an opportunity to get out of the car. I hammered at the glass partition separating me from the driver, until he turned round. Hand over my mouth, I made the universal sign for 'I'm about to hurl my stomach all over your nice clean car', then pointed at a particularly shabby-looking *soi*, one of the alleyways off the main road.

The driver must have been thinking of having to clean vomit off the leather seats, because he pulled over and opened the door. I staggered out, rushed into the bar opposite, one hand on my belly, the other over my mouth.

I lumbered into the toilet and bolted the door behind me. Once inside, I could imagine vomiting for real. The hole-in-the-ground pedestal was cracked and chipped, and from the look of it had recently been used by someone who'd also decorated the walls. The place stank, not just of shit and vomit but mud, blood and God knew what else.

I only had a minute or so before the driver came to find me.

I slipped the burner's SIM card into my shoe and dropped the phone into the murky depths. Anyone who wanted to fish for it was welcome to keep it. On the way out, I poured myself a glass of water from a jug on the bar, sluiced it around my mouth, and, when I was outside and the driver could see me, spat it out into the gutter.

I raised my hands in apology, climbed back into the car.

'Foreign food,' I said, as if that explained everything. The driver gave another of his customary grunts and we moved away from the pavement back into traffic. I was pretty sure I'd be searched again, but thought I wouldn't have to take my shoes off. Keeping the SIM card meant I could buy another pay-as-you-go phone and contact Saltanat when the opportunity arose.

I remembered enough of the buildings we passed to guess we were returning to Quang's villa. This time, I intended to miss out on the hospitality, especially the massage and the food. All I wanted was a quick discussion, an agreement of terms and a provisional start date, a handshake and then a trip to the airport. I was planning to go back to Tashkent; I had no idea what I would do there, or how long I would stay. Saltanat's news had put everything into confusion. I knew I'd have to cross the border to talk to Aliyev, but after that? A lifetime dodging cops and bullets, I imagined.

We made good time, and the driver pulled up outside Quang's gates just before eight thirty. I went through the same procedure as before, the driver paying particular attention to the contents of my pockets. Dumping the burner had been my smartest move since I arrived in Thailand. Finally he was satisfied I wasn't armed, and the gates swung open to admit us.

A servant led me to a small conference room at the back of the villa, spartan and furnished only with a small desk and two chairs. Coffee and water arrived, and then Quang himself.

'Mr Borubaev, I trust your dinner at the Landmark was satisfactory?'

I wondered if Quang had someone in the restaurant report to him; after all, it wasn't as if he couldn't afford to pay off a waiter or two. I decided to play it safe.

'Actually, no. I got there, felt ill, spent the next hour in the bathroom, I'm afraid. Kyrgyz cooking is very plain and simple, so my stomach isn't acclimatised yet. I just had a drink at the bar, and then your driver very kindly took me back to the hotel.'

Quang nodded, as if that tied in with his intelligence reports.

'You're feeling recovered now?'

I smiled, nodded perhaps too vigorously, felt my early morning headache planning a return.

'Quite. One hundred per cent. I'm hoping we can finalise the arrangement we discussed yesterday, so I can send word to Mr Aliyev before the end of the day.'

Quang steepled his fingers, stared at me with unblinking black eyes. Finally, after an uncomfortable moment, he nodded.

'Very well, we shall begin. I share your hopes as well.'

For the next six hours, we danced a complicated series of steps, each offered or rejected with exquisite politeness. Quang was obviously well aware of the financial implications any government legalisation of *yaa baa* would cause to his business, while I was all too aware of Aliyev's punishment if I failed to hammer out a deal.

The major stumbling block was on agreeing the size of the discount we would give when selling the spice. I suggested five per cent was a very generous amount, given he would have no start-up costs, no additional bribes to pay, no import problems. Quang was initially adamant he would only consider the loss of the Russian heroin market for a ten per cent discount of the spice. He insisted that quality had to be guaranteed, along with a set volume each month, to be increased as the market grew. I felt as if I was watching capitalism at its most naked, wondered if communism had been such a bad thing after all.

Finally, we agreed on an eight per cent discount, which was only one point more than Aliyev had instructed me to offer. We shook hands, toasted the arrangement, Quang with lapsang souchong while I sipped strong black coffee.

'What are your plans, Mr Borubaev?' Quang asked. 'I imagine you've no particular desire to go back to your home country. I suspect Minister Tynaliev is not a man who forgives quickly or lightly.'

'He's not a man who forgives at all,' I said, 'so I think I'm going to have to find somewhere a long way away from his reach.'

'As I said before, would you consider staying here in Thailand? I'm certain there will be some teething problems with our new arrangement, and someone who speaks Russian, who understands his home market would be very valuable.'

'Are you offering me a job, Khun Quang?' I said. At that

moment, staying in Bangkok seemed a better option than Bishkek, if only because I wasn't dead.

'Early days,' Quang said, allowing something approaching a smile to move his mouth. 'As I'm sure you know, there's a fine line between rushing in too hastily and missing out on an opportunity. I never do either.'

He drained his cup, placed it on the table.

'Our cuisine and the way we live may be a little spicy for your palate at first, but you'd come to love it.'

'I'm not sure I could cope with living in Bangkok; somewhere a little more rural perhaps, maybe by the sea. As you know, the closest we Kyrgyz get are the beaches at Lake Issyk-Kul.'

Quang seemed set to embark on his newfound role as tourist operator when the driver entered, whispered something to Quang, who looked puzzled, then annoyed. He stood up and stared at me. His face remained expressionless but I sensed anger, perhaps even fear.

'Mr Borubaev, you haven't been entirely open and honest with me.'

'I don't understand,' I said, genuinely bewildered. He couldn't have known about my meeting with Saltanat, or I wouldn't have made it this far. I'd be floating in a muddy water *khlong* while longboats crammed with tourists stared at me and took selfies.

'I go to great lengths to protect my personal security,' Quang said. 'You may consider them excessive, even paranoid. But did you honestly think a simple pat-down of your clothes would be enough?'

'I'm not carrying any weapons, if that's what you mean,' I said. 'I've no way of harming you.'

'There are many ways to harm someone,' Quang said, 'and they don't all involve a physical threat. That's why I have special highly sensitive scanners built into the doorframes of every room.'

He paused, looked over at the driver, who stood awaiting his orders.

'Please remove Mr Borubaev's shoes.'

The driver stepped forward, but I held up my hand to stop him and took my shoes off myself. The driver took the SIM card between finger and thumb, held it out towards Quang for inspection.

'And who were you intending to call?' Quang asked, the veneer of politeness gone, steel in his voice. I looked around for a weapon, saw nothing.

'I use it to contact Aliyev,' I said. 'Not here, obviously, and I buy a disposable phone each time I text him. How else would I keep in touch with him?'

'Why would you need to?' Quang asked. 'Either you have the authority to make a deal, or you don't. If you do, there's no need to contact him until you return. If you don't, he should be here himself. And you would be . . . surplus?'

Quang was a man who believed there are no such things as secrets, and the fewer people with access to information, the better he liked it. In fact, the only way he liked it.

Behind Quang, a door opened and the masseuse Achura walked in, this time not wearing traditional robes but a sweatshirt and jeans. Dressed like that, she looked much more masculine, a great deal more dangerous.

'You remember Achura, of course,' Quang said. 'A person of remarkable qualities. You may think having a *kathoey* as a bodyguard sounds eccentric, their ability to fight merely a spectacle like watching two women wrestling in Nana Plaza. But you obviously never saw Achura fight Muay Thai, our traditional martial art, the Art of Eight Limbs.'

Quang gave a patronising smile at my confusion.

'Muay Thai involves eight points of contact: punches with the fists, kicks with the feet, knee and elbow strikes. Deadly when practised by someone as skilled as Achura.'

I looked as Achura bowed her head in acknowledgement, then folded her arms. I'd never hit a woman before, and I suspected I wasn't going to get an opportunity this time. Achura would have me disabled and dead within a minute.

'Achura, would you escort Mr Borubaev outside?'

As Achura moved towards me, I felt rather than saw the driver move behind me, to block any attempt to move away.

'You'll understand I have many precious works of art in this room. You'll agree it would be a tragedy if any of them were damaged.'

The driver seized my arms and forced them behind my back, pushing me towards the door. Achura gave a smile of anticipation and led the way outside. I didn't think a relaxing massage was on the agenda.

Chapter 41

I'd faced guns, knives, the occasional broken bottle, but never the possibility I might be kicked to death. Tynaliev would weep with laughter, once he'd got over his anger at not being able to kill me himself. Dead may be dead, but who wants to be a laughing stock into the bargain?

'Don't worry, Mr Borubaev, I don't want you dead. Yet. But it will amuse me to watch Achura show you that being a *kathoey* isn't all lipgloss, implants and mascara. You have to know how to survive as well, and theirs can be a cruel world.'

'We shook hands, agreed the deal. Why would you jeopardise that?' I asked, wondering how I could talk my way out of a beating.

'Oh, don't worry about that. I fully intend to keep my word, work with Mr Aliyev. I'm just not sure whether or not our little venture requires your future presence.'

I listened, but all my attention was on Achura as she advanced towards me. I jerked a thumb in the direction of the driver who stood near the gate.

'Put him in a dress and size twelve heels, he'd still look more like a woman than you,' I said, hoping to anger Achura into a mistake, something to allow me a second to take advantage. But the insult passed her by, her stance that of a feral animal waiting to pounce. Suddenly she pivoted on one foot, swung through three hundred and sixty degrees and aimed a kick at my head. I pulled back, felt air move in front of my face.

'She's merely playing with you, Borubaev,' Quang said. 'Much more fun for her and me if the fight doesn't end straight away.'

I moved backwards, feeling my way with my feet, not taking my eyes off Achura. I was learning a new lesson; when you fight someone with Muay Thai skills, you don't just watch their hands. Achura launched an elbow at my face, a knee at my groin, then dragged me forward.

I could smell tobacco on Achura's breath, but the habit hadn't slowed her down at all. Even if smoking didn't kill me, it looked like a smoker would. Every blow was pulled at the last second, leaving me staggering, confused, but so far unhurt. It felt like dancing with a mad person, one whose every move was unpredictable, a choreography from hell.

'Time for the red paint, I think,' Quang called out. A strange way to describe blood, I thought, but stood still, panting, sweat dribbling down my back in the humid air, as Achura stepped back, walked with indescribable grace to the veranda and smeared red chalk upon her fists.

Even as I was puzzling out the significance of the chalk, Achura hit me over and over again, each blow nothing more than a tap but leaving me dazed and confused all the same. I was used to fist-fights in Bishkek bars, watching two men square off, drunkenly telegraph each blow which took an eternity to land. This was like being enveloped in a swarm of bees, impossible to swat away.

After less than a minute, Achura stepped back, made a *wai* of respect and walked away around the side of the villa. I hadn't landed a single blow, and felt as if I'd endured fifty.

'Just in case you were wondering about my thoughts on leniency,' Quang said, mockery and scorn clear in his voice, 'each of the red marks on your clothes and face is a memento of where Achura could have landed a fatal blow, while you were still wondering whether to put your fists up.'

'So loyalty pays off,' I said, hearing the tremor in my voice, hating myself for it.

'And disloyalty pays the price,' Quang said. 'In your case, humiliation, rather than pain or death. This time.'

I nodded. There didn't seem to be anything I could say.

'Please, go into the guesthouse and clean yourself up. There should be clothes there that will fit you.'

As I walked past him, Quang pulled a theatrical face of disgust.

'And shower, Mr Borubaev,' he said. 'You stink.'

Chapter 42

I spent as little time as possible getting clean under a hot shower, wondering how to get revenge on Achura, dismissed my thoughts as grudge fantasy. The clothes I found hanging in a wardrobe were a size too large, so the mirror showed me a burly man who'd recently undergone a serious illness. At least I was still wearing a suit, so I looked roughly respectable.

My face was still on fire with humiliation as I rejoined Quang in the conference room.

'Anyone who works for me offers total loyalty,' he said, his voice calm, dispassionate. 'In return, I offer immense wealth, complete immunity from the forces of law, and the opportunity to live as you've always wanted.'

I sat down, feeling shrunken and insignificant in the too-large suit. I suspected that was deliberate, and it didn't make me feel any better.

Being beaten in a fight by a woman drove any self-esteem I might have once had into the ground. I knew losing to a martial arts expert was only to be expected, no one could have done any better, but I also knew people would snicker behind their hands once my back was turned.

Perhaps Quang sensed something of that. He leant forward

so his face was close to mine, and I could smell the sweet tea on his breath.

'Achura is a phenomenon, a one-off. Growing up with five older brothers, she learnt how to defend herself, studied Thai boxing. If you're from a poor family, success in the ring can feed your entire family. So she turned professional, around the same time she decided the world had to take her on her own terms. As a fighter, she was undefeated in over a hundred bouts. No one survived more than a few moments in the ring. If I had ordered her to, she would have killed you in less than a minute. There is no shame in being beaten by someone supremely gifted at their skill.'

I nodded, as if accepting the wisdom of his words, but deep down, I knew how I felt.

I once found the body of a homeless man, frozen in a grave-yard set back from the north shore of Lake Issyk-Kul. The rats had emerged from deep in their nests, sensing fresh meat. They stripped away his face, the flesh on his arms and legs, feasting until nothing remotely human remained, then bur-rowed deep into his belly for the last pockets of warmth. My defeat would eat piecemeal at me in the same way, working its way deeper and deeper into my thoughts, relentlessly chewing away at me until the only solution was to eat my gun.

I knew I had to go along with Quang's demand for subser-vience, so I nodded.

'Forgive my stupidity, Khun,' I said. 'Obviously I'm used to Kyrgyz ways, and we don't assume loyalty as a given. For us, it's every man for himself and every man has his price, for which he'd betray his own mother.' Not true, but there was no reason to let Quang know we were proud and independent, not bowed and broken.

Quang picked up the SIM card which still lay on the table, held it up.

'I had this examined,' he said. 'I'm sure you'd expected me to do nothing less. It appears there is only one number in the memory, a Bangkok number. And when we tried to call it, the other phone remained switched off. Perhaps you'd care to explain?'

'Like you, my colleague Aliyev is meticulous about privacy and security. I never speak to someone on the other end. I leave a text message, which is then bounced around various telecom companies worldwide until it reaches someone he trusts, who then relays the message face to face. It's time-consuming, but impossible to trace. Even then, we use a code system, so an innocuous-sounding message tells Aliyev what he needs to know.'

'For example?' Quang asked.

'If I write, "Grand Palace an amazing place, you'd love it here", that tells Aliyev we've reached a deal. "Food far too spicy" means that the proposed deal isn't going to happen. Even if someone read it, they wouldn't know what it meant.'

'And the phone?'

'I buy a disposable mobile every time I send a message, get rid of the old one.'

Quang looked at me, his eyes searching my face for lies, prevarications.

'What message will you send today?'

'That the deal is on,' I replied.

Quang nodded.

'I'll have my driver take you back to your hotel. Buy a mobile on the way: I want him to see you send the message. After that, he'll destroy the phone and the card, you understand?'

I tried to hide my concern at not being able to contact Saltanat, but disguised it as concern over reaching Aliyev. I only hoped Saltanat was watching out for me, efficient as always.

'I have my own methods for contacting Mr Aliyev,' Quang said. 'Surely you didn't really think I would rely solely on you? I'm afraid you have a lot to learn about doing business, especially one like ours.'

'I spent twenty years trying to put this sort of business out of business,' I said, and was surprised at the genuine bitterness in my voice. 'But the money is too big, too many people bought. Maybe you haven't seen the consequences of selling drugs, protected as you are, shielded and invulnerable. But for twenty years it was people like me who had to do the cleaning up.'

'Then why get involved now?' Quang asked. 'You've already attempted to murder one of your major politicians, and that didn't change anything. All you've done is make yourself an outcast. Now you're selling drugs yourself. But don't worry; after a while the money will ease your conscience.'

Quang shrugged; my feelings were of no importance to him.

231

'You can always give your money to charity, if you feel so strongly about it. But such a course of action would make me think one day you might betray me, and then Achura will come knocking at your door.'

Quang paused, looking across at the trees by the courtyard wall and the shade they provided. He waved a hand towards them, as if to reinforce the idea that a life under his protection far outweighed the alternative.

'It's not expensive to dispose of a nuisance here in Bangkok. A pistol shot from the back of a motorbike. A green pit viper hidden in your bedding. Even a simple ordinary accident when crossing the road. The Buddha stresses the impermanence of life. When necessary, so do I.'

I said nothing, head bowed, a neophyte humbly awaiting instruction.

'Time for you to report to your master,' Quang said, the scorn in his voice apparent. 'I imagine your encounter with Achura may have dissuaded you from living in Thailand. That's between you and Aliyev, and the duties he considers you're fit for. Your flight will be organised for tomorrow; I don't expect we shall meet again. In fact, I recommend we don't.'

Quang beckoned to the driver who was standing a respectful distance away. One of the servants appeared carrying a bag; my clothes, I assumed. The driver took me by my upper arm, not hard, but just enough to steer me towards the gate.

As we reached there, Achura reappeared, calm and poised as ever, hands washed clean of the red chalk. Come to gloat over my defeat, no doubt. I patted the driver's hand to release me, and walked towards Achura, arm outstretched to shake hands. Quang watched, amusement on his face, like someone watching ants scurrying at his feet.

'No hard feelings?' I asked, smiling as I took Achura's hand. It felt surprisingly smooth, feminine, but with a core of steel along the fingers and the edge of the palm. Then I pulled her towards me even as I moved forward, smashed my forehead into the bridge of her nose, saw the surprise and shock blossom in her eyes, even as the blood blossomed across her cheekbones. My face was warm and wet, and I knew it wasn't from my tears. Flecks of blood stung my eyes, spattered a scarlet pattern across my shirt; I knew it was time to go, and fast, before Achura recovered and decided to retaliate. I held up my hands, as if to apologise for an unfortunate stumble, an accident. I didn't look across to see Quang's reaction. From what I'd learnt of his persona, he probably didn't move a muscle.

'Next time,' I whispered, the smile never leaving my face as I stared at Achura, 'next time, I'll fucking kill you.'

Chapter 43

As we drove back to the city, the driver looked at me in the mirror and shook his head. Obviously, nutting Achura was a bad idea. A better idea would have been to head to the airport straight away, but I needed to see Saltanat, even if it meant encountering Achura once more. As Quang had said, there are dozens of ways to die in Bangkok.

The bombshell of Saltanat's pregnancy still sent echoes through my mind, tremors of fear, elation, terror. Did she want our child or would she simply head for an abortion clinic, a scrape, a day in bed, then back to work?

Did I want a child, and how could I look after it, on the run and most likely dead before it was even born?

I shut my eyes, tried to find some peace, but my life nagged at me like a broken tooth, persistent, insistent. I hadn't lied to Quang; I used the phone to send coded messages. But they were to Saltanat, not Aliyev. And the message I intended to send said 'Visiting the floating market'. Which meant 'Run'. Even if I couldn't escape the shit I was in, there was no reason why she should die. Or, now I thought of it, our unborn child. If Saltanat decided to terminate her pregnancy, there was still Otabek back in Uzbekistan to consider. He'd been traumatised enough by his ordeal at the hands of Morton Graves.

Saltanat had helped him come out of his self-imposed silence, but without her presence, he would surely sink back into a fear and despair from which there would be no escape.

I barely noticed the buildings on either side, until I realised we weren't taking the normal route back to the hotel. I tapped on the glass partition, caught the driver's attention.

'Where are you taking me?' I said, but he ignored me and carried on driving. I began to get seriously worried: I remembered the gun under his jacket, wondered if this was a trip to somewhere quiet followed by a sudden execution. If so, I'd walked into it like a halfwit. Out of my depth, out of my skills, and if I was right, soon to be out of breath.

We turned off the motorway onto a slip road leading into an area full of decaying warehouses. Rusting signs in Thai hung lopsided from shutters and roofs, doors and walls had graffiti sprayed upon them like neon-bright worms squashed by a giant fist. If I'd had a god to believe in, this would have been the time to start praying.

I was surprised at how calm, perhaps even resigned to dying I was. After all, between Tynaliev, Aliyev and Quang, no one in their right minds would bet on me reaching old age.

Finally, the car pulled up surrounded by derelict buildings, the kind of place where businesses die a lingering death. Mine would be a lot quicker. The ground was littered with twisted pieces of steel rebar, broken bricks and bottles and rotting cardboard boxes. Weeds struggled through cracks in the concrete, puddles of water lay in hollows, staring up at the sky like black eyes. The air was foul with the smell of smoke, rotting timber, decay.

The driver clambered out of his seat, beckoned for me to do the same. He held up the phone and the SIM card, placed them on the roof of the car, then stepped back, motioning for me to install the card. I held the mobile up, stabbed at it with one finger. He nodded, watched as I sent Saltanat the code to get out of Bangkok as quickly as possible.

The driver nodded approval, reached under his jacket for his gun. It was then we heard the motorcycle, powerful, aggressive, approaching at speed. Both of us remained frozen as a Royal Thai Police motorcycle raced into view, the wheels bucking and twisting on the uneven surface.

Killing me would be an everyday occurrence; the mysterious death of a *farang* wouldn't make the TV news. But murdering a police officer would bring down nine levels of hell and trouble. So the driver paused, fingers millimetres away from his gun, waiting for the motorcycle to stop.

The policeman stopped the bike, straddling it with his feet on the ground. His face was unreadable behind mirror sunglasses and a full face helmet with the visor raised. I didn't know if he'd followed us, whether he had spotted something wrong or was just following a cop hunch. But it was my only opportunity.

Picking up the brick at my feet was easy; throwing it so it hit the driver's head took a little skill, a lot of luck. The brick bounced off his skull with a dry thud and splintered, like dropping a sack of rice on the floor. I watched as he staggered, half-fell, then pulled himself up, shaking his head the way a dog shakes off water. He felt for his gun, pulled it out of the shoulder holster, finger already dancing towards the trigger.

The cop's gun was aimed halfway between us, and I had no doubt he'd shoot at the slightest sign of trouble. So we both stood absolutely still, statues captured in mid-motion.

Then the driver made a decision. He pulled out his gun and fell backwards as the cop's bullets took him in the throat and jaw, arterial blood a jetting fountain that splashed through the air and onto the ground. As his body fell, I saw the man's tongue, newly exposed in the gap where most of his teeth had been, splayed out like a slice of raw liver. His gun clattered to the ground but I knew it would be suicide to reach for it. At that moment, death by cop seemed as sensible an option as any.

'Pick up the gun, hurry.'

Saltanat's voice, as usual calm and assured.

I stared as she took off the cycle helmet, shook her hair free, gave me one of those smiles that speared my heart.

'We need to get out of here,' she said, dismounting from the bike and heading towards the car. She paused only to wipe the side of my face nearest the driver's body and give me a peck on the cheek. I checked the driver's gun; fully loaded, though I'd expected nothing less.

'A little blood on your face, don't worry, it's not yours,' she said.

'Where did you steal the bike?' I asked.

'There's an unlucky cop who thought he was going to get a blow job down an alleyway; he should be waking up about now with a bruised neck and a very sore head,' Saltanat said, giving a ravishing smile.

237

No question who was going to drive. Saltanat slid behind the wheel, began to reverse and turn around. The rear of the car rose and I heard a horrible crunch and squelch.

'Relax, he didn't feel a thing. Or if he did, he doesn't now.'

As we headed back towards the motorway, I wondered how it was possible to love a woman who could take a life without a second thought. The times I've had to kill, the moment returns to me, mainly in dreams, but also when I see a face, a walk, a look, that reminds me of the dead. The difference between being an amateur and a professional, I suppose; I hope I never go from being one to the other.

'Once we get a little further away, we'll have to ditch the car,' I said. 'No way Quang wouldn't have installed a tracking device and we don't have time to find it.'

Saltanat nodded. 'We dump this at Nana Plaza, leaving the keys in the ignition. Some low life is bound to think it's his lucky day and go for a joyride. I wouldn't like to be the one who has to explain to Quang he'd only "borrowed" his car.'

'And then? I've seen enough of hookers, ladyboys and *farang* drunks for one trip.'

'Taxi to the airport.'

'I don't have my passport with me,' I said.

She reached into her jacket, passed me an envelope.

'You do now.'

The green Uzbek passport looked genuine; with Saltanat's connections, it probably was. I flicked through the pages. Whoever forged the paperwork had been thorough – a dozen visas from as many countries filled as many pages.

'So now I'm called Alisher Nabiyev. And I'm thirty-six years old.'

She looked sideways at me, narrowly missing a tuk-tuk, smiled.

'You must have had a very hard life,' she said.

'The way you drive, I'll be ten years older when we arrive,' I replied.

'Shut up, keep your head down, don't stare out of the window like you've never seen cars before,' Saltanat ordered, forced her way though an impossible gap between an elderly bus and a truck overloaded with vegetables.

I winced in anticipation, shut my eyes, decided that was the only way to travel until we got to the airport.

Chapter 44

Suvarnabhumi International Airport is one of the biggest in the world; however, Saltanat knew her way, led me through several levels towards passport control.

'We've got diplomatic passports,' she explained, 'so we get priority and entrance to a special lounge until our flight takes off.'

'Where are we going?' I asked. 'Not that I have any say in it, obviously, but I'd prefer to go somewhere where no one will look for me. The South Pole, maybe.'

'Kuala Lumpur,' Saltanat said. 'Our tickets say we're coming back tomorrow; that explains why we don't have any luggage. But, of course, we won't be returning.'

'Surely Quang's men will be on their way here,' I said, 'and I don't think they'll want us to leave.'

'Our flight goes in ninety minutes. They won't expect you to be travelling with a woman, and you've got a diplomatic passport under a false name. Unless you think you've got time to shave your head as a disguise, there's not much more I can do.'

As we joined the queue to go through passport control, Saltanat turned to me.

'You got rid of the gun, right?'

I looked around, spotting the universal symbol for a men's bathroom.

'Back in a minute.'

I disassembled the gun in the relative privacy of a cubicle, dropped the pieces into a large cleaning sack, rejoined Saltanat.

Once we were through all the formalities, Saltanat led me to one of the business class lounges. Any other time, I would have been delighted to look around, eat and drink, relax away from the crowds. But all I could think of was getting on the plane, wondering if Quang had the influence to get us dragged off the plane and out of the airport. I looked over at Saltanat, sipping her second glass of champagne.

'Drinking?' I said.

She raised an eyebrow, put her glass down and gave me a look that pretended to be serious.

'Worried about the baby?' she asked, the mockery in her voice all too evident.

'I was thinking more that we ought to get out of Thailand before you set a course for getting drunk,' I replied.

'So you don't want me to have an abortion, then?' she asked, all mockery in her voice gone.

'Can we talk about this later?' I asked. 'I'm tired, stressed beyond all belief, I've just headbutted a ladyboy, I've watched you kill a man, and then sat through some of the worst driving since the car was invented. Right now, I'm not capable of a serious conversation about anything.'

'Kairat's a nice name for a boy, don't you think?' she asked. 'And Aizat if it's a girl.'

I decided not to answer, treating myself to a freshly squeezed orange juice. For a split second, I could almost taste the vodka

I would once have decanted into the glass, half juice half Stolichnaya, cubes of ice chiming against the glass, chill on my lips, the burn at the back of my throat. I used to drink vodka most evenings to calm my nerves after a murderous day. Chinara didn't approve, but she understood my need to escape the day's blood, brains, stupidity and hate. I hadn't had an alcoholic drink since her death, but right then, I couldn't remember why I thought that was a good idea.

'You're worried about Quang finding us here,' Saltanat stated, sipping once more from her champagne flute.

'You're not?'

'Why should I be? I've only just met you, don't know you, just striking up a conversation to pass the time if anyone asks. If they drag you away, I'll just say, how strange, he seemed like such a nice man.'

'And they say romance is dead.'

Saltanat finished her champagne, held up a hand to beckon the waitress to top up her glass.

'Right now, Quang's got more important things to worry about than some Kyrgyz nobody killing one of his staff and disappearing into the night.'

I looked at her, saw the slight smile on her face.

'You've fucked him over somehow, haven't you?' I accused.

'Put a temporary spoke in his wheels, put it like that,' she said, and this time couldn't resist grinning. The shock of just how beautiful she was hit me afresh, the way it did every time when she let drop the mask of professional indifference.

'What did you do?'

242

'You've heard of Photoshop, I suppose?'

'I may be an old-fashioned ex-cop but I do sometimes live in this century,' I said. 'I'm not living in a yurt up on the high jailoo in the mountains. I've even got a mobile phone.'

'Since you're so up to date on computers and world affairs, you can tell me: what do the Thais respect more than anything else?'

'Money?' I ventured. Saltanat shook her head.

'Majesty. The Royal family. The King,' she said. 'It's one of the bonds that holds their society together, perhaps the biggest, and the punishments for criticising, mocking or suggesting the Royal family be abolished are truly punitive. It's a crime called lese-majeste. Up to fifteen years in prison for each offence, and believe me, a Thai prison makes a Kyrgyz penal colony look like a holiday camp.'

The idea made me shudder; a few years ago, the Kyrgyz prison system made worldwide headlines when the prisoners stitched their mouths closed with wire to protest at their conditions. How could a Thai prison be worse? I wondered, then decided I never wanted to find out.

'What have you done?' I asked, slightly terrified at the deviousness of the mind of the woman I loved.

'About two hours ago, someone sent an anonymous email to the chief of police here in Bangkok. From an untraceable address via a privacy-guaranteed foreign server.'

'Go on.'

'There were several grainy photographs attached, all of which showed a very well-known and powerful drug dealer at

243

home. Taken from a distance with a telephoto lens, without the subject's knowledge. Terrible photographs, but at least they're in focus.'

Saltanat held her hand up to her mouth and did her best to look shocked, and I couldn't resist a smile myself.

'They won't show them on TV, for obvious reasons: they would risk criminal charges themselves. Photographs of Quang proudly standing in front of a poster of the King and Queen, on which someone had given them both a huge moustache and beard. Another which showed the King's head transposed onto the body of a porn star at work. A female porn star. And others; you get the idea. Completely offensive, completely insulting, completely fake.'

'All Photoshopped?'

'What do you think?'

'The police will act upon this?'

'They have to, since the email also went to the editors of all the leading newspapers, including the *Royal Thai Government Gazette*, with the threat to send them to foreign newspapers if Quang wasn't arrested.'

'And the images were Photoshopped? By you?'

'Do I look like a computer geek to you?'

Saltanat gave me another of her 'what an idiot' looks, then bestowed her most ravishing smile at the approaching waitress, pointed at the TV, asked for the news channel. The sound was muted, but since we didn't speak Thai, that didn't matter: the images were more than clear enough.

Chapter 45

A tank lumbered up to the gates of Quang's villa, looking like some squat metallic elephant, and didn't stop when it got there. The gates disappeared under the tank tracks as if made of butter, and the walls on either side disintegrated. Two trucks filled with armed policemen pulled up and we watched as Quang's villa was stormed with all the methodical precision of an invasion. The tank reversed away, and more of the walls shuddered, shook, collapsed.

A senior army officer held his hand up in front of the broadcaster's camera, then decided to let the crew continue to film. After a few moments, Quang was led out of the rubble surrounding his home, handcuffed and wearing shackles around his ankles. His normally immaculate suit looked stained and torn, and a bloody bruise on one side of his face suggested he'd been subdued 'while resisting arrest'. He was frogmarched to the nearest truck, manhandled into the back, disappearing from sight under the green canvas. Several soldiers jumped in after him, and the truck rolled down towards the motorway and out of sight.

'I don't think Quang will be looking for you for a while.' Saltanat smiled. 'A few nights in Klong Prem Central Prison should keep him out of your hair. We should be long away by then.'

I was silent, wondering just how many bridges I'd burnt, how many I could still cross.

'You'd better hope you're worth more to Aliyev alive than dead,' Saltanat added, putting down her half-drunk champagne. 'Who knows, you might even be part of their future deal; your head in exchange for a handshake.'

It wasn't a reassuring thought.

A screen on the wall told us it was time to board our flight. We showed our boarding passes and headed down the tunnel to find our seats. For me, it was still a novelty to turn left on a plane instead of right, but Saltanat handled it with the effortless charm that suggested she'd been born to wealth and privilege. I knew the truth about her growing up in an orphanage, but had to admire the way she slipped into a role with no hesitation. I also wondered if I would ever truly know what lay behind all the façades she adopted to protect herself.

My heartbeat slowed from a frantic drumbeat to a relaxed rhythm as I heard the wonderful clunk of the aircraft door being shut. I watched through the porthole as we slowly began to reverse from the terminal. Even so, I didn't feel at ease until I felt the wheels rise up from the runway, saw the million lights of the city sprawling below me.

With just over two hours to go before we landed in Malaysia, the tension emptied out of my body, and I fell asleep even before the plane had reached cruising altitude. Saltanat woke me a moment later as we started to descend. For a second I wondered if we'd had to turn back to Bangkok, if there would be a police reception party waiting for us on the tarmac. But

Saltanat nodded towards the window. 'KL,' she said, and smiled. Perhaps she was as relieved to be out of Bangkok as well.

The diplomatic passport got us through immigration in quick time, and with no bags to collect, we were in the taxi rank in just a few moments. Just to be on the safe side, Saltanat let three people behind us take the next taxi, before crossing the road, with me in tow, and taking the second of the black limousines that hoped for rich customers. I would have been content with a regular taxi, but I knew Saltanat was cautious about any possible danger. The fact she was always alert impressed me yet again.

In the limousine, she made a hotel reservation, using the driver's phone, with what looked like a black credit card to pay for the booking. I sat back and shivered in the air conditioning, knowing that once I was outside, I'd be drenched in sweat in minutes. The constant changing from tropical to sub-zero temperatures was exhausting: at least in Kyrgyzstan I understood the changing seasons.

'I need to eat,' Saltanat said as we paid off the limousine and walked into the elegant lobby of the Concorde Hotel. 'You?'

I shook my head, the rush of adrenalin had left me too exhausted to do anything but fall onto a bed and pass out into a coma. She spoke to the concierge, received an envelope, headed to the lift, beckoning me to follow, not looking behind to see if I did. And I did; perhaps I really was that tame.

In the lift, I stared at the haggard man who gazed back at

me. An ill-fitting suit that looked as if I'd slept in it (which I had), cheap shoes, hair that needed cutting, dark circles under despairing eyes. I was amazed the hotel had let me through the revolving door.

My mood wasn't improved by the opulence of the suite we let ourselves into. It brought home to me the bitter truth I'd spent my entire career sleeping in flea palaces, paying for tasteless food out of my own usually empty pocket. The Uzbek Security Service obviously had a more generous attitude towards expenses than the Bishkek authorities, maybe because they were guarding rich and influential people. I just spent my time hunting down nobodies who'd murdered other nobodies, usually for the most stupid or trivial of reasons.

I lay on the bed as Saltanat announced she was going to shower and disappeared into the bathroom. I felt exhausted; more than that, sick at heart. I felt I was on a ride that could only end in death at someone's hands. Too many enemies and too little worth fighting for. Even if Saltanat decided to keep our child, there was no way we could ever be a family. Too much blood and too many deaths, including my own, stood between us and any future. Neither of us were likely to change our ways. Perhaps I'd abandoned any chance of that when I joined the police force. The best I could offer Saltanat was to keep away from her, and I suspected that would suit her just fine.

Out of curiosity I looked at the envelope Saltanat had placed on the bedside table, noticed the flap had come undone. I looked inside, half expecting to see what was there. I wasn't wrong. A PSM pistol, presumably fully loaded. Saltanat must have had amazing contacts to get an illegal gun delivered to her so quickly. But then, if you're an international assassin, how else could you do the job? I put the envelope back on the table, lay down on the bed once more.

The sound of the shower running was soothing enough to begin to lull me into sleep when there was a knock on the door. Room service; Saltanat had clearly ordered food. I pulled myself up, opened the door, dazed with sleep. Found the very last person I expected to see.

Achura.

Chapter 46

'Pleased to see me?' Achura said, pushing her way into the room, kicking the door shut behind her. She was wearing some kind of maid's uniform, presumably so she could walk around the hotel without attracting attention. I wondered if a naked dead woman was stuffed into a laundry basket deep in the bowels of the hotel; that would be Achura's style. She kicked off her black stiletto heels, flexed her feet and started to walk towards me.

'Clever trick with Quang. But I'm not stupid. I knew you were coming to Malaysia ten minutes after you checked in. We have friends at the airline, in immigration, even at the front desk downstairs.'

I noticed the singsong pidgin had vanished, replaced by an American accent. Clearly, I'd underestimated Achura's determination and loyalty, dismissed her as a *kathoey* and therefore of no importance. It was a mistake that was probably going to kill me.

I backed away and rolled onto the bed, landing on my feet on the other side. Achura advanced with all the effortless grace of one of the snow leopards that hunt in the Tien Shan mountains. The sticking plaster across her nose gave her the look of some ancient tribal warrior, wild and untameable. She touched the tip of her nose, grimaced.

'I didn't expect this. And yes, it hurts. But nothing compared to what you're going to suffer. I know you're expecting it. Then once I've dealt with you, I'll see to that bitch in the shower. I'll show you just how kind and considerate I can be; she won't even know what hit her. Just blackness for ever.'

I looked around for something to throw, a vase, a lamp, anything to slow her down, found nothing. Saltanat was quietly singing in the shower, the water drowning any noise I could make to alert her. In a few seconds Achura would kill me, then Saltanat would emerge from the bathroom to meet the same end.

Achura feinted a few blows at my face, a kick to my chest, but I could tell she was toying with me, the way a cat does when killing something weaker and smaller. Achura side-stepped the punch I threw as if I'd blown smoke at her, kicked me again. I felt a rib crack, knew that in a couple of minutes it wouldn't matter.

'Maybe I should break your nose,' Achura wondered, jabbing at my face with those merciless fists. 'Or kick your balls up into your spine. Gouge out an eye.'

I retreated for a couple of steps, felt the edge of the bedside table on the back of my legs, prepared to die.

And that was when my hand touched the envelope.

I've never moved as quickly as I did then, knowing that if I fumbled the envelope, knocked it to the floor, I was dead. But years of practice had given my muscles the memory to grab the gun and aim it at Achura's face.

'Kick my balls up into my spine?' I managed to say. 'I'm sure you'd like yours removed altogether.'

I resisted the temptation to point the gun at Achura's crotch and fire. It wouldn't be immediately fatal, and that would give her all the time she needed to kill me.

'I don't think you've got the guts to kill a woman, Borubaev,' she said, her voice low, hypnotic.

'Wrong,' was all I said, and pulled the trigger.

The shot took her just above her left cheek, a sudden red-black hole appearing as if by magic. The look of anger drifted into nothingness as she fell back to the floor. The sound of the shot had been appallingly loud, and Saltanat rushed out of the bathroom. She took the situation in at a glance, grabbed the TV remote, found an action movie and turned up the sound so more gunshots echoed around the room.

Saltanat stared at the corpse, then at me. Her look was accusing.

'Why didn't you call me?'

'I was a little busy,' I said, pissed off her first response had been to criticise me. She must have recognised I had a point, because she didn't reply, knelt down beside Achura.

Apart from the hole in her forehead, there was remarkably little blood. Low calibre bullets tend to create a small entry wound, then bounce around inside the skull, turning the brain into porridge before coming to rest.

'You ever think of looking before you open the door?' she asked, switching on her mobile and uttering a string of instructions in Uzbek.

'Let me get dressed, we go and eat. When we're back here,

she won't be. Another mess of yours my people have to clean up. And we need to talk about the rest of this mess as well.'

'I don't want to disagree with you,' I began, 'but you decided we would come to Kuala Lumpur, decided which hotel we would stay at. And if Achura had killed me, what would you have done, unarmed and naked?'

'If you want to argue, you can stay here,' Saltanat said, refusing to lose the argument, picking up her bag and heading for the door, 'but I'm going to eat.'

I've had more companionable meals; Saltanat savaged a piece of semi-raw meat the size of a plate, while I picked at an omelette. Neither of us spoke, and the waiter could tell the temperature at our table hovered somewhere around absolute zero. Finally I pushed my plate aside, reached over, took her hand. She started to pull away, but for once I didn't let go straight away.

'You're pregnant,' I said, in my most matter-of-fact voice, 'and I'm the father. So we both have to act like grown-ups and make some serious decisions.'

Saltanat looked at me, and for a second I could have sworn she had tears in her eyes. Or perhaps it was just pollen from the rose on our table, and I was giving her the benefit of the doubt.

'You think I haven't thought about that?'

'I'm not saying that,' I said, waving the waiter away as he came to clear the plates and probably eavesdrop, 'but once we're out of this mess, we have to decide what to do next.'

'Akyl, you're the one in a mess, not me,' Saltanat said. 'I'm not the one on the run, I've got a country, a home to go to. You've got nothing, except a life expectancy you could time with a stopwatch. And you want to know what I'm going to do about this baby?'

Her laugh combined amusement, anger and sorrow in equal doses.

'If I keep it, and if it's a boy, I'll name him Akyl, after his late father. There; happy now?'

'And if it's a girl?'

'Then I'll call her Akyla, because of her lack of balls.'

'Why do we have to fight about this?' I said, reaching for her hand again, watching her pull away.

'Because you're going to be dead soon, and that will break my heart.'

And with that, she pushed her chair back and stalked out of the door, leaving me to pay the bill.

Chapter 47

As Saltanat had organised, Achura's body was gone, perhaps transported in a laundry basket. There was going to be hell in the morning when it was time to wash the sheets and pillowcases.

'Do you wish you and Chinara had kept your baby?'

We were lying in bed together, close but not quite touching, having wordlessly agreed on a truce once I got back to the room. It was a question I'd often asked myself, both before her death and after, and I'd never been able to resolve the issue in my mind.

'Hard to bring up a child without a mother,' I said. 'Almost cruel, even.'

'And what if there is no father?'

'That's a little different,' I said. 'Look how many Kyrgyz fathers don't see their children from one year to the next. I don't mean the ones who just get divorced once they get bored of the sex and the responsibilities, I'm thinking of the ones who go to Moscow to work shit jobs for shit pay, so they can send roubles home. They've got no choice, so the kids grow up under their mother's influence. Is the absence of a father good or bad? I don't know, but for most people there isn't a choice.'

'So you think I should keep it?'

'I can't tell you what to do, Saltanat, I never have been able to do that. It has to be your choice, but I'll support you totally in whatever you decide.'

We lay there in silence, until I felt her hand reach over, take mine. I rolled towards her as she did the same, our heads colliding in the dark. I winced, awakening the bruise from the headbutt I'd given Achura, then felt Saltanat's hand on the back of my neck, her breasts soft against my chest, her thighs tight and determined against mine.

We kissed, hesitant at first, the way you do after an argument, when you're not sure if the bond between you has fully returned, then with more passion as the memory of being a couple surged back again. And then all memory dissolved into the moment . . .

It was still dark when Saltanat shook me awake from a dream in which Achura kept advancing towards me, a grim smile on her face, while I pumped bullet after bullet into her with no effect.

'I've put the do-not-disturb notice on the door, so we've got at least until noon to get out of here, and out of Malaysia,' she said. 'Don't worry, I've already booked our tickets while you were asleep.'

I sat up and looked around the room. I knew that half an hour after we left, I'd remember nothing about it, and it struck me I'd lived a lot of my life in just such a fashion. And the things I did remember were precisely those I wanted to forget.

'You've got time for a shower,' Saltanat said, throwing a towel at me, 'or I'm not sitting next to you on the plane.'

'Where are we going?' I asked, heading for the bathroom door. 'Or is it a secret?'

'It's time to end this. I'm sure you'll be pleased. You're going to Kyrgyzstan.'

'I wonder how Quang enjoyed his first night in captivity. A very different Bangkok Hilton to the one he's used to,' I said, with a certain malicious satisfaction.

'Money talks, you know that, sometimes in whispers, sometimes by banging on the table, shrieking in indignation at the top of its voice. A comfortable cell, food brought in from outside, a lawyer arriving to negotiate his release,' Saltanat said. 'He'll be out and organising repairs to his property while we're still in the air. Getting the army to do the work, I wouldn't be surprised.'

With our diplomatic passports, we were through and sitting in a coffee shop in a matter of minutes. I was pretty certain there wouldn't be anyone from Quang's team stalking us; presumably they'd be waiting until Achura reported the two *farang* problems had been suitably disposed of.

'You still haven't told me why we're going to Kyrgyzstan. You said yourself I'm going to end up in a grave there.'

Saltanat sipped at her coffee, pulled a face.

'How do people manage to make coffee as weak as this?'

'I'm sorry the coffee isn't to your liking, but to get back to what I was asking . . .'

Saltanat put her cup down with a clatter that almost made the barista drop his mobile phone.

'Simple. Quang will be out of his cell and back in business in a few hours. He agreed a deal with you, and for all he knows, you've passed that information on to Aliyev. Right?'

I nodded.

'Well, he has to honour that agreement, or his reputation gets a hammering. Once suppliers, dealers, his whole network get the impression he can't be trusted to keep his word, then it's only a matter of time before he's deposed.'

'OK,' I said, not entirely sure Saltanat wasn't looking too much on the bright side.

'Then there's the problem he faces if the government legalise *yaa baa*. He needs a new product, and the simplest, cheapest and most profitable way to get that is through Aliyev. So Quang might be pissed off with you, especially after you killed his girlfriend, but as far as Aliyev's concerned, everything went well.'

'Suppose Quang decides he wants my head in return for keeping to the deal?' I asked.

'Aliyev needs you as well,' Saltanat said. 'Think about it. You're famous as the ex-cop who shot the Minister of State Security. You're living proof Aliyev can go anywhere, do anything, with complete immunity. The government can't stop him, the army can't catch him, and the security forces are too busy wondering who'll be blamed for the assassination attempt.'

She finished her coffee. The waitress came to collect our cups.

'How was your coffee?' she smiled.

'If it hadn't been so weak, it would have been disgusting.'
Saltanat smiled in return, stood up, shouldered her handbag.

The waitress gave me a puzzled look, unsure whether she'd
just heard a compliment or an insult. I stood up, shrugged,
and joined Saltanat. It was time to go home.

Chapter 48

The journey to Tashkent gave the sense of being trapped out of time in a miniature world, an identikit copy of every flight I'd ever taken. Saltanat was quick to fall asleep, her hands folded over her belly, protecting a child that wasn't yet showing. I couldn't spot any signs of her pregnancy, but then I wasn't any kind of expert. I envied her the ability to simply shut her eyes and lose the world. I just stared out of the window and felt the minutes drag along like dying men. A seven-hour flight, followed by a long drive to Bishkek to put my head in the lion's mouth, didn't cheer me up.

We were picked up at the airport and driven into Tashkent by a burly man in his thirties, who, judging by his deference, was one of Saltanat's junior colleagues. I'd been to the city before, but never spent time there. I wondered if I was going to get an insight into how Saltanat lived when she wasn't on a mission. But it wasn't to be.

'Akram will drive you towards the border,' Saltanat said as the car pulled up outside the massive Chorsu Bazaar. Even outside the blue-domed building, I could smell the perfume of spices and herbs in the air, the sense of being back among people I understood, whose food I ate, whose hopes and fears I shared.

'Arrangements have been made for you once you're across the border at Osh, and you're booked from there on an internal flight to Bishkek. After that you're on your own.'

'I was wondering about staying with you for a couple of days,' I said.

Saltanat shook her head.

'I don't want to upset Otabek,' she said. I understood; when Saltanat and I rescued the little boy from the paedophile who meant to kill him, he'd been mute with terror. Seeing me might only revive memories best forgotten.

'This is where you live?' I asked, keen to find out more about her, but she shook her head.

'I'm taking the metro home; it's the fastest way to get around the city, and I have things to do. I'll see you in Bishkek in two days' time. Noon, by the statue of Kurmanjan Datka, not too far from the White House. I'll text you to confirm.'

As always with Saltanat, there was no discussion, merely a statement of intent. I didn't have any choice in the matter. I wound down the car window as she started towards the station, never looking back, determined as ever. I wondered if this was yet another of her ploys to ensure I knew as little about her as possible.

'I love you,' I called out as she plunged into the crowd.

I wasn't sure if she heard me.

It's an eight-hour journey from Tashkent to Osh, but we broke the journey at Angren, where I found a back-street barber, had my hair trimmed to a coarse stubble. It wasn't much of a disguise but the best I could do. We crossed the border without any problems, my fake passport simply held up and waved through without even being examined. As we drove towards the airport, Akram spoke his only words of the journey.

'She gave me this to give to you,' and handed me an envelope. I opened it, finding nothing but a one-way plane ticket from Osh to Bishkek. No note, no message, no slip of paper with a mobile number. I felt as if I'd been summarily dismissed from her life.

At Osh Airport, Akram nodded a curt goodbye and drove away back towards the border. I felt more nervous on home soil and at an airport. Security is always more stringent there, and there was the chance a vigilant police officer patrolling the building might recognise me. It was only when we were in the air on our forty-minute flight that I was able to relax a little.

Outside Manas Airport, I looked around for the most dilapidated taxi I could find. The driver had been one of a handful who gathered outside the arrivals hall; international flights with their collection of rich and gullible tourists offered much better pickings. I gave him the address of my apartment on Ibraimova, haggled for a few moments over the price, with much swearing and threats to walk away, finally reaching an agreement. In some countries, haggling is almost a game; in mine, it's done in all seriousness, the difference between a meal on the table or hunger.

It was only as I was getting into the taxi that I realised someone was staring at me from the pavement. Staring hard.

Kenesh Usupov.

I'd worked too many times with Bishkek's chief forensic pathologist to have any hope he wouldn't have recognised me. The look on his face was one of shock, even fear.

I made the 'I'll call you' gesture with my fingers, looking back at him as we drove away. I only had one question: would he tell Tynaliev I was back?

We drove down Chui Prospekt, maybe not the quickest way home, but one that reminded me of how much I'd missed simply being able to walk around the centre of my city.

The apartment smelt musty, unloved, but as far as I could tell, there had been nobody watching the building. I put water on to boil for tea, remembering how Chinara would always have a cup ready for me when I came home from work and I hadn't had too much vodka on the way. I took my tea into the main room and stared at the framed photo of her I'd taken at Lake Issyk-Kul a lifetime ago. Hers, and perhaps mine.

I wondered what she would have made of the news about Saltanat's pregnancy, the disappointment at it not being our child, resignation at the thought I'd found someone else to love while she slept cold in her grave.

'I never planned to meet someone,' I said out loud. 'I still miss you more than I can say. You'll never leave me, I'll never forget you, but life's a river that carries you along.' But in the silence, I found no sign of acceptance, heard no whisper of an answer.

Chapter 49

Chinara always came to me when I least expected her. And that's how it was that evening, when she woke me with her fingertips stroking my face, her breath warm on my cheek. I tried to sit up, felt the palm of her hand pressing me back down to the mattress with surprising strength.

I tried to speak, but no words came. All I could do was put my arm around her shoulder, pull her head against my chest, and stare up into the darkness only broken by car headlights on the road, their beams like searchlights hunting for me.

She took my hand and pressed it against the warm skin of her stomach where our baby had lived for so short a time. She gave a barely heard sigh that might have been sorrow, regret, or merely resignation. Then I felt her slipping out of my arms, and I knew she would never return, that the link remaining between us had dissolved like mist into night air. She knew another woman had replaced her.

The fridge was as empty as my heart, so I decided to go out for breakfast. A couple of *samsi*, hot tea, then it was time to face the music. The only question was who would be playing the tune: Tynaliev or Aliyev.

I debated spinning a coin, made a phone call. I arranged a meeting under the giant Ferris wheel in Panfilov Park at seven that evening, after dark, when the spokes of the wheel light up with flashing colours. A meeting in the open air, with people around, seemed a little safer, unless someone organised a sniper from somewhere under the trees. If I didn't make it to the meeting the following day with Saltanat, she'd know I wasn't ever going to turn up.

The rest of the morning and early afternoon passed in a haze. Wondering if you're still going to be alive that evening has a curiously disorienting effect, as if all the minutes have drained out of your life and the only thing left to do is wait for the end. Sometimes hours pass while you think only five minutes have gone by; sometimes the minutes become hours. When the walls of my apartment closed in I knew I had to get out.

I looked around at the apartment that had housed my marriage, at the photograph of Chinara. I debated locking the door behind me, decided it didn't matter one way or another. There was nothing to steal I'd miss, and if I didn't return, someone else would live there soon enough.

The weather had turned cold as I walked down Ibraimova and turned on to Chui Prospekt. The park was a good forty minutes' walk away, and part of me relished the idea of exercise after being cooped up for so long. A glance at the darkening sky hinted at snow in the near future. Autumn was coming to an end and the death of the year was at hand.

I avoided the cracks in the pavement as I walked, in much the same way as I'd skipped over them as a child, hoping to avert bad luck, not wanting the demons who lurked there to spring up and snatch me away. Maybe I was trying to avert my death, habit being so strong.

I reached the edge of the park after a brisk walk that somehow raised my spirits. I was unarmed; there hadn't seemed much point in bringing the gun I kept in a lockbox in the apartment. Dead is dead, as I kept reminding myself.

The wheel loomed above everything else in the park, the spokes moving slowly, lifting the carriages in an endless vertical circle to offer a view of all Bishkek before bringing their occupants back to earth. As a summing up of life, I thought it was pretty accurate; at the end of your ride, you have to get off, whether you want to or not.

There aren't many lights in the park, so there are long stretches under the trees where all you can see is the outline of benches, each with its couple of lovers with nowhere else to go, impervious to the cold in the warmth of each other's company. I'd sat there myself, a lifetime ago, when a lifetime seemed to last for ever, a future filled with promise.

As the lights on the wheel's spokes danced up and down, turning from white to green, blue to red, pulsing like some giant heartbeat, the leaves on the trees turned matching colours. I passed a couple deep in some silent argument, the girl weeping, the boy trying to comfort her. I thought of Saltanat back in Tashkent, wondering if she was considering terminating her pregnancy.

The wheel was surrounded by railings, with one gap leading to the entrance. It was there I could see the outline of the man I was due to meet, dark against the ever-changing lights.

A little way away, two other figures waited, watching, their body language telling me they were bodyguards, poised for violence. If there were to be any trouble, it would come from them, and it would be coming my way.

I walked up to the waiting man, bulky in a thick overcoat, hair hidden in a fur *ushanka*. I didn't try to hide my footsteps, watched as he turned round to meet me, his face unreadable as it turned white to green, blue to red.

I stopped a couple of metres away. He stood motionless, arms by his side, his body solid, square. He could have been one of the statues dotted around the park. I waited for some kind of acknowledgement, a sign he was aware of my presence. Finally, I spoke.

'Hello, Minister. *Kak dela?*'

Chapter 50

Tynaliev merely grunted, fumbled in his overcoat pocket, pulled out a hip flask and took a deep drink. I was pretty sure it wasn't hot chocolate. He didn't offer it to me.

'Those blanks really bruised me,' he said. 'I had the marks for weeks. And the fake blood bags ruined that suit as well.'

'You wanted it to look authentic,' I pointed out. 'No point in it looking like something in a fifties Mosfilm shootout, where you clutch your side and carry on as normal.'

'Usupov told me you were back, said he'd seen you at the airport. I don't think he would have the balls not to tell me.'

'He's got a wife, children, a career,' I said. 'None of which I have. And as far as he knew, I was an enemy of the people. Or at least, an enemy of you.'

'Isn't that the same thing?' Tynaliev said. I didn't reply.

'Didn't you ever wonder about putting proper bullets in the gun, Inspector? It's not as if you and I are friends. You can bring me down if you want to, if you live long enough. And vice versa. A couple of slugs in my back and you'd have had one less enemy to worry about.'

'And then all the might of a vengeful government to hunt me down,' I said. 'This way, you kept them off my back so that I could hook up with Aliyev.'

Tynaliev nodded.

'For a Public Enemy Number One, you kept yourself well hidden.'

'You'd given orders to shoot on sight,' I reminded him. 'And I know there wouldn't have been a posthumous rehabilitation and a ceremony honouring me at my graveside. "Borubaev, A, died in the line of duty".'

Tynaliev shrugged. The life of one police officer, more or less, didn't tip any scales as far as he was concerned. What mattered was the success of his plan.

'You know what I wanted; to set my enemies against each other, then behead them at their point of weakness.'

With me as the axe, I thought.

'Yusup got taken off the board, so the Chinese will be looking around for someone they trust to negotiate future drug sales,' Tynaliev went on. 'There's a success right there.'

'But Aliyev is still on the scene,' I said. 'It's just a momentary blip in his business, a nuisance, that's all.'

'Maybe so, but he still has to find new markets in South-East Asia. That's why tying up with the Thais would have been a perfect fit, with access to Malaysia as an added bonus. And I'm sure he's still wondering who tried to kill him with the bomb in Derevyashka. Before you ask, it wasn't me. Killing him would have just moved his second in command into the top spot.'

Tynaliev took another drink, lit a cigarette, stamped his feet against the cold.

'Winter's coming, and it's going to be a harsh one,' he said.

'You still haven't explained why you wanted Aliyev and Quang to team up,' I said, taking a cigarette from the pack he offered. I saw one of the bodyguards take a quick step forward, then settle back as Tynaliev sparked a flame for me.

'I didn't,' Tynaliev said, blowing smoke into the air, watching it flower white and green, blue and red, before dissolving into the night air. 'I want them to destroy each other. Aliyev dependent on selling, the Thais dependent on buying, both of them unwilling to trust the other. How long do you think a partnership like that will last?'

'Depends on the money,' I said. 'A few hundred million can mean true love.'

Tynaliev snorted and threw away his cigarette. The sparks scattered along the ground, then died.

'It's not about money,' he said, 'not really. I could have retired years ago, fucked off to somewhere warm, sat on a sunny beach, cold beer in one hand, hot tart in the other, no looking over my shoulder to see which bastard wants to plant one in my head.'

'But you didn't,' I said, 'because that way you keep the money, but lose the power.'

'I think you're starting to understand the ways of the world, Inspector,' Tynaliev chuckled. 'And about time too.'

So you've got Aliyev selling spice to the Thais, the Thais selling spice to Russia. And then?'

'Isn't it obvious?'

'Maybe I'm not devious enough to understand all the intricacies,' I said.

'If they do that, it puts both of them out of their comfort zone, puts them at risk,' Tynaliev explained, as if deciphering algebra for a particularly stupid pupil. 'The Russian mafia that have been dealing with Aliyev for years aren't going to like him supplying anything that might threaten their monopoly, their profits. Especially if those profits are going to end up in the pockets of the Thai mafia.'

Tynaliev ticked off each point on his fingers as he made them.

'The Russian government isn't going to want spice arriving on their doorstep, as if they didn't have enough problems with *krokodil* already. So they put pressure on the Thais, the Thai authorities clamp down on Quang, Quang stops buying, and Aliyev runs out of money. And that won't please the Circle of Brothers.'

He paused, transformed his outstretched fingers into a fist, slammed it into the palm of his other hand.

'And once you run out of money, you run out of power. Even you know what happens then.'

I nodded; this part of the equation I knew by heart.

'A new *pakhan*. A new realignment of the troops. Some promotions, some demotions, a lot of unpleasant dismissals.'

'Plus the need to renegotiate with all the other *pakhans*,' Tynaliev added. 'All of which weakens the structure and causes uncertainty.'

'So they all start killing each other, you announce that the Circle of Brothers is being smashed, and you shyly take the credit and have your backside measured for the president's chair.'

Tynaliev gave me an old-fashioned look.

'Why the fuck would I want that?' he said, genuinely puzzled. 'I already know who the most powerful man in this country is.'

'So you just gain more prestige and power,' I said, watching as the lights turned the minister's face a sinister red.

'Oh, a little more than that,' he said. 'Perhaps you'll even be able to work that out. I doubt it though.'

Tynaliev waved his bodyguards to draw closer.

I suppose your Uzbek tart is hanging around somewhere,' he said. 'Well, she has a Get Out Of Jail card this time. But tell her not to linger here.'

I hadn't thought Tynaliev would let go of every advantage he could seize; perhaps he was getting sentimental in his old age, but I had my doubts.

'Assassinating me got you into Aliyev's camp,' Tynaliev said. 'Shooting me guaranteed your credentials, and after that, following the money was child's play.'

Tynaliev had an odd idea of playground adventure, I thought, but kept it to myself.

'What made you so sure Aliyev would send me to negotiate with Quang?' I asked.

Tynaliev favoured me with another of those shark smiles.

'I knew he was setting up a deal. And who better to send than a man whose history as a smart guy gone rogue couldn't be questioned? Learn to play chess, Inspector, then you can always see a few moves ahead.'

The bodyguards surrounded Tynaliev, and the group set off

towards Frunze, where I knew a long black car with tinted windows would be waiting. Tynaliev turned with a parting shot.

'One more thing, Inspector. I'm sure Kanybek Aliyev is looking for you. I suggest you find him first.'

Chapter 51

Autumn mist still drifted through the tops of the oak trees as I walked through the park, tendrils hanging from the branches, lingering the way strangers and the homeless do as if uncertain of their destination. The life-sized statues of people set around the park paths wore the mist like diaphanous gauze scarves. It was almost noon, and I could see the statue of Kurmanjan Datka in the distance.

To the Kyrgyz people, Datka symbolises the best in courage, by the way she led the Kyrgyz people. When the Russian Empire finally annexed what was then called the Alai region, Datka realised resistance was futile. When her favourite son was sentenced to death, she resisted the temptation to plead for mercy, refused to allow the Kyrgyz to rise up against the Russians on her behalf. She even attended her son's execution in the hope conflict would be avoided, at a terrible personal cost.

I reached the statue, looked around, lit a cigarette. Kurmanjan looked stern, her jaw jutting forward, hair hidden by a traditional scarf. Her impassive stone face suggested a joke would be treated as a sign of frivolity, maybe even impertinence. I guess ruling a country is no laughing matter. There was no sign of Saltanat, but then I was slightly early. My tobacco smoke drifted in a thin blue haze into the air.

Something about the air told me winter was not far away, that in a few weeks, snow would cover where I was standing.

I looked at my mobile; ten minutes after noon. I'd never known Saltanat be late, but I told myself busy traffic, a foreign city, a cross street missed. After another five minutes, a sense of unease gnawed at me, and I glanced back in the direction I'd come through the park. Kurmanjan stared down at me, impassive, resigned to whatever was going to happen.

I saw the figure walking towards me, knew immediately it wasn't Saltanat. The stride too masculine, the carriage of the body aggressive, not graceful. If Saltanat moved like a ballet dancer, this man lumbered like a bear, uncertain on its back legs. A little way further back in the distance, a black SUV coughed smoke, its windows tinted an impenetrable black, like a hearse with four-wheel drive.

The man arrived at the statue, a good head taller than me and twice as broad. His broken nose and misshapen ears told me he'd once been a boxer, but not a good one. He looked at me the way a mugger assesses his next victim, spat and jerked his thumb at the waiting car.

'Boss wants to see you.'

'Then Boss can get his arse out of his status symbol and walk over here,' I replied. He gave me the hard eye, not knowing I've encountered villains who made him look like a toddler's doll. He paused while his punch-drunk brain assimilated the new information.

'He won't like that,' he finally said.

'I think you're mistaking me for someone who gives a fuck.'

He stared at me for a moment longer then walked back to the SUV. I lit another cigarette, making sure I could feel the weight of the Makarov I'd collected earlier. The smoke tasted acrid in my mouth; sweat dribbled down my back. The bear reached the car, opened the rear door, said his piece. After a moment, Aliyev stepped out, brushing the shoulders of his coat, dapper and fastidious as always. When he reached me, he didn't offer the Kyrgyz double clasp handshake but kept his hands in his pockets. So did I, and maybe for the same reason.

Aliyev stared up at the statue, his gaze as unwavering as hers.

'She knew when to cut her losses,' he said. 'She knew when she'd encountered a force she couldn't beat. She was smart: you could do worse than learn from her.'

'And where's the Russian Empire now?' I said. 'Not much sign of it here in the Kyrgyz Republic, if you don't count the monuments to Soviet realism.'

'You're a man of action and a philosopher,' Aliyev said, nodding his head as if in realisation. 'Hidden depths, Inspector, maybe I've misjudged you.'

I didn't reply.

'Just out for a morning stroll, were you, Inspector, taking the air? Or were you planning on meeting someone? A lady perhaps?'

I touched the cold metal of the gun with my fingertips, wondered which one of us could outdraw the other.

'What have you done with her?'

Aliyev feigned a look of confusion.

'Her?'

'You know who I mean.'

'Don't worry, Akyl. I can call you that now we're such close friends? She's perfectly safe. Maybe a little bruised, but then she did kick one of my men so hard in the balls that he's gone looking for them over in Kazakhstan.'

'He may have to go a bit further afield for that,' I said.

'Well, the villages are full of stupid young men looking for a pocketful of *som* and the chance to look hard and impress the local sluts. Replacements are never hard to find. Keeping them alive? That's another matter. But a minor one.'

He dusted off the shoulders of his still immaculate coat once more, dismissing the whole matter as hardly worth discussing.

'Moving on to more important matters, perhaps you can explain what happened in Bangkok,' he said.

I held out my hands, palms up, shrugged.

'The Orient; it's a delicate situation,' I said. 'Confusing, but we got the deal made.'

Aliyev looked directly at me, eyes probing my face for signs of weakness, traces of lies.

'I heard what happened to Quang. Quite a coincidence that he got raided just as soon as you left. And after he'd paid so much for protection over the years as well.'

'Nothing to do with me,' I said.

'And one of his men, found dead, the one who was taking you to the airport?'

'Again, nothing to do with me. I suppose life is even cheaper there than it is here,' I answered. 'He must have had enemies. Or maybe someone sending a message to him.'

Aliyev took one hand out of his pockets, gave a maybe yes, maybe no gesture.

'I'm not entirely sure what's going on, Inspector,' he said, 'and then I become nervous, and I tend to get violent. So people suffer. Along with their families.'

He paused, not blinking, eyes never shifting from mine.

'Of course, you don't have a family,' he continued, 'which means in order to intimidate you, I have to hurt you even more than I would most people. Unless, of course, your girl-friend means more to you than you let on.'

I shrugged.

'Uzbek, you know what they're like.'

'Good in bed though.'

'I'll take your word for it,' I said.

'Well, maybe tonight I'll find out. I like a bitch with some fighting spirit.'

I nodded my head as if I agreed with him. I already knew I'd have to kill Aliyev at some point. The difference now? I wanted to.

Chapter 52

'So how did you get the girl?'

'Simple,' Aliyev said. 'We feed a little bird back in Tashkent a few dollars every month. It wasn't very difficult to hack your girlfriend's mobile. So when you sent a text asking her to meet you by the statue?'

He shrugged at my folly.

'Lots of statues in Bishkek. Leaving it vague like that was smart, except for one flaw. Knowing what a romantic idealist you are, we were pretty sure you'd meet here. You obviously have a thing for strong women.'

It was my turn to shrug.

'We saw her walking down Chui Prospekt, obviously arriving early to scout the territory, check it wasn't a trap. A smart woman, your girlfriend. We grabbed her, not without some collateral damage, and here we are.'

'So she's in the car?'

'Bound and gagged, but otherwise unharmed. For the moment.'

I thought about our situation, knew what I had to do.

'You know what one of the benefits of being left-handed is, Kanybek?' I asked, in as sweet a voice as I could manage. 'Everyone takes it for granted you're right-handed. So they look at your jacket to see if you've got a knife or a gun, they watch the movement of your right hand. And that's all very sensible. And very convenient for me.'

'Explain.'

'Well, while I've been telling you that, I've been aiming a gun about ten centimetres above your belt buckle. With my left hand. I don't even need to draw my gun. This is an old jacket; a couple of bullet holes won't make a difference. Right now I can blow your spine into toothpicks before you can get your gun out of your pocket.'

I watched him assess the situation.

'I want you to take your hands out of your pockets, Kany-bek, but slowly, as if your fingers were poisonous spiders you don't want to frighten.'

I watched as he did what I'd ordered. His hands were steady, calm.

'I think you're bluffing,' he said.

I shrugged. He could see the bulge of the gun barrel pointing towards him.

'Very possibly. But then again ... I'll even contribute towards the cost of the wheelchair. A comfortable one so that you can spend the next thirty years being wheeled around.'

Aliyev's expression didn't change. I had no doubt he'd be a brilliant poker player. But I was holding the best cards. And his stake was his life.

'How long do you think that crew of *gopniki* and *myrki* will stand to take orders from a cripple? A month? Two months? They don't even need to shoot you. They'll just wheel you outdoors one winter evening, jam the brakes on your wheel-chair, go back indoors to smoke and drink. A *pakhan* freezing to death? Well, that would be a first.'

'You want the girl?' His voice was empty of all emotion. He might have been reciting the weather forecast.

'I think of her as a woman,' I said. 'I don't need to belittle her, the way you seem to have to. You're not in her league, Kanybek. She'd have you dead while you were still wondering whether to scratch your head or your balls.'

'We can get beyond this temporary unpleasantness,' Aliyev said. 'All I need to know is what really happened in Bangkok, and then we can get back to being partners again.'

'Kanybek,' I said, 'I think this is the end of a beautiful friendship.'

'You don't trust me?' he said, looking downcast.

I laughed harder than I'd done in months, maybe even years. But I made sure the gun was still pointed at his belly. And my hand wasn't shaking either.

'I won't kill you now if you release her,' I said. 'And if she's been harmed, well, I'll do some harming myself. Of the permanent kind.'

'You sound as if you've been watching too many Hollywood films,' he said. 'No need for all the threats and melodrama.'

Aliyev turned and made a circling motion towards the SUV. After a couple of moments I saw Saltanat emerge from the car, rubbing her wrists and with a look like hell unleashed. She walked towards us in a circle, making sure she didn't get between the gun and my target.

'You know I'll find you, don't you, Akyl?' Aliyev said, his voice so measured you could almost miss the not-so-hidden threat. 'And it will be me holding the gun that time.'

'Neither of us needs or wants this shit,' I said, weariness filling my throat. 'We'll leave now, and you don't follow us. I'll be in touch later and we can meet somewhere on neutral ground and I'll tell you exactly what it is that Quang wants. You start supplying him, I stay away from the whole thing and disappear, and we're even.'

'How do I know you'll keep your word?'

'I want to live. And I don't want to be looking at every car that drives by, every stranger strolling towards me, wondering if the shot is going to come from there. I've got enough information on Quang for you to put the pressure on. It's a good deal for you, a good one for me.'

'We're both reasonable men, Akyl, one hand washes the other. If we can do that, and you decide silence is your best defence, I've got no reason to come looking for you. Bigger fish to catch, and believe me, you're a minnow so small I'd throw you back in the water.'

'Well, that seems a reasonable compromise,' I said. 'But just to seal the bargain, let's the three of us stroll down to Frunze. Once we're there, we take a taxi, you walk back to your gas guzzler, and I'll call you later to arrange a meet.'

'Why bother with the walk?' Aliyev asked, but I could tell he already knew the answer.

'Because you might just have an excellent shot with a sniper rifle in the back seat of your car. As long as you're beside us, and no one can see if there's a gun trained on you, we're pretty safe.'

I nodded at Aliyev's jacket.

'Saltanat, would you oblige?'

She reached into Aliyev's pocket, pulled out a gun. She unloaded it, checked his other pockets for spare bullets, gave him back the gun.

'I don't believe in putting temptation people's way; I'm sure you'll agree.'

'Let's walk,' Aliyev said. 'I'm getting cold, and I'm a little bored with the company, to be honest.'

I waved to the watching men in the car, and Aliyev gave them the signal to stay where they were. I wondered if they expected me to kill him once we were out of sight in the trees, realised Aliyev knew me too well. My white knight syndrome: don't lie, don't do anything underhand. As Saltanat always said, one day it was going to get me killed.

Chapter 53

We walked back through the park, not talking, feet kicking through the swathes of leaves that had fallen from the branches overhead. It felt like walking through a church crumbling through neglect, through lack of love.

We came out onto Frunze, just by the football stadium. I knew we'd be able to catch a taxi from outside the maternity hospital on Logvinyenko, with its endless supply of young women clutching infants bundled up in coats, blankets and scarves.

I turned to Aliyev, held out my hand. To my surprise, I realised I didn't entirely dislike the man. His chosen path was against everything I believed in, but I also knew he wasn't the kind of *pakhan* who believed in slaughter, drive-by shootings, humiliation and rape. Unless they were necessary, of course.

I think he was as surprised to see my outstretched hand as I was in offering it. We shook hands, briefly, and I kept my left hand buried in my pocket.

'I'll be in touch tomorrow,' I said.

'Don't try and play every side against each other, Akyl,' he said. 'Try and ride more than one horse and you're sure to get thrown, maybe even trampled.'

He gave Saltanat the barest of nods – not risking shaking

her hand – and turned, walking back the way we'd come, never looking back. If I had been going to shoot him, a bullet in the back would have told the world I was a coward.

I turned to Saltanat, felt my heart turn over at the sight of the line of her jaw, her full mouth, her eyes the colour of mountain slate, that saw everything and gave nothing away.

'I don't think going back to your apartment is a great idea,' she said.

I waved at a couple of taxis that drove past, then watched as Saltanat raised an arm and a black Audi screeched to a halt. I guess taxi drivers are men after all, despite behaving like bad-tempered bastards.

She hadn't booked the Presidential Suite at the Hyatt Regency, but it was still several notches above my pay grade. She gave the bedazzled man at the concierge desk strict instructions we weren't to be disturbed, then led the way to the lifts.

'Why didn't you shoot Aliyev and take our chances?' Saltanat asked as we sat down on the edge of the bed.

'It might have been a little difficult,' I said, and took my left hand out of my jacket pocket, the first two fingers stretched out, the way children imitate guns when they're playing cops and robbers.

'Bang!' I said.

'What a very good idea,' Saltanat said, and pushed me backwards onto the bed.

Afterwards, we lay in the delicious drifting half-sleep that follows making love. I knew I had to talk to Saltanat, knew

285

she'd object, but I couldn't see any way out of it. I made us tea, putting off the awkward conversation, joined her back in bed.

'You think I should have killed Aliyev earlier?' I asked.

'You had a gun in your other pocket, didn't you?'

'I wouldn't have had time to draw it and aim before one of his boys shot me,' I said. It was the simple truth, unadorned by any pretence at being a tough guy.

'So he gets to kill you instead?'

I sat up in bed and turned to face her.

'The day I joined the force, I knew I could be killed. But I've survived so far. Dying isn't what worries me.'

Saltanat sipped at her tea, her eyes never moving from my face. I paused, hunting for the words the way a crow scours the ground for food.

'Go on.'

'I'm worried about the collateral damage.'

'You mean me, I suppose.'

I nodded. 'And not just you.'

She took another sip of her tea, delicate and poised. She paused, as if unsure how to reply.

'I haven't decided whether to keep it or not, you know.'

'For what it's worth, and if my opinion matters, I think you should keep it.'

'A state assassin for a mother, a late and much unmourned cop as a father? Talk about giving a child a great start in life.'

'OK, I'm looking at the wrong end of a gun barrel,' I said, 'but don't you think you're pushing your luck as well?'

'Retire and take up gardening, that's what you have in mind for me?'

Her tone was light, but I could tell she didn't find the conversation amusing.

'There are worse things than roses,' I said, 'and some of them have sharper thorns.'

'So what are you suggesting?'

'I think you should get on the train to Moscow tomorrow morning. Aliyev's men are bound to be watching the airport, but there shouldn't be a problem with the train.'

'You want me to sit on a train for forty-eight hours, while you turn into Clint Eastwood?'

'Travel first class, a sleeper to yourself. I'd like to do that myself, but I have to sort this stuff out first.'

'With Aliyev?' she asked.

'And with Tynaliev. It was him who threw me into this shit in the first place. If I don't deal with him, I might as well glue rear-view mirrors to my forehead. And then he'll attack from the front.'

I put my empty cup down, took hers, held her hand.

'The fake assassination for a start.'

She nodded.

'It had to be fake. I knew you were a bad shot, but even you couldn't have missed a fat bastard like that at point-blank range.'

'So then I'm on the run, top of the Most Wanted charts, a smash hit. Shooting Tynaliev was the only way I could get into Aliyev's team and win his trust. Since every one of his men has to take off their shoes to count past ten, that wasn't too difficult.'

'He didn't suspect?' Saltanat asked.

'Of course, that's why he sent me off to Bangkok. If I managed to draw Quang out of his regular activities, Aliyev could set him up, let the Russians know who was poisoning their children. Then all he had to do was stand back and let the Spetsnaz go to work. With Quang sidelined, Aliyev could own the spice routes into Russia. Big-time money.'

'While Quang prepared to sideline Aliyev.'

'You've been paying attention,' I said, 'I like that,' and I kissed her to prove I meant it.

'So Aliyev and Quang commit mutually assured destruction. And the resulting vacuum is filled by none other than the Minister of State Security,' Saltanat said.

'You have a very devious mind, even for a woman,' I said, dodging the blow I knew would follow.

'I'm still not going to Moscow,' she said, jaw set in that 'argument is futile' mode.

'I've got tickets for both of us,' I said, and reached into my jacket inside pocket to show her. 'You go tomorrow, I follow two days later, meet you outside Lenin's mausoleum, then we go into the GUM luxury store for the world's most expensive cup of coffee.'

'And then?'

'Then we decide where we're going to live, when we're going to get married, what names we're going to give our children.'

I patted her stomach. Too early to feel life, but I knew it was there, preparing to emerge on an unsuspecting world.

'What makes you think I want to marry you? Or marry anyone?'

'After everything we did an hour ago? How can you resist?' I said, with my most winning smile.

Saltanat looked suspicious, perhaps even a little sad; I couldn't say I blamed her.

'Why do you want to marry me?' she said. 'It can't be because of this,' as she pointed to her stomach.

I felt scared, no, terrified. Terrified of exposing my inner self, or being rejected, of being left alone again, with no one and nothing to live for. I looked at her, and she could sense my fear, watched me struggle to overcome it.

'Because I love you,' I said, my voice hoarse, my throat choked, my words stumbling over each other as if drunk.

Saltanat simply stared at me. I had no clue as to what she was thinking. Finally, she spoke.

'I know.'

And the way she said it splintered my heart.

Chapter 54

'You swear you'll meet me in Red Square?'

'You saw my ticket. I'll even take you in to see Lenin embalmed in his glass box.'

'That's not the most romantic offer I've ever had.'

'I'm out of practice,' I said, and kissed her again. Somehow, her tea managed to get spilt all over the Hyatt's pristine white sheets, but at the rates they charged, I figured they could afford a little laundry bill.

In the morning, showered but unshaved, I watched Saltanat get dressed. She looked at me as she fastened her bra at her waist, turned it round and up, sliding the straps over her arms. At that moment, she had the grace and poise of a ballerina, each movement instinctive and perfectly judged. I smiled as a wave of tenderness, not desire, swept over me.

'Let me show you something,' she said, and pulled at the side of her bra, exposing the end of a thin metal wire which she then pushed back out of sight.

'Ground to a point at both ends. Push this into someone's ear, you can watch it come out the other side. Always prepared, that's me.'

The smile slid from my face, remembering Saltanat's

existence as a perfect killing machine. It didn't stop me loving her, but it reminded me ours was never going to be a picture-book romance.

'Clever,' I said.

'Good for picking locks too,' she said, and a smile danced across her face.

I looked at my watch. Eight o'clock: time to head down to the lobby. I'd called Usupov the night before, asked him to meet us, take us for a drive. I didn't say where. Saltanat paid the bill with a credit card I was certain didn't have her real name on it. The clerk gave an uninterested smile, wished us a pleasant journey, hoped to see us again. Not if I'm paying, I thought as we stepped out into the crisp morning air.

Usupov was waiting, the car exhaust coughing smoke. We climbed into the back seat, and Usupov pulled away.

'I told Tynaliev you were back in the city,' he said, his voice thick with apology. 'If I hadn't, and he found out I knew . . .'

'I understand, Kenesh, I'm sure he has the airport watched full time,' I reassured him. I hoped the use of his first name would tell him I was on his side. And I knew the risk he was taking in being with us, a reminder there are still decent people in the world, pressured, intimidated, afraid, but pre-pared to do the right thing.

'Where are we going?'

'The station,' I said.

'No luggage?'

'Travel light, move fast,' I said. 'It's kept me alive all these years.'

Then I sat back, slumped down in my seat to minimise the risk of being spotted, watched Bishkek stretching and yawning as it woke up . . .

I've known men who've told me it's possible to love more than one woman at the same time. I've even put a couple of them behind bars when their romances turned sour, and one of the women had to go. The truth is you can love two women, but in different ways, for different reasons.

Sometimes it's just hoping you can still attract women, that they're willing to overlook the sagging jawline or beer belly because of your wonderful personality. Or the size of your bank balance. Other times, it's having so much money you can buy what passes for love and desire. Or maybe it's just a need for company and comfort as the years scurry by and the long night approaches.

I knew I'd loved Chinara for all she had been, loved her still. And I hoped she would have approved of me finding someone after she left me. A professional assassin wouldn't have been her ideal choice, but then we can't dictate the future, no matter how much we might try.

Bishkek railway station is a big place, considering how few trains actually run there. From the outside, it could pass for the town hall of a rural *oblast*, built with civic pride for some district far from a capital city. Built in High Soviet style, with a tall three-storey central building flanked by two extended wings, it proclaims the power and invincibility of the USSR. The Union has long gone, but the station remains.

Inside, massive windows light up the floor, while overhead, intricate paintings weave an elaborate design around a single silver six-pointed star. The walls are splendid with painted bas-relief plasterwork, as if modelled upon Tsarskoe Selo, the Catherine Palace outside St Petersburg. In another life, the room could have been a grand ballroom, a string quartet high above in the gallery, aristocratic ladies and gentlemen dancing a minuet. Now, in place of violins and violas, the gallery houses a neon timetable board showing the times of the few trains that visit here.

The grandeur of the interior is rather let down by rows of those uncomfortable metal seats you find in airports everywhere if you can't afford to visit the business lounge. Under the high interior, the benches are grouped together in one corner, huddled together as if for warmth. Like so many of the buildings of that era, it looks impressive at first sight, before you notice the peeling paint, the half-hearted repair jobs, the corners where decades of dirt and dust lurk.

It wasn't the starting point of a great journey. But I knew it was Saltanat's best hope of getting out of Kyrgyzstan, with Aliyev's men watching the airport and the border crossings into Uzbekistan and Kazakhstan.

I gave her the last of the roubles from my lock-up so she had enough to bribe any border guards that showed too great an interest, held her hand as Usupov pulled up by the little park opposite the station entrance.

I kissed her on the cheek, felt her breast against my arm.

'I booked you a four-berth compartment,' I said, 'so you'll have all the privacy you want.'

I knew people would try to push their way into her compartment, pitied anyone foolish enough to try it. I wanted to catch Saltanat's eye, but she looked away, unwilling to show her feelings.

'Here's to meeting in Moscow. I'll text you when I'm on my way. Pay my respects to Vladimir.'

Saltanat got out of the car without saying anything, walked across the road to the ornate entrance. She didn't look back. Right then, I wondered if I was making a catastrophic mistake, whether I should have been on the train with her, travelling towards a new future.

I watched her disappear into the entrance, tapped Usupov on the shoulder. He turned around to stare at me, puzzlement and pity plain in his face.

'You're letting her leave? Just like that?'

'Just like that,' I said. 'Safer for her.'

Usupov shook his head, disbelieving. 'You need your head examining.'

'You'll have to wait until I'm dead before you get the chance,' I said as he drove back towards the city centre. But being on Usupov's slab in the near future seemed a distinct possibility.

He dropped me at the top end of Ibraimova, near the Blonder pub. I could walk back to my apartment from there, check if anyone was watching the building, maybe even manage a couple of hours' sleep before contacting Aliyev. I had a very vague plan sketched out in my head, but plans have a habit of falling apart when bullets start slicing the air.

I crossed the footbridge near where I'd found the butchered body of Tynaliev's daughter, his beloved Yekaterina. That felt like decades ago. No sign anything had ever happened there, the trees as indifferent to human suffering and death as always. Only a few faded scraps of police crime tape fluttered from the branches. As a rule, the murdered dead aren't commemorated with a plaque; perhaps to do so would be to show the world how vile we are to each other. But I remember them, if that's worth anything.

I passed a battered trash can, the sort that swivel over and turn upside down so they can be easily emptied. Someone had emptied it all right; the ground was patterned with crushed beer cans and an empty vodka bottle like a drunk's carpet on a Sunday morning. Someone's idea of an al fresco party, or a wake. I reached into my jacket and dropped the train ticket with my name on it into the trash can. I knew I wasn't going to be travelling to Moscow.

And I was pretty sure I'd never see Saltanat again.

Chapter 55

The one good thing about Bishkek apartments are the front doors. Solid steel, impregnable unless you can squeeze a battle tank up the narrow stairs. They're fitted to keep burglars and other undesirables out; your apartment might be bare of everything but a bed and a kettle, but no one else can get inside unless you invite them.

Somehow I doubted Aliyev, with all his resources, could get hold of a T-90, so I could sleep for a while, drink tea and smoke while deciding what to do next.

The afternoon drifted towards dusk, grey skies holding back all but a little light that slithered in through the kitchen window. Elbows on the Formica table, I watched my cigarette smoke bloom in the air, surprised by the meaning and intensity my familiar surroundings took on with the approach of death.

I stubbed out my cigarette, shook the empty pack. It was time to make the call. The voice that answered showed no emotion at my request, merely ordered a time to meet. I put my phone down, remembered what Leonid Yurtaev, the Kyrgyz chess grand master had counselled: 'When you reach the endgame, remember your opponent is looking to kill you. If your defence is poor, or your attack is weak, he will do so.' I knew I was a mere pawn, but even a pawn can topple a king if the moment is right.

Tynaliev's house was as imposing as ever, the security just as strict, the guards surly as always. I wondered if they were that way when the president made an unexpected visit, decided they probably were.

My Makarov locked away, I was led to the front of the house, where a guard tapped in the lock code and I was admitted into Tynaliev's lair. The house was ferociously overheated, and I could feel sweat begin to form at my hairline. I told myself it was the heat, not fear.

After ten minutes of perspiration, the door to Tynaliev's study opened and the minister appeared. He put out a hand, massive and calloused. I knew Tynaliev had killed people with his bare hands, but I took it just the same. It felt like trapping my hand under a steam hammer.

'What?'

Tynaliev had never been a man to stand on ceremony, but this was terse, even for him.

'I'm sorry to intrude, Minister, but there are just a couple of things to clear up with you. Then I'll leave you in peace, I swear.'

Tynaliev took two steps forward, so we were face to face. I could smell the vodka and pickled cucumbers on his breath. His face was borscht-red and I wondered how long it would be before a stroke or a heart attack made his government post vacant. I couldn't say the prospect depressed me, but perhaps better the corrupt, hard-liner psycho you know . . .

'Get on with it,' Tynaliev half-snarled, sitting down at his desk. I noticed the conveniently placed pistol, wondered how sharp the letter opener was if it came down to it.

'I'd like to clarify my return to the police force,' I said. 'I've gone through a lot of shit, risked being shot by anyone and everyone, including my own side. Now it's time for my re-habilitation, don't you think?'

Tynaliev sat back in his chair.

'If you think I'm going into a dark alley one night wondering whether I'm going to get shot in the front by a criminal or in the back by a cop who thinks I'm dirty, you don't know me very well, Minister,' I said.

'So what do you want?'

'A statement that says I was acting on your orders to help break a major crime syndicate, and I've been restored to my former post of Inspector, Murder Squad. Further details to follow in due course.'

'Which, of course, they never will,' Tynaliev said.

'Which they never will,' I agreed.

'I'll sign the release tonight, have it issued to the press. It should be in tomorrow's papers, but I can't guarantee you'll be front page news.'

'As long as the right people see it and know who it's from.'

'Which leaves us where?'

I looked over at a side table, empty except for a photo of Yekaterina Tynalieva, the way she was in life, smiling, happy, not the disembowelled carcass I'd encountered. I made sure Tynaliev saw me looking as well. We both knew the pain of losing someone you loved, and in that moment I felt a degree of sympathy for him. I'd brought the man responsible for her murder to a summary and brutal justice at Tynaliev's hands. I was too cautious to mention it, but Tynaliev owed me and he knew it.

'Quang thinks I set him up with the Thai police,' I continued, 'which, of course, means he thinks I was acting under orders from Aliyev. Aliyev thinks I deliberately set Quang up to sabotage the deal, probably because I wasn't offered a big enough slice of the cake. So they'll battle it out, maybe wipe each other out.'

Tynaliev gave the kind of smile a shark does at the split second before it hits its prey.

'Which we've agreed would be a good result, Inspector?' he said, emphasising the last word to reassure me of my regained status.

'Of course,' I agreed. 'Although there is one thing that still puzzles me. I can understand why you want to break Aliyev and his organisation. A threat to state security, a major source of corruption and crime, a threat to the harmonious relations we enjoy with our neighbours.'

I paused, decided it wasn't the time to ask if I could smoke. Instead, I adopted my most innocent and puzzled expression, the look of a small child when told where babies come from.

Tynaliev poured himself a giant vodka, threw it down his throat.

'Getting rid of two criminal gangs, even if one of them is based abroad, well, that's a good thing, isn't it, Inspector?'

Even more emphasis on the last word this time: what's been bestowed can also be taken away.

I had a pretty shrewd idea someone else would soon be filling the gap, but I wanted to live, at least until Quang or Aliyev, or both, caught up with me. After that, all bets were off.

'If that's all,' Tynaliev said, waving a finger at the door behind me. I thanked him once again. I had my hand on the door handle when he spoke again.

'I expect your silence on this, Inspector.' No mistaking the threat. 'And don't try to pull the "information lodged with people in case of my death" stunt, like you did after our business in Dubai.'

'I wouldn't dream of it, Minister,' I said. 'You can never rely on most people to do as you ask them, particularly when you're past caring.'

Tynaliev nodded.

'On the other hand, when someone one trusts implicitly hears of one's death, well, they're bound to take it very personally,' I said. 'I would hate to think of walking around wondering if that headache is from a sniper's cross-hairs, that sudden stabbing pain in the ribs from a hunting knife. After all, what's the point of having a bank vault full of money if you're not alive to enjoy it?'

Tynaliev recognised the threat, shrugged it away.

'Then we'll have to keep you alive, won't we?' he said. 'You've already quit the vodka, maybe time to bin the smokes as well?'

It was time to show my hand.

'I've never found it easy to give up,' I said, and he knew I wasn't talking about nicotine, 'and I'm not the only one.'

'The Uzbek woman,' he said.

I nodded.

'No parables, no unspoken meanings, Minister. If you kill me, she'll kill you. She's the very best at what she does. You probably won't feel a thing.'

I stood up, headed for the door, watched Tynaliev reach for the vodka bottle. I suppose we all take comfort where we can find it. I only wished I knew where to find mine.

Chapter 56

There are always taxis loitering outside Tynaliev's house, dogs waiting to be thrown scraps from the master's table. They all know how to reach central Bishkek, and a few of them will have taken reluctant passengers to Sverdlovsky station for further 'discussions'.

I waved to the nearest one, clambered into the back seat, lit a cigarette to soothe my nerves. Meeting Tynaliev always had that unsettling effect on me, like crossing a field and hoping the bull is in a good mood. The driver glared at me as I lit up, said nothing when he saw me stare back. As a concession, I cracked open a window, let cold air take my smoke away.

The driver continued to glare at me until I told him my destination: the Kulturny Bar. His attitude immediately dissolved into fawning obedience, at the thought of being behind the wheel for a gangster who could give him a thousand *som* note or a bullet behind the ear, depending on his mood. I couldn't say being mistaken for a thug made my day worthwhile, but at least it meant I didn't have to listen to the radio.

I paid the driver off with a five hundred *som* note, and before he could say he had no change, told him to keep it, left him staring after me still unsure whether I was a mobster or not. He watched as I kicked at the graffiti-smeared door until it opened a crack, then drove off, leaving a thin trail of exhaust fumes to remember him by.

I didn't recognise the guard at the door, but he'd obviously done enough stints as face patrol security to recognise me. A grunt, a nod of his head, and I was inside, looking down the staircase into the darkness. I'd been inside this shithole too many times, seen too much trouble there, wondered if I'd ever have to traipse down those stairs again, my feet sticking to the soiled concrete.

I walked past the torn and faded poster of the heroin-addicted girl still staring at the camera in dead-eyed opioid despair. Underneath, someone had scribbled a new phone number and 'ALL HOLES AVAILABLE'. Romance, Kulturny-style. The door didn't have 'Abandon hope' written over it; anyone who entered here had disposed of that luxury long ago.

The main bar stank of sweat, spilt cheap beer and fried chicken, although I'd never seen anyone risk the food. There are limits, even when you're an *alkash* putting away two litres of vodka a day. The barman saw me, started to fumble under the counter. Maybe he was just reaching for a clean towel, if the place had such a thing. Maybe. He paused when I raised a warning finger. Perhaps he saw the Makarov under my jacket.

The room was almost empty, apart from a drunk in the far corner, staring into space, trying to remember who he once had been. I pulled up one of the bar stools, inspected the seat for stains, sat down.

'Inspector.'

No love lost, but no change to the status quo. It felt good getting my old title back, but I thought the gun had more to do with any respect I'd been shown.

'Vodka?'

'Two small bottles,' I said. 'The good stuff. Unopened.'

He nodded, his face giving nothing away, a good Kyrgyz. He pulled down two half-litre bottles, set them in front of me. I pretended to reach for my wallet, he pretended they were free, shook his head. I picked one bottle up, took it over to the drunk, placed it within reach. He didn't acknowledge the gift, but I knew if I tried to take it back, a chicken claw of a hand would reach out and stop me. I sat back down at the bar, slid the remaining bottle into my jacket pocket.

'You don't want a glass?'

I shook my head.

'Just get on the phone, you know who to call,' I said, made my voice brutal and set for violence.

'You know who he'll hurt if he doesn't want to talk to you,' the barman said, his face taut with anxiety.

'You know who I'll hurt if I don't talk to him,' I said, gave him the hard stare.

Using his body to hide the number he dialled, the barman listened for a moment, looked increasingly worried as the ringtone continued, finally whispered into the mouthpiece for a couple of moments, handed the phone to me.

'Inspector.'

Aliyev's voice was measured, precise, perhaps even a little amused.

'*Pakhan*,' I replied. We were obviously going to be formal. 'Time to meet.'

'Better sooner than later, don't you think?' I said, listened to the silence for thirty seconds.

'You know Mr Quang is no longer in police custody?' Aliyev asked.

'Locks everywhere have a habit of springing open when you pick them with a big enough banknote.'

'Of course, there are situations where no amount of money buys you a way out,' Aliyev said. There it was. No veiled threats, no suggested alternatives. I knew he meant to kill me. And he knew I was intent on killing him.

'One of my representatives in Bangkok has already discussed your visit with Quang. I regret to say he holds you responsible for the temporary loss of his liberty. Not to mention the damage to his villa, the kilos of product that were seized and then "disappeared". The death of his "friend" whose reappearance in a basket at a Bangkok laundry created quite a stir. Oh, and he seemed particularly angry that the Cambodian government is taking steps to recover a sculpture stolen from Angkor Wat. They're also threatening to extradite his father for the theft.'

'No point in telling him I'm not to blame,' I said.

'No point at all,' Aliyev agreed. 'In fact, he's offered me a substantial reward if I can manage your return to Bangkok.'

'Drugged and in a packing case, I suppose.'

'It may have to be something uncomfortable and disagreeable like that,' Aliyev said, 'but then again, not as disagreeable as you staying here.'

I looked around the bar in all its cheap, shabby decay. Chipped Formica tables decorated with beer rings and scarred by cigarette burns. Mysterious stains on the threadbare carpeting. A subtle hint of vomit mingling with the scent of piss from the toilets. I didn't think I'd miss the Kulturny, except it was a place I'd known for many years, and the familiar becomes more significant when you sense you're approaching your death.

'Inspector, are you still there?'

'Yes,' I replied, feeling the solid weight of the gun at my belt, the vodka bottle in my pocket, 'I'm still here.'

'Then I suggest we meet at—'

'No, I'll say where and when,' I interrupted. 'And I don't want you bringing that troupe of badly trained halfwits you call your men along.'

'I wouldn't dream of it,' Aliyev said, and I could almost believe he felt affronted. 'Where do you suggest, Inspector? Somewhere public, I imagine. Of course, your Uzbek lady friend isn't invited; I'm sure you understand.'

'She's left the country,' I said.

'Really? Well, a woman like that, she was never going to hitch her wagon to a loser like you, was she?'

'That sounds pretty accurate,' I said, left it at that, wondered for a moment if he might be right.

'You always think you know who your friends are, Inspector, until you look around and discover you don't have any.'

'That's a terrible thought, *pakhan*.'

'It's the way of the world. A lesson I learnt very early on.'

306

'You went to the wrong kind of school,' I said. Aliyev merely laughed.

'I'm the one with several million dollars in my bank account, Inspector. I'm not even sure you can afford to pay for the bottle of vodka you've just bought. Tell the barman to put it on my bill.'

'Maybe we'll share a toast. To old friends. If we had any,' I said.

'Where do you propose we meet?'

Voice smooth as Thai silk, a shark homing in for the kill.

'I've been thinking about that,' I said. 'Not in the city, too many people, we don't want anyone to get hurt.'

'The furthest thing from my mind,' Aliyev lied.

'Late afternoon, say four o'clock.'

'*Da*, but where?'

'I'll meet you tomorrow, at the grave of our fathers,' I said and put down the phone.

Chapter 57

I spent the early part of the morning at the lock-up I keep on the city outskirts, away from prying eyes, people who might disapprove of a serving police officer having a stash of fake passports, unauthorised weaponry, dollars, euros and roubles. Nothing unusual; I'd be surprised if most of my colleagues didn't have a similar arrangement. Governments change or are overthrown, politicians rise and fall, and it's always best to be prepared for a sudden change in your circumstances.

I filled a black plastic carry-all, the sort gym freaks like to be seen with, locked up, looked around for a car to borrow. Technically, I was going to steal it, but since I had no intention of joyriding it to destruction or torching it for kicks, I preferred to think of it as a temporary loan.

I wanted an older model, something unmemorable and reliable. Newer cars are much harder to hot-wire, expensive cars get noticed. After several blocks I found it, a four-door Lada 1200 sedan that looked as if it had been driven three times around the world. The doors were locked, of course – no one in Kyrgyzstan is stupid enough to leave anything unlocked unless it's been nailed down – but it wasn't hard to smash the quarter light. Two minutes later, I was on my way, looking in the rear-view mirror to make sure I hadn't been spotted.

In the summer, driving up to Chong-Tash is very pleasant once you're out of the city. Fresh air drifting down from the mountains, passing through villages where excited dogs chase after your car and the local *babushki* sell buckets of plums, apples and cherries by the roadside. But that's in the summer.

By autumn, the mist clings to the hillsides and haunts the fields, the day darkens earlier, and the mountains take on a menacing look. The villages are empty with only an occasional light shining through net curtains to show the place is inhabited. We're Kyrgyz; we know winter is creeping up on us, stalking us as if we were its prey. Perhaps we are.

Ata-Beyit, Grave of our Fathers in Kyrgyz, is a memorial ground thirty kilometres south of Bishkek, near Chong-Tash. Every few months I go there, listen to the wind blowing from across nearby fields, watch tree branches shiver and their leaves tremble.

In the 1930s, almost a hundred and forty political figures and intellectuals were 'purged' by the Soviet NKVD as 'enemies of the people', shot at night, bodies dumped in a brick kiln. Shamefully, the massacre only came to light when the USSR collapsed and the bodies were moved to a mass grave by Chingiz Aitmatov, our most famous author and diplomat. His father was amongst the victims.

If that was all, Ata-Beyit would still be a melancholy place. But in 2010, during our second revolution since independence, waves of protests and demonstrations against corruption and nepotism flooded the country. Over forty protesters, mainly young men, were shot dead by government forces in Ala-Too Square.

It's a day I would love to forget but cannot. Bullets tearing into flesh, blood from the dead a scarlet flood spilt on the road, the screams of the wounded, smoke from burning cars throwing a black pall over everything. Seeing the bodies stacked in the morgue like so much firewood as their families wept and begged for news was the worst day of my career, the day I realised the dead must always be avenged.

Many of those who died on that day are buried at Ata-Beyit, a reminder of the price we've paid for democracy. They lie in a separate graveyard, two rows of identical black marble stones, each one showing a name, dates and sometimes an engraved likeness of a face.

In April each year, the relatives of the young men killed in 2010 visit and clean around the graves, maybe bring a bouquet or a jar filled with flowers. Otherwise, the place is usually deserted, apart from the woman who works in the small yurt-shaped museum, a guard at the turn-off from the main road, an occasional tourist ticking the site off his list of things to see.

Older tragedies are also commemorated. It was only in 2016 that a monument was built to remember the *Urkun*, the Exodus, when men, women and children fled during an uprising against the Russian Tsarist forces. Perhaps a hundred thousand people and their animals perished trying to escape over the Tien Shan mountains as winter set in and the mountain passes became snowbound killing grounds.

Even now, a century later, at the Bedel Pass, four thousand metres above sea level near the Chinese border, you can wade through icy spring snowmelt and pick up human and animal bones, gleaming white where the water has brought them down and scrubbed them clean.

Not many people visit Ata-Beyit. It's a reminder, after all, of suffering, murder, lives lost. And people are busy, of course, with the day-to-day stuff that fills our lives: fields to plough, livestock to tend, getting the children off to school. Visiting the dead isn't a priority.

It was in this most sombre of places I'd decided to face Aliyev once and for all.

Chapter 58

The clouds were looking ominous as I stopped the car down a rutted path two hundred metres away from the entrance to Ata-Beyit. My watch said it was just after noon. Aliyev and his men would arrive soon, set up an ambush, gun me down as I arrived, innocent and trusting.

I climbed over a fence to avoid the guard at the entrance, walked up to the main memorial ground, where the victims of the purges lie together underneath a symbolic *tunduk*, the round smoke hole at the top of every yurt. Our national symbol, it's a sign of our nomadic heritage; you'll even find it at the centre of our flag. Beyond the mass grave is the memorial and burial place of Chingiz Aitmatov. A metal bas-relief of his face hangs on a white marble wall behind his grave, also capped by a *tunduk*.

I'm not the world's greatest shot with a rifle, but it wasn't as if my targets would be a kilometre away. I'd found the gun when I was searching an old warehouse used in a couple of murders. The decapitated corpses had been removed and all that remained was to find the heads. The gun was hidden under an old paint-stained tarpaulin, nothing to do with the murders. I replaced the rifle, came back that evening, gave it a new home in my lock-up. I didn't imagine I'd ever need it, but in my line of work, you never know what hides around the corner.

Now, with Aliyev coming mob-handed, as I knew he would, I needed every advantage I could get. I'd also got my service issue Makarov, and my Yarygin. If I needed more than the eighteen bullets it held, I was going to be dead by the end of the afternoon anyway. I told myself I'd save the last bullet for myself, if I had to, but I intended to make sure I was the last man standing.

I checked my line of sight, making sure I could see the main road and the turn-off to the complex. There's a small space for parking, with steps leading to the lower level where the gravestones stand in disciplined ranks. If I took up a space among the graves, I'd have a clear field of fire. I thought about shooting Aliyev first, dismissed the idea. Disposing of his troops first was not the sensible option, but I wanted this to be a duel between Aliyev and me.

Black clouds were moving in over the mountains, and I could smell rain in the air. Not yet cold enough to turn rain into snow, but that time was fast approaching. The end of the year, perhaps the end of many things.

I sat down, back to one of the tombstones, where I was concealed but could watch the road. My fingers brushed the incised lettering of the name of the young man who slept beneath me. Twenty-four, his face open and trusting, unweathered by experience, a slight smile for the photographer. Did he have a wife, children? Did they think of him as they played with their toys, sat through boring maths lessons? I've tried to find a meaning to life, to death, but never been able to reach any conclusion other than: it simply is.

313

I wondered about lighting a cigarette, decided against it. Smell carries a long way on mountain air, and I didn't need to give Aliyev any more clues to where as I was than I had to.

I checked both the Makarov and the Yarygin again. I could smell gun oil on my fingers, sharp, acrid, the scent of death.

It was a little before three o'clock when I saw the SUV turn off the main road, stop at the guard hut, then drive on up to the car park. After parking, no one got out for a couple of moments. Looking to see if I was waiting and welcoming with open arms: here I am, come and kill me.

The rear doors of the SUV opened and three men clambered out. No one I'd ever seen before, bulky in warm winter jackets that left their arms free. They stood looking around, stamping their feet on the ground, ensuring the coast was clear before Aliyev left the safety of the vehicle. I couldn't see anything through the heavily tinted glass, but my guess was he'd been driving, taking complete control at the climax of the mission.

My rifle barrel felt like an extension of my arm, the barrel a giant finger pointing towards the SUV. As I watched, finger taut on the trigger, the tallest of the men reached into the back seat, began to pass out weapons. I knew it was time.

The man's navy blue watch cap pulled low over his ears suddenly flowered into a scarlet mask as I shot him in the head. A spray of red spattered the side and roof of the car as he fell back, slumped and slithered to the ground. My mouth was dry, tasted sour and metallic from fear and adrenalin.

I shot again, missed, saw the side window shatter, the remaining men diving for cover. My next shot was luck rather than aim, and I saw one of the men half-sit then roll back, clutching his right thigh, the blood already pouring in a thick stream. I wondered if I'd hit an artery, decided I didn't care.

At this distance, I couldn't hear him, but I watched his mouth freeze open in a long, drawn-out scream. I didn't expect Aliyev to rush to his rescue, and I wasn't disappointed. There was no movement from the guard hut by the road. Aliyev must have made a pay-off; either that or the guard had more sense than to come to investigate.

The SUV rocked slightly as the doors on the side away from me opened, and I put another shot into the bodywork, just to keep things interesting.

Bullets were coming in my direction now, none close enough to cause me any worries. In any case, being shielded by a dead man's tombstone is a great way of ensuring you don't earn one yourself.

The man lying on the ground had stopped moving, and I wondered if he'd bled out already. The SUV was moving forward now, slowly, acting as cover for whoever was left. My guess was Aliyev and the last of his men; the odds were better but still not in my favour.

As I watched, one man broke cover, raced towards the shelter of a statue of three men in chains. I aimed, fired, missed, turned my attention back to the SUV. Their aim was to outflank me, knowing I couldn't watch every direction. It was time to move.

I dropped the rifle, crawled behind the line of tombstones, rose and raced for the upper level of the complex, expecting a bullet between the shoulder blades every step of the way.

Chapter 59

The upper level of Ata-Beyit is dominated at one end by a marble memorial wall behind Chingiz Aitmatov's grave. It was there I took cover, waiting for Aliyev and his men to hunt me down.

The sound of the wind driving the clouds down from the mountains had been joined by a curious melancholy clatter. At the far end, a giant terracotta-coloured arch commemorates the dead of 1916. The top of the arch holds a giant *tunduk*, from which are suspended cables which end in oversized metal stirrups, evoking horses without riders. In the wind, the metal swayed and created the noise I'd heard. The desolation and sorrow of the noise was an appropriate soundtrack to the setting, and the situation I was in.

'Akyl, this is crazy,' I heard Aliyev shout. 'We should talk, there's no need for this nonsense.'

'Walk towards me then,' I shouted back. 'I promise I won't shoot.' Yet, I added to myself.

After a couple of moments, Aliyev appeared, walking down the steps by the 1916 memorial, which was flanked on either side by bas-relief murals showing the suffering and death of the Kyrgyz people a century earlier. His hands were held out before him, to show he wasn't carrying a weapon.

I was watching, expecting Aliyev to shoot me. But when

the shots came, they were from the bridge of the entrance, where the inscription in raised bronze letters read '*Ak iyilet, birok synbait*' – 'The people: bowed but unbroken'.

I felt a force grab me by the wrist, flinging my right arm high into the air and away from me. When I looked at my hand, I realised I'd been hit. My ring finger had been smashed to pulp, the first two joints missing entirely, the rest a sodden mass of tissue from which bone protruded like an insult. It didn't hurt, but I knew that would soon pass. It looked like I wouldn't be getting married after all.

I pumped three shots in the direction of the bridge, heard them whine off marble, a scream of pain as I hit the third man with the second bullet. The Makarov clicked empty. I dropped it, took the Yarygin from my belt. I knew I needed the extra firepower; the killing hadn't quite finished yet.

It felt like an afterthought that a bullet had bitten into my thigh. No pain yet, but plenty of blood, enough for me to bleed out fairly quickly.

'I want to end this, Kanybek,' I said, wincing as the pain began to gnaw at my hand. More blood on the ground now, and a fierce ache in my hand, as if someone had held my fingers to a naked flame.

'You had me fooled, I admit that,' Aliyev said. 'Assassinating Tynaliev was the perfect way to show you weren't a government plant. I give you credit for that.'

'Tynaliev's idea,' I said. 'I couldn't be that devious.'

'Shame you didn't use live ammo; we could all have made a lot of money, lived happily ever after.'

I knew he was dragging things out, waiting for me to grow weak so he could finish me off.

'You don't have the balls to shoot me?' I asked, making sure he saw the Yarygin.

'Do I need to? All I have to do is watch; my hands stay clean.'

My eyes felt sore, the lids heavy, and the blood dripped onto the marble like melting roses.

'You never saw the big picture, did you, Akyl?' Aliyev laughed. 'You were hunting me, I was hunting Quang, he was hunting me, and Tynaliev was out to fuck all of us. You didn't have a clue; "Drunk on reckless might-have-beens", that was you.'

The phrase sounded familiar, nagged at my mind.

'Wasn't your wife a poetry lover?' Aliyev taunted. 'You don't have a memory for such things.'

It was then that the story turned sharp, pieces falling into place as if preordained from day one.

'The dead girl down in Alamedin, the drug overdose, the one with the poem tucked into her clothing,' I said. 'You knew her?'

'From the day she was born,' Aliyev said. 'My daughter, my Roza,' and I could hear the madness in his voice. I said nothing, tried to see the bereaved parent in his face, glimpsed only rage.

'She wasn't a user, not ever,' he continued. 'I'd kept her away from that shit. My team was warned what would happen if it went wrong, if she got mixed up. The best schools, holidays, whatever she wanted, nothing was too good for Roza.'

Now I had a name to fit to the body; Roza Aliyeva, drug dealer's daughter. I wondered if I'd live long enough to tell Usupov he could attach a name tag to her toe.

'Don't get me wrong; she knew who I was, what I was. Hard to pretend with the kind of money I had, with the way we lived. She knew.'

'So what got her started?' I asked. His face twisted into a mask of sorrow.

'She went on holiday. Chiang Mai, Bangkok, the whole thing. She called it "finding herself".'

Aliyev gave a mirthless laugh, the sort that usually means death for someone. I tightened my grip on my gun. Blood pooled on the ground below me; I could smell its metal sweetness, almost taste it on my tongue. I was dying by the glassful.

'Instead Quang found her. Someone squealed, got an envelope under the table. Next thing I hear from her, she's met this wonderful man. Guess who. I find out who it is, I go nuclear. Quang and I had already had some opening discussions about the business, but we hadn't been able to agree. Then I discovered he was using my daughter to get at me.'

Aliyev shook his head, as if in wonder anyone could have been so foolish.

'When I wouldn't give in to his demands, he gave Roza the hot shot that killed her. Not him personally, but one of his employees. Adding to the pressure to reach a deal. He knew I had other children.'

'You saw the autopsy report?' I asked.

'Dollars buy a lot of information,' Aliyev said. 'The blood spatter on her pants was just another humiliation, a defiling, blood from another dead junkie squirted onto her from a syringe, I imagine. One more way to insult me, prove how weak I was.'

That explained the different blood groups, reminded me once again that hate and violence against the weak never rests, never goes away.

Aliyev paused, looked into the sky as a few drops of rain danced across the ground.

'The same with tucking those lines of poetry into her bra. Roza wrote that poem. She always wanted to be a writer.'

I said nothing, felt pity for her, perhaps even for him. I understood what he'd felt: I wrote the manual about the loss of love.

'I was off the investigation almost before it had even started,' I said. 'We never found who gave her the hot shot.'

Aliyev gave a grim smile, and I felt my pity for the bereaved father melt away.

'I did,' he said, said no more. He didn't need to.

'Yet you sent me to broker a deal with Quang?'

Aliyev shook his head.

'I sent you there to fuck him and his business over, not that you knew. Of course, I could have had him killed. But I didn't want him to die fast, the way Roza did. I wanted him rotting in a Bangkok shitpit, his organisation destroyed. I wanted him to know I'd taken over from him, that I was running things, making the money, calling the shots.'

I thought about ripping the sleeve from my shirt to make a tourniquet, knew I didn't have the strength, knew I couldn't put the gun down, knew I had to keep it aimed at Aliyev. I only had a few moments of life left, and I had to use them.

'Tynaliev will wipe you out, you know,' I muttered, my voice thick and sour with pain. 'He'll take over everything you've worked for.'

'He'd like to, I'm sure,' Aliyev smiled, 'but let me tell you a fact of life, Inspector. Politicians rise, politicians fall. Cemeteries are full of men who thought they could have it all, that the names on their graves now overgrown with weeds would never be forgotten. But crime and money? They go on for ever, hand in hand.'

He paused, reached into his pocket, took out a gun, pointed it. One of those .25 Berettas people carry as a hideaway. Tough guys think of them as a woman's gun, but they'll kill you just as dead as a .45. For a few seconds, I remembered the dream where Chinara had mimed shooting me.

The rain on my forehead ran into my eyes, and without thinking I used my hand to wipe it away. Blood joined the rain, and I had to blink to focus on Aliyev.

'You're right, of course. I don't expect to live long enough to grow a white beard and complain about the state of the world. Burn brighter, burn faster. But until then, everything I want is mine for the asking. Or the taking.'

321

'Except for getting your daughter back,' I said, and pulled the trigger of the Yarygin, just as he fired twice. I felt Aliyev's bullets slam like fists into my chest, hurl me backwards, saw Aliyev's mouth gape and his face dissolve into a catastrophe of blood.

Chapter 60

Redemption is always tentative. All you can wish for is that your hopes, your motives and your actions don't make things worse, maybe even improve them. You do wrong, you do your best to right it. A parent dies, their child lives. There's a balance and a harmony in that; maybe that's enough.

I slumped against the memorial wall, the marble chill against my back, shirt crimson and sticky with blood, gun strangely leaden in my hand. I could see the blood pouring out of me, watched with a curious detachment. I coughed, tasted blood in my mouth. The rain was falling harder now, and the sky had taken on an ominous dark as the mountains loomed over me.

I thought of Chinara, at rest in her grave overlooking the valley and the mountains beyond, the poets she loved safe and eternal on a thousand shelves.

Of the dead child I'd found dumped in Yekaterina Tynalieva's mutilated belly like so much rubbish, now both of them avenged and at peace.

And of Saltanat, journeying back to safety and Otabek, the mute boy we'd rescued, the new life in her womb turning and stirring, waiting to enter the light.

For the briefest of moments, I sensed all their kisses on my cheek, light and insubstantial as a moth's wing beating its rhythm on my skin.

And I realised how beautiful and unknowable the world is, in all its mystery and passion and danger, how relentlessly hard it would be to leave it, and how easy it is to die.

Acknowledgements

The previous three novels in the Kyrgyz Quartet thanked the many people who have helped in their creation.

This book is no different, and I repeat my thanks to all of them.

However, four people deserve individual mention.

Stefanie Bierwerth at Quercus; her patience, encouragement and commitment to the series has been immeasurable.

Simon Peters, who has improved my grammar, spelling and plotting throughout; he helped the books gain whatever merit they may have.

Tanja Howarth, my agent and, more importantly, my friend; all I can say is *sine quo nihil* (without whom nothing).

And finally, Sara, who first introduced me to Kyrgyzstan. *Spasibo*.

Everything in this book is solely the product of my imagination. Any flaws or mistakes are mine alone.

Bangkok – Bishkek – London – Dubai, 2017–2018